The Romantics

ISABEL JOLIE

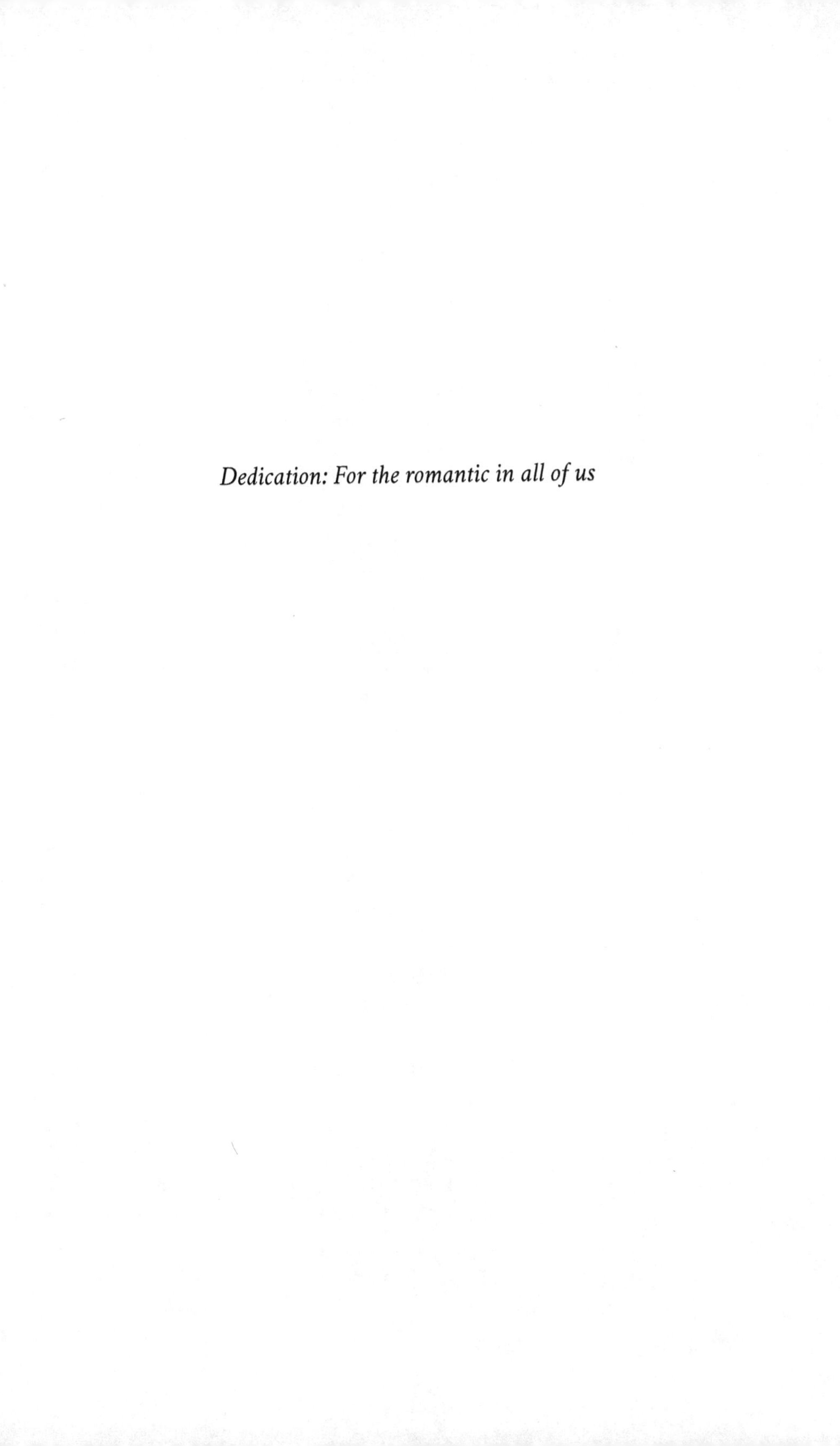

Dedication: For the romantic in all of us

Romantic:

* Belonging to or characteristic of Romanticism or the Romantic Movement in the arts

* A soulful or amorous idealist

* Expressive of or exciting sexual love or romance

The soul, fortunately, has an interpreter—often an unconscious,
but still a truthful interpreter—in the eye.

Charlotte Bronte

One

HARRISON

It is a truth universally acknowledged that status meetings hazard a colossal waste of time. However well-known this truth, my colleagues insist on participating in this farce. To glorify the weekly occasion, an enormous vase of blue hydrangeas graces the center of the sleek conference room table.

The rare blue flower symbolizes desire. The metaphysical striving for the impossible, for the infinite. The ambitious soul reaching for the unreachable.

My mother added aluminum sulfate to the soil in the beds alongside our home to achieve a blue similar to those in the vase of hydrangeas decorating the sleek walnut conference room table. Proving beauty is in the eye of the beholder, a subjective affection, other gardeners add lime for a profusion of pink.

My mother favored blue. The simple glass vase on the table delivers a burst of fond memories. Mom creating an arrangement. Trimming the six-foot-tall border. Dad coming up behind Mom in the garden, kissing her cheek. Tender and devoted.

The arrangement stirs memories, but it's doing so when I don't have the time to waste. The partner status meeting should've begun ten minutes ago. And thus, here I sit, fancying flowers in a meeting that should not be.

Paragon Surgery is Houston's premier plastic surgery practice. Patients fly in from all over the United States, and sometimes from other countries, for our talent and expertise. Yet a punctual start to our status meeting remains elusive. The meeting won't begin until the founding partner arrives, and Joel Lennox, our amiable and jovial leader, thrives on tardiness.

A butter scent permeates the room, thanks to the Olive Garden-catered lunch selected by Dr. Matt Sutton, a.k.a. Glutton. The man loads up his plate like he's at a Vegas buffet.

He claims the chair beside mine and leans in conspiratorially.

"Next time you have a guest pass, please, pick me. I beg you. That place. It's all I've been able to think about."

I scan the room, searching for Dr. Jessica Chandler, one of our partners, to ensure she isn't within hearing range. She's in the corner, her phone plastered to one ear, and her hand to the other. Her brow remains smooth thanks to the muscle relaxing properties of Botox or one of its competitors, but judging from her hunched back, she's focused on a troubling call.

"We don't talk about that here," I pointedly remind Matt.

Matt, like me, is a plastic surgeon, but he can't yet afford the million-dollar membership fee for TMPT. Once in a blue moon, we're granted guest passes. I broke down and took Matt to our soirée last week. If he can't shut up about it, it will prove to be a lapse in judgement.

Some call it a sex club. Others a private club. In an earlier era, it was known as a gentleman's club. But progress begets evolution, and today women can join. Women have always attended, of course, but now they can become equity members. I recently recruited my good friend Amelia, and I believe membership changed her life.

Alfredo sauce drips down Matt's pale blue and baby pink diagonally striped tie.

"Do you know where Joel is?" I ask Matt the question at the precise moment his lips stretch around a mound of pasta.

Chatter from the hall leaks into the conference room. A blend of feminine and masculine intonations. Apprehension stirs.

Something's off.

When something feels off, it is. We can try to tell ourselves it's all in our head. But it's never all in our head. The wise listen to their gut.

A black plastic serving spoon hangs precariously over the side of the alfredo pasta bowl. Dressing drowns the never-ending salad, but chain restaurant cuisine doesn't explain my loss of appetite. I completed a one-hour morning run followed by a three-hour mommy make-over. I should be famished.

And I was.

But now I'm not. I push my untouched plate away. Is it the memories? Blue hydrangeas?

Jessica's call ends, and she approaches the Olive Garden spread.

Something's wrong.

"Jessica, how're your kids?"

Jessica blinks like she didn't hear me correctly. A fair response, given I don't think I've ever inquired about her children before.

"Why?"

"Just making conversation."

The way she looks at me you'd expect nasal hair sprouted from my nostrils.

"I have one child."

"Ah–"

"How's Molly?" Matt asks.

"Not great. She skipped school today. She's throwing her life away." She drops the plate, picks up a breadstick, and paces the floor.

"Everybody skips school at some point."

"Skipping one day doesn't mean Molly isn't going to get into college," Matt says to his alfredo.

Jessica chews on her thumb nail. I shift in my seat. Something's off, but I don't think my loss of appetite is due to Jessica's kid.

"Where did you say Joel is?" At this point, we're running fifteen minutes behind schedule. Fifteen minutes we can never reclaim.

"He's out in the hall. Talking to his niece," Matt answers. The pit of my stomach plummets.

"I'm going to go. I'm not letting her throw her life away." Jessica chomps on one last remaining piece of bread, picks up a napkin and wipes her fingers. "I have a consultation this afternoon. Can one of you cover for me?"

"What time?" Matt asks.

"Which niece?" I ask. Joel has two nieces. Possibly more. It's probably not her. She wouldn't want to see me.

"Thanks, Matt. You're a life saver."

Jessica swings the conference room door wide. Joel's back is to us. The lights glimmer over his thinning scalp and a shiny bald spot the shape of a yarmulke. The spring-loaded hinge closes the door behind her.

Instrumental elevator music flows through the room at a barely noticeable level. As always, the tune is familiar. I can't place the band's name, but my mind fills the missing refrain *never say never again.*

It can't be her. She wouldn't come back.

The paneled door swings open. Time slows.

Her presence sucks the oxygen from my lungs. A bright white light imbues my periphery. She hasn't aged. A classic profile; elegant nose; high cheekbones; angular chin; arresting, movie star violet eyes; wavy dark strands swept up in a clip, half up, half down.

I was never supposed to see her again for as long as I lived. *She promised.*

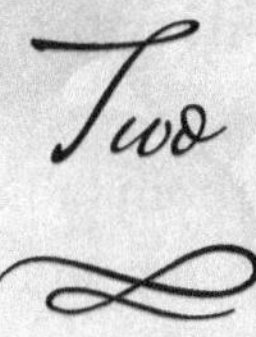

Two

ZURI

Speak. Move. Breathe.

"Harrison, you remember Zuri, right?" Uncle Joel's voice sounds foreign, distant.

Harrison's glare blends ice and fire. He stalks to the door. The conference room door slams behind him. The wall shakes.

Heat climbs my neck. I offer a timid smile I don't feel. The men in the room stare. At me.

His reaction is so much worse than I feared. So much worse than I dared to imagine.

Uncle Joel nudges me toward the table, as if everything is fine. As if his partner didn't just slam the door.

"You didn't tell him?" I ask under my breath.

I assumed Uncle Joel wouldn't bring me down here without giving him a heads up. I also assumed so much time had passed, it wouldn't matter.

My stomach twists. Uncle Joel's words flash by me. *Don't worry. They're gonna love you. A dermatologist on staff is a great idea.*

I questioned him. Did his plastic surgery practice need a dermatologist on staff? *Oh, yes. We've been looking. It's brilliant. A growth strategy. Win-win. An opportunity for us both.*

But I didn't ask about Harrison specifically. It felt a little too conceited to think he'd still have an issue with me. Ten years later. My cheeks and eyes burn, and my throat constricts. He hates me. Still.

Sitting at the conference room table is a man I recognize from Paragon's website. Dr. Sutton appears to be about my height, unfortunately for him, and his dark hair is both receding and thinning. He chows down the remaining food on his plate as if he's in a race to the finish line. Silence descends. I haven't eaten, but I feel like I need the Heimlich.

"He'll come around," Uncle Joel says, as cheery as ever. "Get a plate."

"Do you think maybe," I jerk my head back at Dr. Sutton, "say something to him?"

"Oh. Matt. I'm sorry. I got distracted by lunch. Starving." He rubs his free hand over his stomach. "Zuri here is my niece. You guys are going to love her. She's a dermatologist. She's going to help us with the med spa expansion, and once she gets her Texas medical license, join us."

"We're adding a dermatologist to the practice?" Dr. Narcisse pulls up a chair at the conference room table. He entered moments after Harrison stormed out. He's also featured on the Paragon site. His expansive dark eyes appear mildly interested. Under the lights, his mahogany skin bears a youthful, dewy glow. The man's background is exemplary, Cornell undergrad, Harvard Med School, and residency at Johns Hopkins.

"Sure are. We talked about it. Remember? And Zuri here is the best."

Dr. Narcisse taps the table with his index finger. "Adding a dermatologist was Phase Three in our expansion plans."

"Phase Two," Dr. Sutton corrects, then dips a breadstick into creamy white alfredo sauce.

"Well, this happened a little earlier than expected. It's all good. She's fantastic. You're going to love her."

Dr. Narcisse's jaw flexes, his gaze steady. He's sizing me up. And he's probably concluding that I must be a colossal fuck-up. At least, if I were in his shoes, that's what I'd surmise.

"Doctor…you are a doctor, right?"

"Yes," I answer as Uncle Joel says, "Tim, I just told you she's a dermatologist."

"I can get—"

"Where are you from?" Dr. Narcisse asks me.

"I went to Rice for undergrad, Berkley for med school, and I did residency at Mt. Sinai." My palms sweat and I wipe them on my dress slacks. "New York," I add, but that's unnecessary, because everyone knows Mt. Sinai is in New York.

His dark, studious eyes track the movement, and my armpits swelter. He's going to ask where I worked after Mt. Sinai. *Please don't.*

"She's great," Uncle Joel says as he pulls out a chair. "You're gonna love her. Smart as a whip."

I cringe at the phrase my grandfather loved.

Dr. Sutton stands and gathers his plate. "Joel, Jessica had a personal emergency."

"Everything okay?" Uncle Joel asks.

"Yeah, just something with her daughter. But why don't we reschedule status? I'm gonna go…" Dr. Sutton gestures to the door.

Dr. Narcisse stands, too. "I've got surgery in thirty. I'm going to prep." He doesn't smile or bother with a backward glance. The issue—me—is forgotten.

Dr. Sutton pauses at the garbage can. "Welcome, Zuri. If you don't like the beverage options in here, there's more in the break room."

"And a nice coffee machine. Top of the line," Uncle Joel says.

"And help yourself to anything in the refrigerator. If there's anything I can do, or you have questions about Houston, my office is just down the hall."

"Thank you, Dr. Sutton."

"Oh, call me Matt," he says, but he isn't looking my way.

The door closes behind him, and I let out a long, slow breath. "That did not go well."

"What?" Uncle Joel bites on the end of a pepperoncini, and juice drips onto his plate. "I thought it went great. These guys don't care about the med spa. That's all you're seeing."

"Uncle Joel," I wait for him to raise those rose-tinted glasses up to me and speak slowly so he can grasp the situation. "They cared. And Harrison clearly doesn't want me here."

"Pfft." He dismisses me with an odd noise and waddles over to the table. "He's reactive. Lets his emotions get the better of him. Give him time. He'll calm down."

No, I don't think Harrison will calm down. There was a time, over ten years ago, when I might have bought into that hope. But that was before he blocked me from his life.

"I'm going to have to talk to him." I say it as much to myself as to my uncle. With a plastic fork, I pick at the parmesan cheese dotting the romaine lettuce. My stomach roils uncomfortably. If this doesn't work out, I'm screwed. One flaming dumpster fire.

He raps the table with his knuckle. "Chin up, buttercup. He's gonna come around. They all are. Gina's gonna be so thrilled to have the help."

I lean back against the cabinet and cross my arms. "Uncle Joel…" I can't believe he hired me without talking to his partners. "Why didn't you tell them about me?"

"It's my practice. I founded it. They'll go along with what I want. And besides, seriously, they don't care about the med spa. They see it as a profit center. Now, eat up."

Upon my arrival thirty minutes ago, Uncle Joel took me on a whirlwind tour of his baby, Paragon Plastic Surgery. He birthed her decades ago, and he's nursed her into a sprawling practice with top-notch credentials. He's done the same with his surgical prowess. According to several polls, one or two that don't require payment for placement, he's one of the nation's top plastic surgeons. Harrison joined him on one such list last year.

In under an hour, I met a slew of office assistants and several surgical nurses. It didn't escape my notice that all the office assistants were beautiful and well-dressed. Knowing Uncle Joel, he sees them as branding.

"Which one was Gina?"

"Gina is the one…well, we walked by her desk, and she was on the phone. Dark hair, olive skin, red lipstick."

I vaguely remember her. "And the one we talked to outside of the conference room, Jennifer? What does she do, again?"

She'd been tactile with my uncle, touching him frequently as she talked, but she struck me as a good thirty years younger, so I don't think she meant anything by it. Texas is different than other states. People here are prone to touching and hugging.

"Jennifer is a surgical nurse. Fantastic at her job."

"Well, that's good to know." It could be my imagination, but Uncle Joel's cheeks appear slightly flushed. Broken capillaries crisscross the broad planes of his nose.

Mom used to say they should place Uncle Joel's photo on the Wikipedia page beneath the word philanderer. Of course, she said my dad's photo belonged under asshole. And my dad claims she's a world-class, psycho bitch.

"Don't look at me like that. This heart here," he pats his tie for effect, "belongs to the love of my life."

"You mean the latest love of your life?" Uncle Joel's been married five times.

"Who else would I mean?" He gives a slanted smirk.

My optimism remains submerged by doubt. "Are you sure about this?" He shoves a cherry tomato in his mouth, nods, and scrolls. "I won't be in your way?"

The plan is for me to live with Uncle Joel, in his house. Further evidence my life is solidly in the shitter, to use one of my lawyer's favorite descriptors.

"You'll be fine." He grins. "Besides, we mainly stay at Jolene's."

I arrived last night, after a multi-day drive from Minneapolis, and he greeted me with an ice-cold beer. Jolene didn't come over, but then again, I didn't stay up late.

Uncle Joel gets up to pour himself some more iced tea. "So, what did you think of Harrison?"

"I think we've established he's not happy I'm here." My stomach is a pitiful mess, guilt-stricken to the nth degree with a high coat of nausea. The Muzak running overhead is a familiar instrumental, but I'd prefer silence.

"No, not that. I mean, it's been a while since you've seen him, right?"

"What song is this?" I point upward, although I don't see any speakers.

Uncle Joel's eyes roll upwards thoughtfully. "James Taylor. *Fire and Rain*. Don't change the subject." There's a drip of creamy white alfredo sauce on the table, and I wipe it away with a napkin. "Did he look the same? Different?"

He's so different. Completely different. The Harrison Ramsey I loved was a gawky, nerdy mess, most commonly in movie-themed T-shirts and stained jeans or worn-down, cut-off khakis. The one I studied on the Paragon website bore a resemblance to a GQ model. Perfectly coifed black hair, chemically bleached teeth, and an expensive custom suit with classic detailing.

And in person…I tremble slightly, remembering the ferocity in those enigmatic eyes. I spent hours staring into those gray eyes that once were kind and warm. Today, ice filled those orbs. No, not ice. Hatred. Years have passed, but some things remain the same.

Three

HARRISON

My fingers tremble. My heart palpitates. The only thing that's working correctly are my lungs, which are sucking in air like I've just run a goddamn marathon. *Jesus.*

I charge into my office like a seismic shift occurred and it's the only safe ground. My diplomas hang on the wall to the side of my desk, mocking me. Behind my desk is a black-and-white portrait of a model I fucked.

When I close my eyelids, Joel, as a circus master, materializes with a wide smile and brilliant white teeth. And then I see her.

Get a grip.

A glass wall and a black wooden door separate my professional space from the colorless hallway. I hit a button, and the glass smokes. Frivolous tech, but it was Joel's money. *Fucking Joel.*

What is she doing here? Passing through?

I spin my desk chair and stare up at the model. My gaze falls to the point of her nipple. The photograph is post-breast lift combined with a light liposuction treatment. She sent me the framed art in gratitude. Thanks to the full moon behind her, creating her silhouette, you can't identify her. She's anatomical perfection as defined by modern times.

What a truly phenomenal surgical result.

I rest my head on the back of the chair and close my eyes. Attempt to block visuals. Focus on my breathing. Find my center.

Knock. Knock.

"Hey, there, Ramser."

"Didn't say you could come in." I spin the chair around. Sutton the Glutton lowers himself into my guest chair. The white vinyl squeaks.

"Given you ran out of our status like a burning man, someone needed to come check on you."

"You drew the short straw?"

"Tim has surgery. Jessica left. Joel is eating lunch with his niece." He taps the silver armrest, leaving buttery smudges on the polished chrome. "Normally, it's the women who get flustered around you. Never seen you react." I glare at the fucker. "Where'd you meet Joel's niece?"

I recline my chair and perch my head between my index finger and thumb. If I glare at him long enough while in this pose, in all likelihood his balls will shrivel, he'll cower, and either shut the fuck up or leave.

"Not the club, right?"

Does he really think I'd get worked up over someone I met at the club? That's the entire point of the club. I let out a loud exhale of frustration. "You're not going to leave, are you?"

"Nope." He pokes out his lower lip and lets his hands rest on his flabby middle. A streak of white cream sauce dots his tie. "If you need to rally us together to vote against her joining, fine."

"She's not even a surgeon…" Wait. There's no way. "Is she?"

"If you'd stayed, instead of tearing off like John Wick after his dog died, you would've learned that his niece is a dermatologist."

"And?" My brain's on strike. I need him to lay it out for me.

"He wants her to run the med spa."

Unfuckingbelievable.

"Bringing on a dermatologist was Phase Two. This is slightly ahead of schedule," Matt says, all the while sitting poised like a therapist. Shrink Matt.

"It's nepotism. Why is she here? Where'd she work before?"

Shrink Matt burps. A less than smooth move for a therapist. He shrugs, lifts his hand, and examines his manicure. "Why don't you ask her?"

I spin the chair to face the work of art.

"What'd she do to you?" Shrink Matt asks my back.

"I disagree with moving the schedule up. Is Joel putting any of this to a vote?"

"He can't bring her on as a partner unless we all agree. It's in the partnership agreement."

I spin the chair around. Shrink Matt has a point. I should've thought of that. Joel sold out. We have rights.

"Is she your ex-wife or something?"

I pinch the bridge of my nose, close my eyes, and exhale. "Marriage is relative."

"What does that mean?"

"Not absolute." Arms on the chair rests, eyes narrowed, I explain. "Can have a different meaning to different people."

"I get that…" He cocks his head to the side. "So, she's an ex?"

"We lived together." Matt's hairline is receding. He could use some plugs. And cool sculpting. "A long time ago."

Knock. Knock.

Mena pushes the door open with the side of her body. Her arms are loaded down with something that's wrapped in clear cellophane and a silver glittery bow.

"Delivery," she says cheerily. "Pies. From one of your fans."

"Pies?" Matt whines. "No one sends me food."

"Well, no offense, Dr. Sutton," Mena says to Matt, "but I think they want to thank Dr. Ramsey in a different kind of way."

Matt turns to me with exasperation, and I hold my hands up. "I swear, I'm not sleeping with my patients." He gives me a look that says he doesn't buy it. And maybe he's looking at the framed portrait behind my head. "It only happens when I meet them before they're my patient or a long time after they're my patient."

Mena's hands fall to her hips. She's wearing a tight skirt that flatters her assets, high heels, and dark red lipstick that contrasts well with her olive complexion. It's a good look.

"I call them the romantics," she says to Matt as if I'm not in the room.

"Mena, we were in the middle of a meeting," I tell her, hoping she'll leave.

"The romantics?" Matt asks, completely ignoring me.

"Yeah, it's like his little fan club. They seem to think if they fawn over him enough, he'll ask them out on a date. Or, if he takes a bite of their cherry…" Mena pauses for effect, "pie, he'll leave his playboy ways behind. At least, that's our theory."

"That's enough, Mena." I gesture to the door. "And next time, if those windows are frosted, please don't enter until I say it's okay. Patients disrobe in here during consultations."

"I saw Matt come in."

"Mena," I snap my fingers and point to the door.

"Are you guys done with lunch? Can we go in and eat the leftovers?"

"Sure," Matt says.

"You can take the pies," I say. I'm not sure how she knows they're pies, as it's a stack of pale pink boxes, but I don't eat bakery goods, so it doesn't matter what's inside.

"Really? Oh, thank you."

"Like you didn't know I'd give them to you."

She smiles and bats her long eyelash extensions. "Oh, don't you want the card?" I shake my head in the negative, and she gives me a mom look. "So you know who to thank?"

"Fine. Give it here."

She sets a small black envelope on my desk.

When the door clicks closed, I set my gaze on Matt. Of all the partners, he's my closest friend.

"How long ago did you guys break up?" Matt probes.

That's not important. I point my finger at his nose, which, now that I'm looking closer, needs a good wax. "You've got to work with me on this. Do not make her feel at home. I don't want her staying. Joel probably thinks she'll win us all over." Everyone likes Zuri. If it comes down to a vote, I don't want to be the single vote blocking her. That'll make me look like an ass. "This will be hard for you, but do not be her friend. Do you hear me? Do. Not. Pull. A. Matt. Understand?"

"When did I become a verb?"

I blink him down.

"What?"

"It's in your nature to be friendly." *Too fucking friendly.* "But in this case, you're my friend. Not hers." And yes, I sound like a middle school boy, but survival trumps maturity.

"When did you guys break up?"

The light on my phone blinks. I check the time and press the intercom button.

"Yes, Mena?"

"Your one o'clock is here. She's a little early. Just wanted to let you know. And by the way, one of these isn't a pie. It's a Mississippi mud cake, and oh, my god, is it to die for."

I click to end the call.

"I can't believe women send you food. It's clear you don't eat." He holds an arm up at me as if I am evidence.

"You get out of your body what you put into it."

Why is she down here? Where did she end up? Does she even have a Texas medical license? What the fuck is going on?

Matt gets up and smooths his tie.

"You got food on it."

He glances down. "Shit." He steps to the door as he licks a

thumb and dabs his tie.

"Don't be nice to her, Matt."

"How could I forget? I'm a verb. Being a decent human being is now a verb."

"Please don't clean your tie with your thumb in front of me."

He pauses at the door. "What's wrong with that?"

"It's gross." That really should not need explaining.

"Anything else you'd like me to do?"

I exhale, giving his wrinkled slacks a once over. "The list is too extensive. Just don't be nice."

"Got it. Be mean."

"No." I grab the doorknob and wait until he looks me in the eye. "That won't work. You don't know how. Just don't speak to her. The silent treatment. You can do that. Silence." It'll make her feel uncomfortable. "You think Tim will play along?"

"He's a prick. He'll be an ass without you having to call in a favor."

That's an accurate assessment. "And Jessica—"

"Is going to bond with the only other female. You're screwed there."

"But Gina will be a bitch."

"She'll have your back."

A woman and her husband, both approximately mid-sixties, glance up from their magazines. Her glance is one of recognition, and she hastily sets the magazine down and picks up her black patent Louis Vuitton.

"Mrs. Fitzgerald?"

"Yes, that's me."

She and her husband both struggle to stand, and I point at Matt as he walks away, wanting to send one parting reinforcing request, but his attention is back on his tie.

I'll figure this out. Maybe all I need is to confront Zuri. If I lay it all out there, maybe she'll leave. Or she'll tell me I'm being child-ish. Even though she's the one who violated our agreement by coming here. With the right approach, I'll convince her to leave. She promised me. I'll leverage the broken promise angle if forced.

I sit down on the loveseat across from the matched pair of chairs opposite my coffee table and stretch my lips into a cordial smile.

Mr. Fitzgerald sits uncomfortably beside his wife. There's a good twelve inches between their thighs. His gaze falls to the ground. He bears the look of a cornered man. Mrs. Fitzgerald looks at me through Christian Dior glasses with a gold chain that dangles. The diamonds on her manicured, wrinkled hands sparkle. She could use an eye lift, really, an overall facelift, and some time in the gym. Her silk blouse is too loose for an accurate assessment, but given the downward slope of her breasts, she could probably benefit from a breast lift.

"That's a beautiful blouse. The color flatters your complexion."

She smiles and leans forward as she spreads her fingers across her throat.

I link my fingers and lean forward to better listen.

"Thank you." She glances at her husband, but his gaze is on the portrait behind my desk.

"Now, Mrs. Fitzgerald, how can I help you today?"

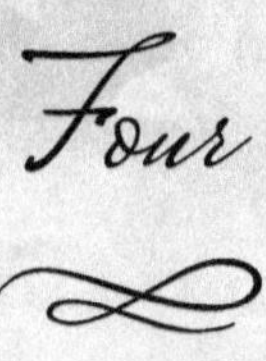

Four

ZURI

A lifeline. For some, it's a rope tossed out in rough seas, for others, it's a phone call in a trivia game. For me, it's my jolly uncle and his recently re-invented plastic surgery center. Maybe if I explain to Harrison, he'll understand.

My savior, my one phone call from the Hennepin County jail, strides across the lobby floor in his clickety-clackety dress shoes, smiling as brightly as his navy and pink polka-dot tie, gesturing for me to follow him. He beams like it's a brand-new day. No issues here, folks.

A woman in khaki dress pants, a matching silk blouse, and gleaming gold, easily five-inch heels, approaches. She looks past my uncle, to me. Her gaze glides down my suit and snaps back to the general vicinity of my face.

"Gina, this is my niece I was telling you all about."

I offer a polite, first-day-on-the-job smile. She returns a restrained, my-boss-is-beside-me smile.

"Zuri is my little genius. She's one of the best dermatologists in the country. Did I tell you?"

"Yes, you mentioned it once or twice." There's a coldness to those brown eyes with long, curled eyelashes. The bun her black hair is pulled tightly back into accentuates her no-nonsense, you-are-wasting-my-time demeanor. Given the Houston humidity, it's a look I should probably mimic to avoid having corkscrews attached to my head by the end of the day. Or worse, a mushroom. I pat my head, evaluating shroom status. "You sound like a proud uncle."

"Well, I am." Uncle Joel beams. "She's a coup. Lured her down to Texas, the place she always swore she'd never live."

As Uncle Joel trumpets what he perceives as my successes, I struggle to relax my facial muscles. Plenty of thirty-somethings struggle under a mound of debt that screams for bankruptcy protection.

And as a member of the desperation cohort, I must win over Gina and all of my uncle's partners. Less than two hours in, winning over his partners feels about as realistic as qualifying for the Tour de France.

Gina, Uncle Joel, and I stand awkwardly in the center of the marble lobby, beneath a sparkling chandelier monstrosity.

Persuasion begins with graciousness. "Gina, I read about you on Paragon's website. You're the Master Injector and Laser specialist, right?"

"I'm the director of the medical spa." She crosses her arms over her midsection. Her breasts rise beneath the V of her blouse. Everything about her, from the spread of her legs to her pushed back shoulder pads, says *I-am-the-queen. I will expel you from my domain, you pea-sized crumpet.*

"Well, I'm looking forward to working with you. The expansion plans are exciting. I love the ideas so far." The inner critic cringes. My professional kiss-ass persona needs work.

"We should be breaking ground soon. Unless, of course, you

make changes. That could put us behind schedule." Her smooth forehead might as well bear a neon flashing sign that reads *do-not-fuck-with-me-or-my-plans. This is my baby.*

"Well, I'm sure—"

"We created our plans without a certified dermatologist on board. If improvements slow us down, so be it. It'll all get done in good time." Uncle Joel's twang comes across as native Texan, but really, he's Long Island through and through. Her glare won't so much as exfoliate his tough, oblivious skin.

My uncle guides us through the lobby and down a brightly lit hallway with twelve-foot ceilings and ten-foot doors. He chatters away to Gina about plans and my role, which is a consultancy role, but listening to him you'd think partner is a done deal. I trail the two of them, taking in the black and white abstract framed art on the walls and the spotless interior.

Troublesome nausea swirls. It's first-day job jitters augmented by near financial catastrophe. Plus, somewhere behind one of these massive interior doors, is my ex. My ex who hates me. Coming here was a bad idea.

Dr. Harrison Ramsey's headshot is predominantly displayed on multiple pages of the Paragon website. Time has transformed him into Mr. GQ. In his headshot, he's sexiest man alive material, with piercing gray eyes and a chiseled jaw. In person, he's hotter. The man is a powerhouse with broad shoulders, towering height, and stormy, elusive, brooding eyes. Successful, driven, confident.

Back when we lived together, I never doubted the slightly nerdy, lovable goof's future success. But I never expected my life would spiral downward while his shot up.

A dozen years after our breakup, and I'm a hot mess, with all the emphasis on "mess" and "hot" as an amplifier, not a descriptor. He's a partner in a prestigious group, virtually right out of residency. I'm unemployed and technically unemployable, leaning on an uncle to sidestep homelessness.

Harrison won't buy my doting uncle's line about me being the best dermatologist in the country. He's too intelligent. Only a desperate doctor would accept a consulting position out-of-state. True, doctors can and do move around. You can get certified in other states. But if Harrison remembers anything about me, he'll see right through a move to Texas as last-resort desperation.

"And this, honey, you're going to want to pay attention to this." We've stopped in an office kitchen. There's a small black device with a listing of coffee types. "You can select your favorite coffee, cappuccino, latte, whatever you want, push the button, and...magic."

Uncle Joel presses a button, and whirring noises sound from within the machine. Free fancy coffee. Undeniably, a nice perk.

Gina stands at my side. In her heels, the top of my head reaches her collarbone.

Uncle Joel turns, his amenable smile ever-present. "Here you go. Try it," he says, completely disregarding Gina's frown.

He passes me a jet-black coffee mug with the Paragon logo emblazoned on the side in shimmery silver. I raise it to offer the first coffee to Gina, at the same time her arm unlatches from her side.

Her forearm hits the coffee mug and, much like my life, the mug spirals downward, crashing on Gina's pointed gold shoe. Which, looking closer, might be a Manolo Blahnik.

"Oh, my god. I'm so sorry."

Dark brown splotches spot from her thigh down to her drenched foot.

There's a stack of napkins by the coffee machine, and I snatch a handful.

She plucks them out of my hand and dabs away at her thigh. "Dammit, that hurt."

"I'm so sorry," I repeat, attempting to dab her as she swats my hands away.

"You okay there, Gina?" Uncle Joel asks.

Fire blazes from her eyes.

It's official. I'm a walking disaster.

"Fine," she snips, gazing down at her ruined outfit.

"I'm so sorry."

She holds her hand out in a get-the-fuck-away-from-me gesture, and mortification swallows me whole.

"You know, I've got a consult shortly. Let me finish showing you around," Uncle Joel says brightly, like I didn't dump hot coffee on a living, breathing human being who is seething before us. "Follow me."

"I'm so sorry," I repeat before obediently following my uncle down another hall. Gina stands there, frozen, like she can't believe what happened.

Me too, Gina. Me too.

Uncle Joel stops in front of two double doors with smoke colored glass. "Allie, come meet my niece. Zuri Lennox."

A woman in teal scrubs and light gray Crocs stops and extends a hand and a genuine smile. "Nice to meet you. Are you in town visiting?"

"Oh…" I glance at Uncle Joel. "I'm here—"

"She's coming on board. At first as a consultant, but eventually she'll join us." He winks.

"You're a plastic surgeon?" Allie looks at me with renewed interest. Her brown eyes are warm and…friendly.

"No, I'm a dermatologist. From Minnesota, actually. I'm here to help with the expansion of the med spa. Eventually I'll go back to…" The words that should come out scrape the raw wound. I'm not sure at all if I'll go back. I'm board certified in Minnesota, but I did a lot worse than spill coffee back home.

"Well, welcome aboard." She smiles wide and shifts to the exit. "I'm off to get lunch." She pauses and directs a question to my uncle. "You want anything?"

"No, we had lunch during the status meeting."

"That's right. The bigwigs get lunch." Her smile softens the bite of her words. She waves her fingers in my direction. "Welcome aboard, Zuri."

"What does she do?" I ask as she speeds through the lobby doors into the asphalt parking lot.

"Oh, she's one of our surgical nurses. Good at what she does." He taps my arm. "Want to go see Harrison?"

"Seriously?" Thanks to the coffee catastrophe, my insides are in quiver mode.

"You think he needs time?"

I'm not sure if there will ever be a good time to approach Harrison, but quiver mode isn't the right time. Uncle Joel reads me.

"I know. Let's go find Jessica. She's gonna love you."

There's a rap against the wall, and I glance up from the computer. I'm reading about laser machine leasing agreement options.

The friendly nurse with warm brown eyes from earlier today, the one who wore teal scrubs, stands in the doorway. Only she's wearing a knee-length floral skirt, a T-shirt, and flip-flops.

"Allie, right?"

"Yep. How was your first day?"

The last three hours passed as quickly as three months. Jessica did not, in fact, love me. Uncle Joel said, "Jessica, I'd like you to meet Zuri." She looked me over, stuck her hand out, and said, "Dr. Chandler," meaning I'd better call her Dr. Chandler, and promptly closed the door in my face.

Gina went home early on account of her stained clothes, leaving me to flounder through folders, attempting to figure out how I can contribute to an expansion that's already underway.

In the history of shitty first days, this one is record-breaking. I swallow and push on a smile that's comparable to Allie's. "Great."

"Bullshit." She grins and rocks back on her heels. "I heard you spilled coffee on Gina. Wish I'd seen that."

"No, you really don't."

"She'll come around."

The fury in those dark eyes comes to mind. Not to mention, I'm stepping all over her toes in this role Uncle Joel concocted. "No, she won't."

"Meh." One corner of Allie's lips rises, and she waves her hand dismissively. "She's got no choice." She adjusts the strap on her backpack. "You look like you could use a drink. There's a place we walk to, right around the corner. Mena and I are heading there now. Want to join?"

"Really?" Alcohol is exactly what I need. "I'd love to."

Allie and Mena do most of the talking on the short walk to the bar. Music flows out the door, welcoming us. I brace for country, which isn't my favorite, but relax when I recognize the band. Soundgarden. I can work with that.

It's not until we're sliding into a booth that Mena asks, "So, what's your story?"

"Ah...I..."

"We don't mean to put you on the spot," Allie gushes, kind as ever.

"The heck we don't," Mena says. "Did you move down here for Dr. Ramsey?"

"What?" Mena's smile reminds me of a sorority girl. Bright, hopeful, conceivably void of deep thought. "Why would you say that?"

"Just something Dr. Lennox said. That, and I noticed you both went to Rice in undergrad."

"How—"

"Dr. Lennox had me update your information on the website."

"But I'm a consultant." Bulldozing me into the firm will not win friends.

"It's an additional doctor on staff." She shrugs like it's no big deal. I suppose it isn't. But I'm not licensed in Texas, so I'm not even sure it's legal. "So, did you follow him down here?"

"Noooo." The pad of my thumb cuts a path through the condensation on the side of my glass. "We haven't seen each other since undergrad. Haven't spoken in a dozen years. Not sure what Uncle Joel said, but…" Exhaustion washes over me with the effectiveness of Valium. I'm tired. So tired of fighting. Of being alone. I need friends. So I take a long swallow of cheap, frosty Sauvignon Blanc and admit, "My arrival here has nothing to do with Harrison."

Allie and Mena look at me expectantly. With eagerness.

"At my old practice, I dated a partner. Things went badly." It's the understatement of a lifetime.

"Oh, shit," Mena says.

That's an apt deep thought. "You can say that again. It got ugly. Let's just say I won't be getting a good job reference."

My lawyer says if Warren wins in court, my downward spiral might continue. The medical board could request a review, which would be problematic for my pursuit of a Texas medical license. Another element of proof that my life is one gigantic cluster fuck.

"I see," Allie says cheerfully.

I don't get the cheer. The cheap wine is overly sweet, but I swallow it down in gulps.

"You've probably got a ton of student loans," Allie correctly surmises.

"Over half a million." With each slow nod, my anxiety rises.

"Jesus," Allie says. "That's why I'm a nurse and not a doctor. And I've got a pile of loans myself, but not that high."

"Yeah." My gaze falls to my wine glass and my insides sink into the sticky vinyl booth seat. So many bad decisions.

"Well, thank goodness you didn't move here for Dr. Ramsey," Mena says.

"Mena, would you shush? You don't know a thing."

"Oh, yes, I do," she sing-songs.

"Do not," Allie argues.

"Women love him." Mena places a dramatic emphasis on the word love, and I have to say, I'm not at all surprised. "But I don't think any of those women would be as interested if they knew his kinks."

"Mena. Shush." Allie raises her voice. Eyes wide.

"I'm in the office, remember?" Mena says to Allie. "I saw the paperwork. He's a member of TMPT. Actually, so is your uncle." She taps my hand and lifts her beer, like she's explained all.

"What's tempt?" She's not making any sense. *Kinks?*

"It's spelled T-M-P-T." She leans forward and whispers, "A sex club."

"What?" I try to imagine Harrison in his faded black Matrix T-shirt entering a sex club. "Like with whips and chains?"

"That, I don't know. But it's pricey." She rubs her thumb and index finger repeatedly. "People say they have giant orgies."

Allie lets out a sigh. "Mena, you're spreading rumors. There's also a bar there. It's a networking thing. And neither of us," she looks to Mena, "have ever been inside. No one we know has."

"Well, I knew Harrison a long time ago." I'm hit with a flurry of sensations, not so much the visuals, but long forgotten memories of how we used to be. The friendship. Our connection. But we were different people then.

"Even if he's not in a sex club, he's a total manwhore. You wouldn't believe the number of women who call to check to see when he's expected out of surgery because they know he can't answer his cell when he's in surgery." She sets her drink down and leans forward like she's eager to spill all the tea. "There's something about him. He makes women desperate."

Her words deliver an onset of dizziness. "Really?"

"Yes. I call them the romantics," Mena says, beaming at her clever nomenclature. "You do not want to be one of them."

"Mena...we brought her out to let her day end on a good note. Let's talk about something other than her college ex."

"It's okay." I say with a deep, stabilizing breath. "It was a lifetime ago." People change. He's a different person now. So am I. With a swallow of my wine for fortitude, I push forward. "So, why the romantics?"

"Oh, because they never give up. Every single one of them believes they're going to be the one who changes him. The one with the magic pussy that turns the beast into a prince."

"The beast? Is he a jerk to them?" That's not who the old Harrison was at all. But if present-day Harrison is a jerk, maybe what happened this morning doesn't have as much to do with our past as I assumed. Which would be a shame, because while Harrison has always been attractive, his heart, his love…those were full of beauty.

"I don't really see him interact with them. I only get the phone calls. Because he doesn't seem to ever call them. Which is why, in their desperation, they end up calling me. The receptionist. Where he works. The man has zero social media presence, so I'm literally the last tangible contact point." She sips her wine and then holds the stem of the glass daintily between two fingers. "They never give up. Always so hopeful. For months, they drop off baked goods and leave messages. Sometimes flowers. Plants, even. That's why I call them the romantics."

"He might call them back. You don't know," Allie chides.

"Oh, I know. I'm friends with a couple of them now. The ones who moved on to dating other people. Saturday night, I'm going on a blind date one of them set me up on."

Allie swirls the liquid in her glass thoughtfully. "I guess we've all got a little romantic in us, right? Otherwise, why get up in the morning?"

"What about you?" I ask Allie. "Are you dating anyone?"

"Allie here is living with the love of her life."

Allie side-eyes her. "I wouldn't call him that."

"Since when?" Mena seems genuinely affronted. But thank the

gods the conversation is no longer on me, or Harrison and his sextourage.

"I don't know. Maybe he is, and I just don't know it yet." She looks directly at me, but it's like she's seeing through me. "Things are good. For now. But I believe in evolution. And that means you don't get stuck in the past. Some of the best things might be in the future. A product of the past, sure. But the future is better thanks to the past."

"Are you going to break up with Milo?" Mena asks, head slanted and eyes bulging with disbelief.

"His name is Milo?"

Allie pulls out her phone and shows me a photo of her and a blond guy with thinning hair and spectacles. "Milo Javonovich."

"He's cute."

"He's a professor. English lit."

"Oh, even better," I say.

Mena reaches out to touch Allie's arm. "Tell her how you guys met." She wrinkles her nose and grins as she adds, "It's the best story."

I feign listening, but inside my head, my thoughts circle to Harrison and this rumored sex club. Talk about life details absent from my thirty-something bingo card.

Five

HARRISON

When I pony up to the bar at Jack's, my intention is to forget. More accurately, to forget one particular person.

Drinking in pursuit of amnesia is a dumbass move. One I will most definitely regret in the morning. When Gray slides the bourbon across the bar, I gaze at the gilded substance as if it's a lagoon, and I'm on a cliff towering above at a life-threatening height. Should I dive?

To escape…what? I'm not in pain. No, the visceral pain dissipated years ago. I'm thrown. Discombobulated. Confused. Flustered. Offended. Pissed.

Tomorrow morning, I'm performing extensive facial reconstruction on an automobile accident victim. For months, Jared's surgeries were of the emergency variety, saving his life. The guy is one unlucky bastard. When I met him, his teeth were wired together and plaster casts covered him. He was a living, breathing cartoon caricature of an injured person. Jared the unlucky doesn't

29

need a surgeon who got blitzed the night before over a girl from a decade ago.

The amber liquid swirls in waves against the glass. I close my eyes and hear her honeyed southern lilt as if it happened hours ago.

Ending things is for the best. It's the best for both of us.

She broke up with me by phone. We lived together, and she called me. I suppose I should be thankful it wasn't via text. Text is her go-to for controversy, and she at least phoned. So, there's that.

A hand clasps my shoulder, jarring the glass in my hand.

"Watch it," I warn as Sutton asks, "Whatchu drinking?"

"What're you doing here?"

"Amelia texted. She's stuck at work. Wanted me to check on you."

"Why?" My glass clinks against the bar when I set it down. The liquid sloshes close to the edge but doesn't surpass the rim.

"Your text worried her, I guess?"

I pinch the bridge of my nose and try to recall the text I sent to my gal pal. I'm pretty sure it just said to meet me for drinks.

"Hey, Gray, I'll have whatever he's drinking." Sutton reaches over, touching me again, and I shrug him away. "All right, man. Let's hear it. What's the story?"

"Already told you. There's no story." I lift the glass and sip. The bourbon soothes my tongue and the back of my throat.

"Well, let's see. You didn't meet her at this club of yours. In fact, she's pre-club. And seeing her has you cutting out early from the office and sitting at a bar. How many of these has he had?"

"Just the one," Gray answers as he slides a matching glass to Sutton.

"Thanks, man. Can I get the dessert menu?"

"There's no real…" Gray begins, flustered, probably because we come here all the time and it's a bar. "We've got a cheesecake and a chocolate cake."

"I'll take the cheesecake," Sutton says.

I squint at the Glutton.

"What?" he asks.

I position myself to face the bar because the guy just packed on thousands of calories in creamy alfredo at lunch and is about to have a pre-dinner snack of cheesecake, and tomorrow morning he'll be complaining to me about his slowing metabolism that must be responsible for his mysteriously expanding waistline.

"I like to eat dessert first."

"I didn't say anything."

"Could hear you just the same."

The funny thing is, I get that. I've spent enough time with Sutton that I don't doubt he can interpret my expressions. "Did Amelia say what time she'll get here? Or is she not coming?"

Since meeting a guy at our club a few months ago, Amelia's become as reliable as rain. I'm happy for her, but at the same time, I'm looking forward to when things end with them. It'll be good to have my drinking buddy back.

"She's gonna make it. But before she does, can we talk about this thing with Joel's niece?"

"What is there to say?" I forced her into the farthest recesses of memory years ago.

"Well, if we're going to go to Joel and ask that he not hire her, don't you think we need a solid reason?"

"First, the history doesn't matter. Second, the fucker is aware. If he'd honestly thought what he was doing was okay by bringing her in, he'd have told me beforehand. I'm a partner. You're a partner, too. Joel is new to having partners, and he clearly doesn't get that he can't run Paragon like he's a one-man show. We both need to go in there and insist she leave."

"Ah, I'm not so sure that's true."

"It's in the by-laws."

"That's for bringing on a partner. Not a consultant."

Dammit. Sutton's probably correct. I swirl the bourbon and ask Gray for a glass of water.

"It's been a long time since you dated her, right?"

"Lived together." The distinction might be negligible to some, but to me, it meant we envisioned a future. Back when I was naïve.

"You're still messed up over her?"

"No. I am not *still messed up over her.*" I spit his venomous bullshit words back at him. "Besides, she looks totally different." Lie. "Didn't she look old to you?" I pointedly stare at my drink. "Wrinkles." I point at my eyes. "Around the eyes. Loose skin around the jowls." Lies. "I didn't bother to look closely, but I'm sure she's gained weight." Lie.

Zuri's more Type A than I am. Like me, she's probably healthier now than she was back then. But I didn't have time for a close examination. I'd been too shocked to look at anything other than her face, the violet irises, and then everything blurred.

"Well, I mean, yeah, she wasn't what I would consider your type."

"Exactly." She's not at all like the women I typically fuck. The women I go for are tall, with sleek, glossy, straight hair, brown eyes. Daring, provocative women. Zuri's not my type at all. "But I still don't want her at Paragon."

"Right." Gray delivers a slice of cheesecake to Sutton, and he stabs it with a fork. "Well, if you don't want her working with us, we shouldn't hire her. Nepotism be damned."

"Right. That's the angle." I snap my fingers. That's a good strategy. "We should move to ban nepotistic hires. That might even be in the by-laws, but if it's not, we can move to add it. Dr. Harvard probably won't read the changes. He'll just pass it by his lawyer, and any good lawyer will approve. Probably the same for Jessica." I clink my glass against Sutton's sitting one. "That's the plan. That's the angle we'll take."

"We can try it," he mumbles, his mouth full of high-fat, high-calorie cheesecake. He swallows it down with bourbon, which I imagine doesn't blend well. My stomach twists at the thought of such rich, sugar-laden food. "I'll back you. Worth a try. We'll do anything you want. Just evaluate the consequences and make your choice. That's our motto, right? And I don't see a downfall to this plan. Do you? I mean, it's a change to the by-laws. Might appear a little shady if we tried to change the by-laws without a verbal discussion."

I push up from the bar, wanting to get away from Sutton's droning. Amelia should've never called him. I really just need to sit and absorb and be. I'd be fine if I hadn't been sideswiped. *Fucking Joel.*

On the way through to the restroom, my gaze drifts to the wall of booths. Allie, Mena, and, fuck me, Zuri are clustered together in the same booth we occupy when we come here as a group. One day and she's found a tribe. The trio remains lost in conversation.

Blonde highlights twist in curls along her shoulders, but her roots are dark and natural. Her body shape is unidentifiable in her bland, conservative pantsuit.

I continue to the restroom.

When she ended our relationship, I asked for one thing. A survival thing. A critical request. To never see or hear from her again. Why the hell is she here? The last time Joel mentioned her, he said she lived in Minnesota.

It's nonsensical. And yes, it feels like an attack. Cognitively, I recognize Zuri isn't attacking me. She assumes we meant nothing. That enough time has passed that she can overlook my request. She didn't care about me, so she assumes the reverse is true.

As I dry my hands, I check my reflection. I don't look a damn thing like I did a decade ago. Thanks to personal trainers, private chefs, a nutritionist, and a personal shopper, I have improved. Women love me. So why the hell am I letting myself get discombobulated over a girl from college? A girl who lived in oversized sweatshirts and short shorts.

I toss a napkin in the trash and swing the door open, only to come face to face with my past.

Startled violet eyes blink up at me. My chest quakes. *Jesus.* I had one simple request. Anger surges. "I'm fighting this. You're not staying."

You promised me. I bite the whiney thought back. Even though it's fucking true.

Her small, pale hands ball into fists at her side. Defiant, she thrusts her slim shoulders back, and her angular jaw, the cherry on the top of a textbook sweetheart facial shape, juts out.

I expect her to throw a verbal punch, one that knocks me down. A sick part of me eagerly awaits whatever she's going to launch my way. She's cut me before. Let her slice me again.

"I need this job."

Candor. Not at all expected. I focus on her fists, because my quivering insides can't bear to look anywhere else on the slight pixie.

"Fifty states. Pick another one."

"You can't be serious? Harrison, come on. It was—"

I leave her. We're not having this discussion. She's going to tell me it was years ago, and I should be over it and she's over it and I don't want to hear it from her callous, hard-hearted lips.

I am over it, dammit. Doesn't mean I'm going to cave on our agreement.

Amelia's standing at the bar with Sutton.

Thank god, Amelia's here.

Amelia's eyes are full of worry as she glances between me and Zuri, who I assume must be standing nearby based on Amelia's expression and the way my skin prickles.

I knock back my drink in one long swallow and slam the glass down on the bar.

"You okay?" Amelia's question is soft, meant to be between the two of us. Maybe Zuri walked away, maybe she didn't.

"Come on." I look to Sutton and Amelia. "Let's get out of here. Up for the club?"

ZURI

My head throbs.
A revolting soundtrack plays through my head.

Yes. Right there.

Ohhhhhh.

That's it.

Ahhhhhh.

Oh, yes! Yes!

. . .

Oh. Oh. Oh. Oh. Oh.

Stop it. All I want is to crawl back into bed, pull the covers over my head, and go back to sleep. But, in the wise words of Mindy Kaling, "Sometimes you just have to put on lip gloss and pretend to be psyched."

So here I am, second day on the job, slightly hungover, a few strands of hair stuck in my lip gloss, entering the shiny glass doors of Paragon Plastic Surgery and wishing for music streaming EarPods to drown out the nightmare of last night. Mena smiles from behind reception, flashing a set of perfectly straight pearly whites. "How're you feeling, sweetie?"

Did she sound that southern yesterday? Thinking back to the booth, and our cocktails, yes, by our third drink, we were all rocking a southern drawl.

"Feeling great." My cheek muscles strain from my Kaling-inspired smile. "Is Unc—I mean, Dr. Lennox in?"

This morning, things were quiet in the house. Either he's already in the office, or he's back at the house catching up on the sleep he didn't get last night. I need to give him a heads up about Harrison's plans to block my being hired.

Truthfully, I'm not angling for partnership. Paragon isn't my first choice. But I need an income. Student loans and legal fees must be paid. If the medical gig doesn't work out, maybe I can con Gray into giving me a chance behind the bar. Last night, he mentioned he's short-staffed.

"He's in surgery." She glances at her computer screen. "It's both him and Dr. Ramsey. They've got the OR reserved for eight hours. Must be something extensive. They do most procedures here." Well, so much for giving my uncle a heads up. "But, ah, Gina was looking for you."

"Oh, really? Which way is she again?"

Mena gives me directions to her office, and I find my way through the hallway maze. She's not in her office. There's a Starbucks cup with a lipstick stain on her desk, and a briefcase rests on the floor on the side of the desk.

I trudge to the kitchen for the free coffee. Uncle Joel has a Keurig at home, and lots of interesting pods, but no milk. Today after work, instead of going to a bar, I'll visit a grocery store.

In the work kitchen, I swing open the refrigerator door. There's a black bowl with a lid and a yellow post-it with the name Tim written neatly in architect-style print. One shelf is filled with Diet Coke cans. But thank the gods, the door shelves hold both dairy and non-dairy products.

"Nice of you to come to work." I raise my head from the door, milk carton in hand.

"Gina. Hey. I stopped by your office, and you weren't there."

Her dark gaze travels from my feet, up my body, and back down again. Her disgusted expression has me doing a double-take, searching for a stain or wrinkle. She's in four-inch-tall black leather heels and a magenta skirt suit. I almost put on scrubs today, because that's the most comfortable outfit I own, but given I'm not seeing patients, I chose one of the four pantsuits I own. Mena's skirted suit belongs on the set of *Suits*. Professional yet sexy. In comparison, my tan suit with ballet flats looks like a Hillary Clinton wanna-be suit.

"You missed the meeting with the contractor."

"I did?"

She crosses her arms, and her finely plucked eyebrows knit together into a disapproving scowl.

"I didn't know about a meeting."

"The contractor's day starts early. We met at eight."

"Oh, well, why don't I follow you into your office and I'll get all the meetings down? I won't miss another one."

The milk carton slips. I grip it, but there's condensation. It slides down. Out of my grip. Tumbling forward. Onto the floor.

White splatters over Gina's pointed black leather shoes and up her legs.

"Oh, my gosh." *Holy fuck.* "I'm so sorry."

She steps back. Swallows. If those dark brown eyes were lasers, I'd be an incinerated pile of ash on tile.

Napkins. I scan the counter. Lift a box of sweetener. Napkins. Christ on a cracker, where are the napkins?

Ever so slowly, she bends and picks up the milk carton. A white river coasts across the square graphite tiles. With two fingers, she picks up the carton and holds it out to me like it's toxic.

"I am so sorry."

"I can see why you didn't go into surgery."

I pause at her feet where I'm dabbing at her expensive looking shoes. She snatches a fistful of paper towels and begins cleaning herself up.

"I really am, Gina, I'm so sorry."

"Don't worry about it," she says, but her stern tone implies I really should most definitely worry about it.

"I'm so sorry. I'm such a klutz."

She leaves followed by a *Click. Click. Click.*

What the hell is wrong with me? I never spill on people. And I spill on Gina twice? Is it some subconscious desire to dig the deepest hole and bury myself in it?

Back in my office, coffee in hand, I sit staring at the screen. Gina has the layout of the new space underhand, and they are probably too far along for me to make any changes without incremental expense. To an untrained eye—my eye, that is—the addition to the building looks lovely.

Research. Business isn't something they teach in med school. But I can do this. I need to learn about income streams for med spas. If there's one thing I learned during med school, it's how to study and how to research. The computer comes to life, and I set about learning.

~

Knock. Knock.

Harrison fills the doorway. He's in scrubs, his dark hair is ruffled, and a five o'clock shadow darkens his jaw. It's mind-blowing how handsome he's become. His broad shoulders and wide stance convey confidence and pride, two traits I never thought I'd envy so much in another person.

He's come a long way. He deserves his swagger. Life on top of the world.

My gaze travels to the clock on the corner of the monitor. Four o'clock. I worked through lunch.

He's staring. I should say something. "How'd the surgery go?"

He narrows his eyes to a squint and his lips purse into a disapproving glower, and I straighten, the discomfort too much to endure sitting frozen.

"Your uncle and I talked."

Fantastic.

I push back from the desk, wheeling the chair to the side so the monitor isn't between us. Dread fills me. But it shouldn't. If I've lost this gig, I can wait tables. Or bartend. There are backup options. And once I get my footing and apply for jobs, Uncle Joel has connections. He'll handle my recommendations. *Breathe. It will all work out.*

Harrison crosses his arms over his chest and leans against the open door, which is pressed against the wall. "Why'd you come here?"

My eyes burn. From exhaustion? Shame? Both?

Doesn't matter. Hold it together. Do not cry in front of Harrison.

"I didn't have a choice." That's as much as I will share, and I lift my chin, daring him to push for more. He's the one who blocked me. He doesn't get access to the shit show.

"You didn't think it might be…" his jaw flexes, and his neck shifts forward, "considerate to call and check in with me? Give me a heads up, at least?"

"Honestly…" I let the word fill the air for a beat and force myself to swallow. "I figured you'd be married with kids and you wouldn't even care."

He bites down on his tongue, and the tip of it shows near his upper lip. It's what he does when he has something hurtful he wants to say, but he's holding it in.

"I knew you'd become a partner here. Uncle Joel told me. But I refused to ask questions about you." A lone ant crawls across my desk calendar, and I smoosh it under my thumb. "I'm sorry." Jesus, I say that a lot. "I just…you didn't…" I let out a sigh. The truth is, I was too much of a coward. I didn't want to ask my uncle because I didn't want to appear interested in Harrison, and I didn't call Harrison because I didn't want to appear interested. And I told myself he didn't want me to call him, but that's faulty, shitty logic because if I didn't call him because he told me not to, then I had no business showing up here. "I'm sorry."

"I read the employee manual." I glance up because his tone is slightly softer, but those gray eyes of his remain cold and impenetrable. "You can't have an office."

"Are you firing me?" The room wobbles a little, and I lean against the desk for balance.

"I can't fire a consultant. The partners don't have to agree on a temporary consultant. But someone thought it appropriate to stipulate that only partners of the firm or those at a director level or higher get a closed-door office. All nepo hires get a cubicle. There's an available cubicle with the reception staff." He looks ever-so-pleased with himself. "And you'll also need to punch in with a timecard. The same as our receptionists use."

"But I still have a job?"

"Yes." He releases a pained sigh. "But the partners get to vote before we hire you. You won't get a permanent job in this practice. You should look elsewhere."

"I know." Air flows through my lungs a little easier. This is good. There's a paycheck that will pay my bills as I piece my life together.

"Hi, ah, Zuri?" Mena shows up in the doorway with a puzzled expression.

"Yeah?"

"There's a Mr. Shelton on the line? He says he's your lawyer. You're not answering your cell, but he says it's urgent that he speaks to you?"

My stomach drops like I'm on a freefall ride at the amusement park.

"Ah, well," I glance at Harrison, arms still crossed in judgment. If I show him I hear him, that I won't fight him, he'll take it as a victory. So, to Mena I say, "I'm moving out of this office."

"Oh, why? Is there a problem?"

I wave Mena's concern away. "No, just a misunderstanding." I lift my phone, which is dead. *Fuck.* I must not've charged it last night. "Can you send the call to the conference room?"

"Sure," Mena answers with the brightness of someone who has a promising future before her.

I open my tote bag and pull out my notebook, the one I've been using to document every single thing in this horrid affair.

"What's going on?" Harrison asks.

I sidestep him and say as sweetly as I can with my insides churning, "I didn't punch in, so you don't have to worry about me punching out. After this call, I'll clean out my office and then I'll punch in."

I hurry to the conference room, because time is very much money. Mr. Shelton charges a whopping twelve hundred dollars an hour. Which is insanity because law school only lasts three years.

"Mr. Shelton?" I answer as the pen in my hand drops to the floor and bounces.

"Dr. Lennox?"

"Yes, sir. That's me."

"Good. We've heard from the district attorney's office. He's decided to pursue charges of destruction of property as domestic violence. The judge also granted a domestic violence protective order to Dr. Evans. You are not to come within five hundred feet of him."

"No problem. I'm in Texas."

"Yes, but I need to make you aware. Even if you see him in Texas, just stay clear of him. Do you understand?"

I let out a sigh. My blasted eyes burn, and I close them and hold my head in my hand. I should've just stayed in bed.

"Yes, sir." Why am I saying sir? That's not me. But this whole situation isn't me. It's a nightmare I can't seem to wake up from.

"You don't have a court date yet, but we'll need you to return when we do. I need you here for the case."

"Of course." If only I could go back in time. If only I had stopped with the first headlight.

If convicted, I could lose my medical license. All those years of hard work, all that debt, all the personal sacrifices, poof. A lone tear leaks, and I swipe it away. Crying solves nothing.

Mr. Shelton's voice softens. "I'm surprised Patrick pursued charges. First offense and everything."

Patrick Buchanan is one of the assistant DAs for Hennepin County. He's also a good friend of Warren Evans, the asshat whose Ferrari collided with my baseball bat. I wish I could say I'm surprised, but I'm a realist.

Seven

HARRISON

A lawyer? What the hell?

The conference room door closes behind Zuri with a harsh click.

Zuri Lennox isn't my concern. But if her uncle thinks our partnership is going to absorb the expense of a medical malpractice claim from another state, he's dead wrong. Maybe she went for a cheap malpractice insurance package. I could see Zuri doing that. Weighing the risks and deciding to go with the highest deductible and lowest monthly. It's a tempting thing for a doctor starting out, but Joel can't expect our practice to shoulder the burden of her cheapskate mistake.

I charge down the hall to Joel's office. He's finishing up with a client, so I pace the hall, avoiding looking into the room as a professional courtesy. Based on the melodic tones, it's the normal wrap-up spiel.

The second his client passes down the hall and enters the business controller's office to arrange payment, I'm in his space.

"You can't possibly think Paragon is going to absorb Zuri's medical malpractice lawsuit."

His brow lifts, wrinkling the skin right up to his receding hairline, his eyes widen, and his mouth opens into a surprise circle, then morphs into a… What is that? Amused grin?

"What kind of suit do you think would be brought against a dermatologist?"

"What…" People sue for any reason. "Misdiagnosed skin cancer? Scar from a melanoma removal? You tell me. She just took a call from a lawyer. Don't lie to me, Joel."

Joel sits against the front of his desk, one leg crossed over the other, relaxed and chill. The smug bastard grins. *Fucking Joel. Paragon is our livelihood.*

"If you want to know what she's going through, ask her. It's not my story to tell."

"Are you kidding me?"

"It has nothing to do with Paragon. That much I can tell you. But I'd like to point out that you've got a medical malpractice lawsuit, and I'm supporting you one hundred percent."

Joel is too jolly. "We're getting that dismissed. That woman has a body image disorder."

"True. But all the signs were there, and even though I recommended against you taking her case, you did." His lip twitches. He's right on this. I thought I could help her.

"I didn't see the signs."

"Rookie mistake," Joel says matter-of-factly.

"Why do you say it like that?"

"Because we all make them."

The man has a love for riddles that would make you think he's a wannabe poet.

"So, she is fighting a malpractice lawsuit?"

"She's not fighting a malpractice lawsuit." The grin spreads. "You are." I have no idea how to read that grin. "Whatever has you so worked up…you've got to let it out." He spreads both hands in front of his pecs and makes a rolling motion, presumably the hand waving motion represents letting it out. "You still going to the club?"

I have to close my eyes and readjust. I back up and fall into a chair. "Okay, so… No medical malpractice suit?"

"Nope." He's still grinning.

"Why are you grinning?"

"Am I grinning?" He gives me this I'm-an-innocent-boy look. I don't get it. He's too fucking happy.

"Did you see Jolene after we finished up the surgery?"

"Nope." He licks his lips and shakes his head.

"Go to the club?"

"Nope. But that is a thought." He shakes his index finger at me. "Have you been there recently? That might help you with the tension and whatever…" Once again, he spreads his hands over his chest and does the bizarre wave motion.

"What're you up to?"

"Me?" He flattens those meaty hands against his chest. There's no wedding band, so he didn't up and get married for a sixth time. "Look, I should've told you she was coming down here. I owed you that. She means a lot to you."

"She means nothing to me."

"Oh, right. Of course." Now he's looking at me like he doesn't believe me. "Well, it would mean a lot to me if you helped make her feel at home. She's going through a rough time."

I narrow my eyes and study the pudgy man. "With the lawsuit?"

"Yes, but…" he exhales and rounds his desk to his chair, dismissing me.

"It's not your story to tell," I finish for him.

"Right. But I can tell you she could use a friend."

A friend? One thing Zuri Rachel Lennox has never needed is a friend. She re-invented the definition of independent.

"If you won't make her feel comfortable here as a favor to her, please do it for me. You and me…we're tight, right?"

The light reflects on his silver spectacles, and I glimpse my reflection. Until this week, I would've counted Joel Lennox as family. He plucked me up under his tutelage. Gave me opportunities I wouldn't have had otherwise. Introduced me to a whole new world here within Houston. He's who I aspire to be...minus the whole pursuit of a doctorate in divorce.

There's a knock that diverts my attention before I concede to Joel that yes, he and I are tight.

"Dr. Ramsey?" Mena pauses in the doorway, glancing between Joel and me as if she's afraid she's breaking up a fight.

"Yes?" I ask.

"Your four o'clock is here."

"Thanks. I'll come and get them. Main lobby, right?"

She nods and speeds back to reception. I check the time. She's probably been calling my office desk.

Joel beams a radiant smile my way. The man is totally up to something. But I can't concern myself with his machinations. I snap my fingers as I remember what I still need to clarify with him. "She doesn't want to live in Texas. You know that, right? She hates this state. The entire Bible Belt. No amount of being nice to her is going to have her moving down here permanently. We'd be better off bringing on a dermatologist who will stay and grow her practice."

"You're probably right." He's still smiling.

"Here. Grow Paragon here," I clarify.

I don't get him. But I have a client, so I leave, scratching my head on the way to the lobby. Maybe Joel's stoned. We're done with surgeries for the day. It's conceivable.

He got one thing right. I do love the man in spite of how infuriating he can be. He didn't out-and-out say it, but I owe him. It won't kill me to be professional with Zuri. Somewhat welcoming. But I can't have her here for long. Yeah, sure, I told him she means nothing—and she doesn't—but I still have illogical reactions around her. Irrational visceral reactions.

It's not healthy. I can grant Joel's wish and be appropriate around her but encouraging her to extend her stay is ludicrous. And pointless. She won't do it.

Which begs the question—why is she here? What lawsuit can she possibly have?

I round the corner, and Maya's wide smile effectively pushes Zuri Lennox out of my thoughts.

"How's my favorite patient?"

She pops up off the chair and holds up her arms for a hug. It's astounding how much this girl has changed. My first cleft palate operation. She'd been this quiet girl with straight, glossy, black hair, and beautiful dark brown eyes that darted around the floor, incapable of making contact. Her mom said the kids in lower school were nice enough, but by middle school, she became painfully aware of her difference.

Over the years, her mother kept in touch and told me she'd blossomed after her last surgery. But the difference in her demeanor is unbelievable. It's not just the lip that's different.

I give her a hug, then give her mom one, then stand back and take her in. She's glowing. That's the difference. Head held high, those brown eyes stare directly into mine with a sparkle and energy I hadn't seen before.

"Maya, you look incredible." Her cheeks flush ever so slightly. As I look closer, I notice she's wearing lengthening mascara, possibly some blush or rouge, glossy lipstick, and long, sparkling acrylic nails.

I look between her mother and her, then notice another diamond-clad client flipping through a magazine in a chair nearby.

"Let me take you back to my office. I want to hear all about life." As I lead them back to my office, I try to recall what this consultation is for.

They claim the two adjacent chairs, and I take the loveseat. There's a faint white line that extends from her septum to the top of her lip, but it's barely noticeable. If anything, the wispy indentation adds charm. It's a phenomenal surgical result.

"So, tell me, what can I help you with today?"

Maya looks to her mother, and her mother answers.

"You did such a good job with her lip."

"Thank you." She's gorgeous.

I've done dozens of cleft palate configurations since Maya. Looking at her makes me want to get post-operative photographs of patients farther down the line. Request a two-year, maybe three-year follow-up.

"There's one last thing she'd like to touch up," her mom continues, motherly love and pride evident. "Her nose bothers her. You see, it's crooked. Looks like she might have broken it, but she didn't. And it causes her trouble sleeping at night."

Hmm. Sleep apnea. "Let me see." I move closer and sit on the coffee table. Touching her chin, I angle her head to the left and to the right.

"I think we can fix that. We need to do a scan so I can see what's going on with her airways."

"And we can pay," her mother says. "My husband's business is doing well." I completed Maya's first surgery pro bono. It's probably one reason she was willing to take a chance on an unproven surgeon.

Maya's dad owns a landscaping company. I've seen his trucks in my neighborhood and would've hired him, but I prefer to do my yard.

"Maya's going off to college in the fall. She received a full scholarship to A&M."

"That's fantastic, Maya. Congratulations." She beams. And makes direct eye contact, something she never did years ago. This is why we do what we do. We change lives. "Do you have a photo of what you want your nose to look like? Or an idea in mind?"

There's not really much to straighten. But it's possible that is not all she wants.

I've had women with perfect breasts ask me to reduce their size, just like I've had women with a tight ass request an augmentation. As Nietzsche noted, there is no one right way. In our field, subjectivity commands respect.

Her mother opens her Coach handbag and passes me a photo of Jessica Alba.

"Okay. All right." I look back and forth between Jessica and Maya.

"How about this? I'm going to take a photograph and look at what we can do. Before we proceed with an estimate, let's get your scan, and I'll do some visual representations of what I think we can realistically achieve. Does that sound good?"

Mother and daughter nod in agreement, and I study the retouched photo of the actress. There are no pores, so at the very least, it's been airbrushed.

"Do you think you could do it before graduation? What's the recovery time?" the mother asks.

"You wouldn't want to wait until summer?"

"No. We were thinking spring break."

"You're going to be looking at six weeks' recovery time. Swelling. Bruising. Summer would be a better time to recover."

"But my friends, they all supported me after my surgeries. This will be the last surgery, and they can be a part of it."

Hope. That's what I see when I look at her.

I once had a patient come in with a photograph of forty-something Elizabeth Taylor. The woman was seventy-five. That woman was so unrealistic in her desires, I turned her away.

I keep looking between Jessica Alba and my patient. I can alter her nose, but she's never going to be mistaken for Jessica Alba.

Don't do this. That's what my gut is telling me.

"Let me work on this," I say to Maya and her mother. "And let's get you scheduled for that scan."

After I leave Maya and her mother at the front office, I take the long way back to mine. The conference room door, the one where

Zuri took her call, is open. Spread across the table are index cards with notes.

Zuri loves index cards. For every single test, she used them. And she ordered them with methodical precision. I lift the cards, shuffle them like a playing card deck, and leave the neat stack centered on the blueprint. As I exit the room, my steps feel noticeably lighter.

It's also the end of the day. I should listen to Joel. He knows me well. It's time to go blow off some steam and frustration.

Eight

ZURI

Last night's discussion about Harrison and all the questions about the way Harrison used to be got me thinking about the way I used to be.

Back when the future was wide open. I didn't know which field of medicine I would enter, only that I wanted to change people's lives for the better. I'd read enough blogs, watched enough TV, read enough books to know the path forward would be grueling. Four years of medical school followed by four years of residency. Eight years with little sleep, constant studying, learning, and stress. If I didn't work hard, people could die at my hands. Instead of saving, I could kill.

But I wanted to be a doctor so badly. Blindingly so. Of course, my motivation wasn't solely selfless. In my mind, a medical profession led to financial independence and earned respect.

During residency, I chose dermatology because I thought it was the best of all the worlds. I could alter lives, perform some surgery, and have reasonable work hours. The regular hours meant a normal life with time to sleep and weekends to explore.

And yet, instead of screening for skin cancer or helping a patient with eczema, acne, or lupus, I'm pouring over med spa business journals and websites. Mountains of debt weigh me down. I should've majored in finance. Or law.

There's no sign of Gina in her office. The one notepad and pen out on her desk are square with the edge as if placed for a photo. A thick, furry, white rug in the center softens an otherwise vacuous room. The gold legs on her glass-topped desk and contemporary desk lamp glimmer. The golden framed portrait on the wall is a line drawing with a quote from Coco Chanel.

"Ah, the brilliant niece." Gina breezes past me into her office. "Need some more reading material?" She bends down to pick something up from behind her desk.

I hold out my peace offering, and when she rises, holding a wallet, she eyes my outstretched arms warily. "Aiming to ruin outfit number three?"

"No...I...it's a cupcake. From Magnolia Bakery."

"I don't eat sugar." She crosses her arms and huffs, "Or gluten."

"Ah. Okay. Well, good to know." There's a modern champagne gold clock on the wall and the straight line ticks the seconds away.

"Did you need something?"

Just get it out. "Look. I can see you're swamped. I can't see patients yet as I'm not certified in Texas. But while I'm here, please let me be useful. Let me take stuff off your plate. Use me as your assistant. Just tell me what you want me to do, and I'll do it. We don't have to be besties, but we don't have to be enemies either." She's frozen and unreadable. "I need this job. That's why I'm here. I won't get into it—"

"Good."

"But please let me be useful."

The second hand vibrates with each tick, falls still, then clicks to the next spot.

"Okay. You can do something for me."

"Really?" Annoyance flashes in her expression. "Great. Yes. Tell me anything. Treat me like your assistant."

"First, don't come around me with food." I take a step back, onto her plush, expensive-looking rug, and tighten my grip on the cupcake box. "I need to look presentable tonight, and don't have time to run home to change. There's an appointment this afternoon with a designer. It's picking out countertops and tile. We know the basic look. It's in the designs. But she needs someone to go with her to make final selections. Can you go, meet with her, and come back with samples of recommendations? I have clients all afternoon. Mena didn't block off the time slots on my calendar."

"Absolutely."

"Great. Thank you." She passes by me, wallet in hand, and pauses. "Is there anything else?"

"No. Thank you, Gina."

Gina's heels click against the floor. She doesn't look back, doesn't respond in any way to my gratitude or groveling, but I feel like a flat bike tire with some fresh new air pumped in. Progress.

On my way back to my office, I pass Harrison's. He's not in it, as he spends his mornings in surgery. His laptop lies closed on his desk, centered. The handset phone is perfectly squared to the corner. Neat and orderly, just like Gina's. But unlike Gina's office with a touch of glamour, Harrison's is modern and cold. Devoid of personality other than the one sensual portrait centered behind his desk. There are no photos. There's no sign of the man within. His neat freak tendencies are clinical. I pull open the drawer on the right of his desk. Pens, pencils, and paper all have their own place within the drawer. A small glass jar holds black paper clips. The drawer below is empty.

The trashcan below his desk includes two opened letters, probably solicitations, and a medical journal. He saves nothing.

Back in undergrad, he'd been the one guy who showed up to class without a notebook. Everything went on either his laptop or his phone. Every other person had a pen, notebook, you know, the things students carry. But not Harrison.

On the first day, he sat at the end of my row. There were one hundred and fifteen students in the auditorium style class. And each day, he moved one seat closer. One day, he claimed the space five seats down. The next class, four seats away. To test my theory, on the third day, I took the seat he would have theoretically claimed. He stood near the podium, back to the professor, counting seats.

"Did you change your seat?" Yep, that was the first thing Harrison Ramsey said to me.

For a minute, I doubted myself. Maybe he'd wanted to be close enough to read my handwritten notes, but not so close he was beside me. Maybe I'd gotten it all wrong.

"Did I?" I scratched my head. "Does it matter?" was on the tip of my tongue, but I went for a less confrontational, "It's just the two of us back here. Why don't you sit beside me?"

We sat side by side for the rest of class, but he still made me resume the seat I'd sat in for the first half of the semester. Change grates Harrison's psyche.

For the hell of it, I scoot his laptop six inches to the left and move the phone down five inches.

"What're you doing?"

"Oh, I, ah…. Was looking for you."

"Below my phone?"

"No, I was just going to call Mena and ask when you'd be back."

He doesn't buy that line at all. I lower my gaze to the floor and skedaddle right out of his office. If he wasn't so nitpicky, it wouldn't be so tempting to mess with him.

"What's in your hand?" he calls after me before I cross the threshold to the hallway.

I hold up the cupcake. The item meant to smooth things over with Gina. Self-awareness washes over me. Here I am, trying to make a go of it with Gina, and I'm messing with Harrison.

I'm bigger than this. He's not wrong to be pissed. I broke my promise. Even if it was a childish, ridiculous promise.

Slowly, with care and purpose, I raise the hand holding the gift box with a cupcake inside.

"Would you like a cupcake?"

He narrows his eyes. "No."

I swallow. Okay. Note to self. Bakery items do not go over well in this office. I spin to leave, then stop, and spin again.

"Harrison, I'm sorry I'm here. In your space." I bite back that it was a ridiculous, infantile promise. "But we're adults now. I need this job. It's temporary. Then I'll be out of your hair. Out of your life. For good." Because I will not fuck up again. "So, please, just…" My gaze falls to his feet. Running shoes with a pressed navy pinstripe suit. "We used to be friends. For the sake of that friendship, maybe we can be friends again?"

He's silent.

"At the very least, professionals." He's unreadable. He hates me. The one thing I wanted to avoid, I failed miserably at avoiding. In some ways, he and I are worse than my parents.

Flat, dark eyes lie within an unreadable face. The custom suit augments his shoulders, and his height lends him the air of a lion overlooking his lair. If all the rumors are true, he's now a sex god. And I'm holding a cupcake in rounded flats and pleated slacks.

Head down, I exit his office. With luck, my lawyers will work magic, and our paths will never cross again.

Nine

HARRISON

She could have yelled. Thrown a pink cupcake in my face.
Slammed the door on her way out.

But she apologized.

What am I supposed to do with that?

Her eyes were puffy, like she didn't sleep well. Her skin was
pale, the corners of her lips downturned.

Back at my desk, an uneasiness prevails.

I reposition my laptop. And the antiquated desk phone. With a
tug on the drawer, I inspect the contents. Visually, it's all in order.
It's the innards that are askew.

I open the bottom drawer, deposit my phone, and spin the
chair to look upon the Loblolly pine outside my window.

It's past lunchtime, but I'm not hungry. And thus goes my day.

On the way out, after an afternoon of consultations, I pass the
patch of cubicles in the office center. Files line shelves, because for
legal compliance we maintain both paper and electronic files. My

chest fizzes. She's somewhere back there. I scan the area and locate her. Her head is bowed down, reading. There's a curious shopping bag beside her laptop, along with stacks of square ceramic tiles. Reception closes at five on Friday, and she's the last one here.

I check the time. Scratch my scalp.

She's always worked hard. Pushed herself harder than anyone. Determined. She doesn't do it for money either. When she learned of my family's wealth, she treated me the exact same. She had the chance to marry into wealth, and she'd have none of it. Not Zuri. She's got to do it all on her own.

A haze of fine, unruly hair tops a mass of tendrils, a sign that she's scrunched those curls endlessly. The bottom two inches of her brunette roots appear to have been dipped in golden caramel sporadically. She's in her study pose, immersed in whatever project Joel has given her.

The scene is familiar, but different. Back then, that mass of curls would've been swept up on top of her head, and there were no stringy blonde pieces. Her tortoiseshell frames would've been pushed up on her head, as she only wore them for distance. My guess is she succumbed to contacts. And she's missing the Bic ballpoint pen tucked behind her left ear.

She's no longer the Zuri from college. She's the Zuri who's lived in Boston, New York, and most recently, Minneapolis. Yes, technically, she's the girl who ground my innards to pulp, but time does a number on a soul.

We're different people now. Adults. All grown-up and mature.

What is the adult version of Zuri like? What hobbies has she fostered? Or is she all work and only work?

In our prior life, she dissected my heart. To dull the blade, I blocked her. But now, twelve years later, time has muted the pain. The sensation is so dull it doesn't qualify as pain. No, a more apt description would be bittersweet. A mix of sweet and bitter, which brings to mind poisonous nightshade.

"Are you going to keep staring at me or are you going to say something?" Zuri asks without lifting her head, fingers still on the keyboard.

The woman has superior peripheral vision. Contacts, it is.

Yes, she gutted me, but I learned. She can't hurt me twice. She can't hurt me because I'll never hand her my heart. Never again. Besides, I lead a full life. I have everything I've ever wanted.

"Harry? If you have an issue, get on with it. It's hard to focus with you glaring."

Harry. That's an undeserved level of familiarity.

"Harry?" This time she turns those soulful eyes on me, and that fizz in my chest burns.

"Harrison," I correct her.

Ah, dammit. I am bigger than this. There's a tear in my heart, but it tore a lifetime ago.

"I'll leave. I promise. As soon as I possibly can."

What happened that the diligent, determined, hardworking Zuri Lennox needs to take a job she doesn't want? Why does she have a lawyer?

"Have you got plans?" The question out of my lips surprises me, but I don't want to sit among files on Friday evening, and I have questions.

She flattens her palm against her sternum and dramatically looks behind her at the floor to ceiling shelves. "Me?"

I chuckle. "Yes, you."

It's a scene from an eighties movie she loved. Dated back then. So bad. Probably worse now.

"No plans. Uncle Joel is spending tonight with the love of his life."

"Love?" Joel needs to slow down on the marriages. The man's bound to have mastered the pre-nuptial agreement, but even so, how many times can your heart split in two?

"So he says." She brushes her curls away from her smooth forehead. A smattering of freckles shows across her cheekbones, a sign she's either rubbed away her make-up or put little on. Her make-up application is hardly relevant, so I look away to the lobby, through the glass, to the parking lot.

"I have reservations for three, and one canceled. You're welcome to join if you'd like."

"Three?" Her right eyebrow rises, and the corner of her lip curves upward, as if she's mocking me. I don't quite get why.

"Amelia, me, and a friend you don't know. But he's heading home to his wife." She doesn't trust me. I can tell by the way her brows nearly meet over the bridge of her elegant, pointed nose. Definitely no Botox. "His wife is pregnant," I add, although now I feel like I'm giving too much information. If she doesn't want to join me, that's fine. For the best, really.

"I'll join you," she says, snapping down her laptop lid. "If you think Amelia will be okay with it?"

"She won't mind." I don't bother mentioning that Amelia is only meeting us for a cocktail and an appetizer because she's meeting her sex acquisition at eight.

Amelia is one of my more progressive friends, but she's still somewhat restrained about sharing her private life.

"Where is it?"

"Not far. MacArthur Street." I step outside into the waning light and scan the parking lot. "Did you not drive?"

"I walked."

"Well, hop in. I'll give you a lift."

She closes the car door, and the air conditioning flows at full capacity, the whoosh sound overpowering. A sweet scent invades my senses. I inhale deeply, as much to calm my nerves as to evaluate the aroma.

Zuri favors light, sweet scents. The brand might change, but her tastes haven't. My chest cavity smarts at the realization my car will now smell like her. But it's fine. We've changed. The past is the past.

"This is nice," she says after the whoosh of the air conditioning lessens.

I flick the turn signal and glance her way, unsure what she's referencing.

"Convertible Porsche," she answers. "Beautiful." Her fingers glide over the curve of the black leather seat, and a memory surfaces of those fingers curving around something else.

This was a bad idea.

"It looks like you," she adds.

Again, I don't quite know how to take that. It's an automobile. "What're you driving these days?"

"I'm…" She glances out the window as we zoom by a homeless person on the corner holding a cardboard sign beside a rusted shopping cart. "Nothing like this. Uncle Joel has been urging me to drive his Lamborghini."

"Let me guess. You don't like driving it?"

"Oh, my god, no." Her eyes widen in horror.

She's so predictable. Amusingly so. "You'd probably have a panic attack if you scratched it."

Zuri Lennox worries about money. Or at least, she used to. Whatever she's driving these days is probably a relic. The cheapest thing she could find. Going to the grocery with her was excruciating. She'd step back and check the prices of all the products. Didn't matter if the item was paper towels or canned green beans. She also carried a battered envelope filled with coupons. A shopping trip that took the average person ten minutes took her thirty.

"Oh, I won't drive it." There's a smile playing at the corners of her lips. "I'll Uber before I drive that thing."

"And what about back…where is home?" Joel drops updates occasionally, but as a matter of habit, I deflect the unwanted information shares.

"Minneapolis," she says. There's a wistful quality to her violet gaze, and it piques my curiosity. "And I still drive Miss Daisy."

"No." I lighten the pressure on the accelerator and twist in my seat. "Get outta here. She had over two hundred thousand miles… you bought her what…twelve years ago? Thirteen years ago?"

She lifts her chin and fights a grin. "She still runs. And it's good for the environment."

"Is it?" I flick my blinker to enter the valet line while my brain wraps around this information. "That car is so old. Surely a newer model has better gas mileage."

Miss Daisy is a butter yellow Toyota Camry from the seventies that had seen better days when Zuri bought her. Rust tinged the curve of the metal near the wheels. Foam peeked out of torn vinyl seats. I pull up to the valet and pause. "Is that why you're here?"

She looks at me quizzically.

"Because you need money to buy into a practice? Is that what this project is with Joel?" He loves his niece like she's his own. He'd loan her money if she needed it. "You won't just take the money from him because you're too damn stubborn?"

"I'm not stubborn," she bites out.

There's no one on the planet more stubborn than Zuri Lennox, but I won't touch that with a ten-foot pole. I pass the keys to the valet and catch up to her as things click into place.

"You saved to buy in," I snap my fingers, positive I've got it, "and they hosed you somehow. That's why you've got a lawyer. And you're down here earning money while things get settled."

"Something like that," she mutters.

Amelia greets us near the entrance, looking like the CEO of a Fortune 500 company. In reality, she's the CMO for a Fortune 500 company, although from the sound of it, she might as well be the COO, and she's currently fucking the CEO, so she's simply all the things.

"Amelia," I greet my bestie with a kiss on her cheek. "You remember Zuri?"

The look of pure ice Amelia gives Zuri reminds me why Amelia is my preferred wingman, but at the same time, the part of me that will forever protect Zuri has me running interference. I lean down and whisper in Amelia's ear, "It's okay. Lifetime ago, right?"

Amelia's skeptical, but she's too polished these days to do anything other than extend her hand graciously and smile. "Hi, Zuri. Pleasure to see you again."

Ten

ZURI

Harrison and Amelia stand two steps higher than me at the entrance to the restaurant and tower over me in terms of success. Amelia's business power suit, complete with Prada heels and a matching Birkin bag, leaves no doubt who donates more to the Rice alumni fund.

I'm on the verge of bankruptcy, and yet these two are model success stories. If the rumors are true about Harrison's sex life, are they still just friends? Or are the rumors as accurate as a tabloid?

The way he's touching her exudes fond familiarity.

Ever the gentleman, Harrison holds the door for both of us. With a glance back, I see him touch her arm, then her back. She's gorgeous. If they're together, they make a stunning couple. More so than he and I ever did.

A hostess leads us to a waiting table.

I didn't know Amelia well when we were in school. She'd been in one of Harrison's classes and they'd had a project together. After things ended with us, I'd see the two of them in posts now and then. But his single status never changed. And, eventually, neither of them ever posted, or maybe I just stopped scrolling. Those were busy years.

The small round table we're seated at allows me to study them both.

Harrison asks the hostess to send someone for our drink order. It's conceivable he's not as comfortable with this as he's letting on. I'm still surprised he invited me out, but if I'm going to win him over, a friendly dinner is a proven path forward.

Glancing between the two of them, it's easy to see why they would couple. Harrison's the epitome of gorgeous, a classic tall, dark, and handsome. They're both successful and driven.

It's mind-boggling he was ever into me. He probably can't believe it either. If he had a crystal ball back then, he would've never maneuvered to sit beside me in history class.

When the hostess arrives, I order a gin gimlet, and Amelia orders a gin and soda and a charcuterie board. We exchange a glance at the similarity in our drink orders, and apparently, our taste in men. Harrison orders bourbon on ice.

"So, where is Ian?" Amelia asks Harrison.

"His meeting this afternoon canceled, so he headed back home."

"That's a shame. I would've liked to see him." The implication in her side glance is clear. She wishes their mutual friend, one I don't know, sat in my seat.

"Is Ian a surgeon, too?" I ask, zeroing in on Amelia, because she was a business major.

"He is," Harrison answers. "Amelia here is one of Fortune's forty under forty. Power player in the security industry."

"Security…like finance?"

"Guns. Weapons," Harrison says, but Amelia interrupts with, "It's the defense industry. So, what are you doing these days?"

I half expect Amelia to pull a cigarette out of her Birkin. She's got this master-of-the-planet badass business maven countenance. Not a hair out of place, business suit, high heels, probably an assistant on speed dial. And then I risk a second look at the Birkin. I'm fairly certain concealed weapons are allowed everywhere in Texas.

"Zuri is helping with a project at Paragon," Harrison answers for me, probably because of my delayed response time. "But she'll be returning to…" he pauses, and hits me with a steady gaze, "Minneapolis as soon as it's over."

As promised.

"A project? Are you a doctor?" Amelia asks, understandably confused by Harrison's incomplete explanation.

"Dermatologist."

Our drinks arrive, and Amelia is the first to lift hers, but she doesn't offer a toast. "So, what's your story? Are you married?" She leans for an overt glance at my ring finger. "Divorced?"

The direct inquisition reminds me Amelia isn't originally from the South.

"Never married," I say and lift my glass to quench my thirst and calm my nerves. I'd ask Harrison, but Uncle Joel would've told me if he'd gone down that rabbit hole.

Harrison simply sits there looking smug and amused. *Did he put her up to this?* I glance between the two of them, and ask, "How long have the two of you been together?"

If we're putting it all out there, I might as well get my questions answered, too. Besides, there's a need for diversion. She's a stone's throw away from asking for my dating history, and I'm absolutely not sharing my horrific choices that landed me penniless and unemployed.

Amelia crosses one arm below her breasts and rests the elbow of her drink holding hand on the wrist. I swear, she needs to be holding a cigarette between those fingers instead of a G&T. Her body position combined with her deadlocked gaze on Harrison makes it clear she's putting this in his court to answer.

Back in the day, I remember wondering if she had a crush on Harrison. The two of them met up quite a few times on projects, and he'd always come home slightly buzzed. But I was never inse-cure. Harrison would've never cheated. Not back then. His word was true. I didn't realize how rare that was.

But I can't deny envy, jealousy, and, well, pain, stabbed me when I saw some of their posts that summer after I'd left. They moved on with their lives without me. As they should have. I don't hold it against them, but it doesn't mean it didn't hurt. That summer was hell.

Harrison swirls his glass thoughtfully while setting those gray eyes, dark in this light, on me. A member of the waitstaff passes the table, and he calls out to her, "Can we order now?"

"I'll get your server, sir," she answers.

Amelia smirks, looking far too amused for a woman whose partner hasn't answered an innocuous question. Something in her bag catches her attention, and she bends, lifting a phone.

Her face lights up, clearly pleased with whatever she's reading on her phone. She taps away and Harrison rises.

"Headed to the loo," he says and heads out of sight.

Since when did he start calling the bathroom the loo?

Amelia continues tapping on her phone, and I twirl my drink. The two of them are odd. I'm not sure what I'm doing here. Well, yes, I am. I'm bonding with Harrison so he won't fight my pres-ence and I can pay my legal team.

Amelia crosses one leg over the other and grins, beaming at the phone. It's like she's forgotten I'm here. She never liked me. We didn't hit it off like she and Harrison. Back then, she blended in with the other girls on campus. But now, she's both gorgeous and confident. Far more put together than I could ever be. If she's with Harrison, they make a stellar match.

If I'm honest, Harrison's the most gorgeous man I've ever met. But it's not his looks that I've missed over the years. It's his friend-ship. We'd watch movies or television shows, and he'd tear up all the time. He read more romance for pleasure than any guy I knew. I wonder if he still does that, or if that's a part of his personality he outgrew. There's definitely no evidence of that sensitive side. He's gone from adorably slightly insecure to smug and overly confident.

Ironically, I've probably traveled the exact opposite path. Adult me is a verifiable disaster.

Amelia makes a throat sound, and I glance up. I must've zoned. She's standing with her Birkin hanging from one perfectly manicured hand, her polish a discreet pale pink.

"I've got to head out of here. You'll tell Harrison?"

"Yes, sure." It's a little odd she's leaving. "Is everything okay?"

"Yep." She twists, as if she's going to leave, but then straightens. "You know, you really hurt him." Her words wrap around my ribcage like a vise. "Don't do it again. *Comprende?*"

I nod, too stunned to do more. She leaves seconds before Harrison returns.

"Amelia had to leave." He doesn't seem surprised she's gone, but the server arrives as he's taking his seat.

Harrison orders a salad with steak, and I order a salad. Harrison also orders a bottle of wine.

"I can't drink that much," I tell him.

"I'll cork what we don't finish." He didn't share the wine list, but knowing Harrison, the bottle he selected is extravagantly expensive. The one bottle probably costs more than my monthly gasoline budget.

But, then again, money has never been a concern for Harrison Ramsey, thanks to a trust fund. I always found it appealing that he didn't have to work, yet he worked hard. I suppose now that he has an income on top of his vast net worth, dropping a small fortune on a beverage is something he can do without a second thought. And there's nothing wrong with that. It's simply not something I can do at the moment. The salad here cost nineteen dollars, and I have twenty-six dollars cash.

"What are you thinking?"

I shift in my seat, awareness prickling that he's about to ask me questions. "You and Amelia…you never answered. Are you together?"

The corners of his lips turn up ever so slightly, evidence of restrained amusement. "No. She's a friend. She's always been a friend."

Allie's words from the other night come to mind. He's got a reputation as a player. I believe him when he says they aren't together now. But I'm skeptical about a decades-long platonic friendship.

"Never slept with her?" I ask, studying his response like I'm preparing for a test.

His smile cracks. "We've slept together." He reaches for his drink and smiles at me over his highball glass. "A few drunken times."

That makes sense. They're still friends because emotions didn't factor in. The Harrison I used to know wasn't one for intimacy without emotion. But he's grown up.

"I hear you're a member of a sex club now." He chokes on his drink. "Never saw you as the BDSM kind of guy."

His heated gaze, one that's not anger but more relevant to the topic at hand, lights a fuse, burning from my center to my core. I'll need to drink more water than wine.

"Who told you I'm in a sex club? Joel?"

"He knows?" I ask, wrinkling my nose. *Ew.*

"Knows? He introduced me."

My mouth drops open in confusion. But then again, he and Jolene were vocal last night. And are most nights.

He chuckles, clearly amused by my consternation. "Who told you?"

"Allie."

"From work?" I nod. He adds, "I didn't realize they all know."

"You don't seem bothered by it."

He lifts his shoulders like it's no big deal. If my work colleagues had knowledge of my sex life, I'd be mortified. Come to think of it, when I discovered my work colleagues had knowledge of me and Warren, it put me on fragile mental ground. It was the beginning of a rapid descent to the bottom.

I shake my head, ridding those thoughts from my brain. "So, BDSM, huh? When did that start?" Back in college, we'd had a traditional, or vanilla sex life, terminology I'm familiar with thanks to the movie *Fifty Shades of Grey*.

"You really want to talk about my sexual preferences?"

Now it's my turn to shrug. "I'm curious." The smooth lacquered wood of the table bears scratches from wear and tear. I dig my fingernail into a crevice and let my thoughts pour forth. "Was it… was that something you wanted to do back then, and I held you back?"

"Zuri." The seriousness in his tone draws my gaze from the table to his familiar and stunningly handsome face. "Never doubt what we had. It was the best of my life."

That, right there, is what I miss about Harrison. He's still got it, the words, the way of making a person feel like she's the most amazing person. The pull between us intensifies, and a part of me, buried deep down in the recesses, breathes in oxygen for the first time in a decade. That buried part of me pleads to clamber across the table and climb into his lap and run my fingers through his trimmed beard and breathe him in, but I stay chained to my seat, because what's the saying? That ship has sailed.

"So, tell me about dermatology." His thoughtful, kind gaze tells me he saw I was getting sad, and in that way Harrison has, he's guiding us back to safer waters. "How on earth did you end up in dermatology?"

It's an easy topic, so we spend the next couple of hours trading stories about what we liked and didn't like in residency. He explains that plastics isn't limited to boobs and facelifts. And I explain that I ultimately chose a path I thought would lead to a better quality of life. Fewer emergencies, more normal hours. A combination of quality patient time plus the occasional surgery.

Oddly enough, similar factors weighed in when he chose plastic surgery.

It's what the two of us do. Converse easily.

By the end of the meal, when he's paying for the check, it hits me we've consumed nearly two bottles of wine.

I make a show of pulling out my credit card, since the twenty-six dollars I have wouldn't cover more than my salad, but he dismisses it.

"Thank you." I wish I could fight harder to pay, but I'm not in the financial position to do so. One day.

"Our Uber will be here in five minutes."

"But your car," I say, stating the obvious.

"I'll get it in the morning."

He helps me up, and my head swims. I'm just drunk enough to sway a little, maybe slur a word or two. I'm not drunk enough to climb him like a tree. Or push my nose into his neck and breathe him in.

"Any chance you'll take me to this sex club of yours?" I ask as I lean into his support.

"No."

"But we're friends, aren't we?"

His words from the past play in my mind, as crisp and sharp as ever, sobering me. *Don't you get it, Zuri? I don't just love you. I'm madly in love with you. My soul desires you, my heart beats for you, you are the oxygen I breathe. That kind of love doesn't water down into friendship. It's not possible.*

The next thing I know, he's closing the car door and there's a man wearing a baseball cap behind the wheel.

"How're you getting home?" I ask, confused when he backs up to the curb. But he can't hear me, because the window is up, and the driver pulls away.

Eleven

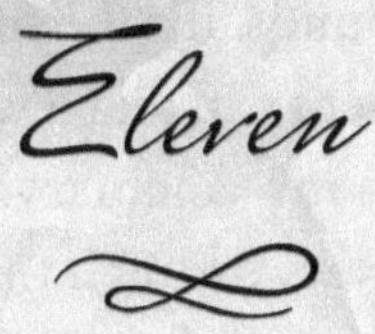

HARRISON

Days have passed since my dinner with Zuri. I spent the weekend in my yard, pruning the lantana, plumbago, and bougainvillea. When I had nothing left to trim, I combed the lawn, head bent, steps slow, searching for weeds. The meditative process of identifying and removing crab grass and nutsedge provided a reflective calm.

Distance preserves my sanity.

Yes, it's been a long time since we ended things. And yes, I am a different person. But I'm also still the same. I thought I was big enough to extend an olive branch, to foster a semblance of friendship. But it's not a matter of age or maturity; the concern is fragility.

After she left, I molded a protective barrier around my heart. Sex morphed into a physical act of release void of emotion. The only souls I let into my world belonged to close friends. Friends who would never choose to leave.

Zuri's presence throws me into the past. A weaker version of

"

myself, a person who fell into a depressive funk, an era only survived thanks to friends like Amelia and Ian.

Since her return two weeks ago, I have yet to go into the back rooms at TMPT, to so much as touch another woman.

And that stops tonight.

The dulcet ringtone sounds. It's the tone I assign to friends to differentiate between a client call and a work call. I pick up the phone and head outside to my sanctuary. It's late in the evening, and the waning sun glimmers through the leaves. The pungent scent of cut grass wafts through the air, and the faint sound of a distant blower mixes into the suburban symphony.

"Ian, how's it going?" I miss him, but his wife, Sunny, seems right for him.

These days, he's back and forth between here and Austin, but soon that will change. I always joke with Sunny, telling her that if she tires of life with an orthopod, I'm ready and waiting and won't charge for the mommy makeover she's going to need.

"Driving home now," he answers.

I check my watch. "You picked the wrong specialty."

He lets out a sigh I recognize as exhaustion. "Tell me about it."

"How's Sunny?"

"She's good. Got back the amnio results. All's good."

"Fantastic. Congratulations." Sunny's over forty, and both of them seemed to have memorized every published statistic out there.

"Yeah, well…" The navigation on his car cuts through the line and he pauses, then speaks over a feminine voice telling him to turn right in five hundred feet. "I'll be happy when she's here and…" His voice trails off.

"Stop with the worrying. She's gonna be healthy. Why're you using navigation? Didn't you grow up there?"

"Yeah, but traffic." He doesn't need to say more. Navigation will guide him through backed up streets. That's why I love Houston. I have a house with a suburban feel within the city limits, and if worse comes to worst, I can hop on a bike and make it to work or the hospital. "How're things with you?"

"Fine." I pull out a chair and sit back. I'm met with the sweet scent of gardenias mixed with a subtle dash of rose.

"You handling everything okay?"

I'm not a disaster, but I'm not quite myself either. "I'm fine. She's promised to leave, but there's no date attached to the promise."

"Does she seem happy there?"

"No." There's no sparkle. Her light has dimmed. "She's not even practicing medicine. I think she has the licensing exam in a couple of weeks. But she'll pass. Once she's licensed, how long will she stay?" Ian's silent. The question weighs down the line because there is no answer. "I actually turned to AI."

"Seriously?" Yes, I hear the amusement.

"ChatGPT. The free one."

"Did it have any answers for you?"

"No. Asked how to convince someone to leave a practice. It was like an HR professional wrote the response. Bullshit about quality of life with work hours, personal fulfillment, burnout, and stress."

"What were you expecting?"

"Damned if I know." The high shrill of crickets sounds, portending nightfall. "I made her move out of her office. She's sitting in an open desk behind reception."

"Taking the high road."

I roll my eyes at Ian's judgment. "I'm open to ideas."

"Sunny's an advocate of capturing flies with honey."

"I'm nice." I'm pretty sure I hear him huff, and it sounds like skepticism, so I add, "I took her to dinner."

"A long time ago, you fell in love with her, which says to me she's not a monster. Tell her it's hard having her around. Tell her the truth."

I grit my teeth, denial on the tip of my tongue.

"Offer to help her start her own dermatology practice. Step

back. Be her friend. Be a part of the solution. Steer her to your desired outcome."

"No one steers Zuri. She does exactly what she wants." Emotions surge in my chest. Friday night, we brokered a tenuous resolution. But I'd be happier if she left. I'd been way too tempted to tell her to slide over, to take her back to my place. I'd wanted so badly to reach across the table, to touch her. And then she reminded me why I used to love her. Direct as always, she asked about the rumors. About the sex club. She's refreshingly real.

"Look, you were there for me. If you need me, just call. Sunny will understand."

Ian hit the proverbial bottom before he and Sunny worked their shit out. "No. I'm fine." It comes out sounding confident, and it occurs to me there's a reason for that bravado. She destroyed me before. I won't let myself go through that again. Emotional deluge aside, it's just not going to happen. The light dims, falling farther behind the horizon, and it's my cue. "Listen, I'm meeting up with Amelia. Let me run. When're you back in Houston?"

"Tuesday."

"Lunch?"

"If I can get away, if not, definitely drinks."

"Sounds good. Give Sunny a mind-blowing orgasm for me."

I can see him rolling his eyes and the vision has me grinning and feeling more like myself.

Twenty minutes later, I enter TMPT, the club I joined. Yes, it is a sex club. The bar up front serves drinks and food. There are several rooms in the back with open play, but on the higher floors there are private rooms. It's a place for those who can afford the membership fee to relax and let off steam discreetly.

Amelia and her lover, Liam, are already seated at a table. His hand is on her thigh, but thanks to the table, I can't tell if his hand is above or below her skirt.

"Already ordered you a drink," Amelia says as I approach.

I give Liam a curt nod and say, "Thanks."

"Thought you might need it."

Her words throw me, and awareness dawns. "Have you been talking to Ian?" She bats her curled eyelashes, and I see right through the shroud of innocence. "I'm fine."

Her nose wrinkles. "No, I don't think you are. You're down. Too quiet."

I lift my glass and knock back the bourbon in one long swallow. When I set the glass down, Amelia's lips purse. "That was a double."

Well, shit. TMPT has a two-drink max.

"Just as well," I say. I don't have a great desire to hang out with Amelia and Liam. Tonight, I want raw and anonymous. "What're you two up to?"

Amelia and Liam met here in an anonymous, masked setting. Discovering her favorite masked man was the CEO of her company set her into a tailspin, but one he quickly righted. Now Amelia prefers the private rooms upstairs. A few times they've come down into the more public areas, but it's something they save for special occasions. They have gone away to exclusive weekends, a benefit of the club I have yet to appreciate, as the events are usually for couples.

"We're going upstairs," Amelia answers. Liam's guarded gaze tells me he doesn't trust our platonic status, and that's fine with me. I'm not seeking a bromance.

"Well, have fun. Do all the things I would do."

Amelia smiles, and I don't even bother with a goodbye to Liam. I like the guy, but Amelia's right. I am in a funk. And it's hard to give two shits about people who don't really matter when you're out-of-whack.

I push the back door open, nod at the person sitting behind a counter to hand out upstairs room keys and push through to the back room. The lighting is dark, the music pulses, and the smell of sex fills the air. I cozy up to a high bar and take it all in.

A hazy fog softens the strobe lights. Seating areas, poles, and furniture designed to facilitate sex are spaced apart in groupings, and a second-floor balcony surrounds the perimeter. I call this the voyeur room. Plenty of couples arrive here and never interact with anyone else, but they get off on the erotic scene. Then there are members like me, who arrive without a plan.

A woman approaches. She's familiar. Black hair, short-cropped bangs, blood red glossy lipstick, black leather harness, and spiked heels. She's here to play. Her hair could be a wig. Or it might not be. Apathy pulses through my veins.

The bass vibrates through the polished concrete floor. The high volume inhibits conversation, but nothing else. She fingers my shirt and questions with a tilt of her head and the touch of her tongue to her glossy plump upper lip. I nod confirmation. She smiles. Steps closer, chin tilted, asking. I give a quick shake of my head, declining.

Plenty of us here opt to not kiss. It's personal. Intimate. And sometimes when we come here, we only want vulgar, raw, and gritty.

She understands. And she doesn't seem to mind. As she kneels before me, I wonder about her intuition. Her powers of deduction. Ian and Amelia picked up I'm out of sorts. Did this woman, this familiar, nameless woman, deduce the same with one glance?

She unzips my trousers and releases my semi-hard cock. Her fingers wrap around me, stroking until I thicken, all the while looking up at me through lidded, horny eyes. She licks her lips and takes me. I close my eyes and grip the edge of the counter. Her mouth is hot and wet, and the grip of her hand at my base is tight.

Behind my eyelids, I envision us. Her on her knees, spiked heels glimmering under the lights, calf muscles soft and relaxed, wavy hair with caramel highlights.

I force my eyes open. Suck in air. Take in the slick black hair. God, my mind. It's one fucked up place. She's not Zuri; she won't be Zuri. Since I can't close my eyes, I pick a woman, arms out, holding on to the back of a sofa for stability as a man pounds into her from behind. Her breasts jostle with each thrust.

Sensations swirl, the familiar tightening at the base of my spine, and I pull back, then finish myself off with three quick, firm strokes. I offer my hand to the woman to help her up. She spins away, licking her lips like she enjoyed a lollipop. She returns with a warm damp towel and leans into me, so close her breath warms my earlobe.

"Feel better, okay?"

Jesus, I really am a walking fucking billboard. I use the towel to clean my hands and myself, put myself together, discard the towel in the bin, and head out.

I pass through the hall, then exit into the bar.

All the air leaves my lungs, as if a wrecking ball slammed into me, shattering my being. Two hundred and four bones splintered, and the soul living in the physical form obliterated.

Violet eyes meet mine. She's drinking a beer in a glass, and Joel sits beside her, laughing.

What. The. Hell?

In three strides, I'm across the room, at their table. "You bring your niece here?"

He smiles up at me, eyes half-closed in a squint, the look of someone who has had far more than two drinks. "Harrison," he booms. "Sit down. Join us."

My stomach twists with disgust.

"Don't…" he protests with a jovial smile. "We're only here for drinks. She wanted to see the place."

Zuri looks to me, then to the door I exited. Shame. Guilt. Sadness. The emotions seep through the floorboards, dispersed by the ventilation. Irrational emotions. Incoherent perception.

I did nothing wrong. She left me. A lifetime ago.

I push out into the night air, sucking in a mixture of exhaust and city stench.

Twelve

ZURI

"Harrison?" I look to my uncle. "I don't think he's happy you brought me here."

Uncle Joel shrugs and glances over his shoulder, scanning the other diners.

This place looks like a high-end, pricey restaurant that caters to affluent patrons. If it weren't for the bouncer at the door, checking for phones and ensuring membership, a visitor wouldn't think anything of it.

"He may think you're still virtuous," Uncle Joel says, returning his attention to me.

My gaze travels to the black door Harrison exited and my stomach twists. No, I'm not sure I buy that line of thought. Whatever goes on behind those doors, whatever his sex life these days comprises…that's all about him and has nothing to do with me.

"Virtuous?"

"I'm going to guess when you were together you were a vanilla couple, right? He might think you'll judge him."

Yes, we were a vanilla couple. I suppose I'm still a vanilla person. Whips and chains and whatever else have never been my thing. But I don't buy he's worried about what I think. Since our night out with Amelia, if I didn't know better, I'd say he's been avoiding me.

"What goes on back there?" I tick my head toward the black door. I'm sitting here because I asked about this place. Uncle Joel told me he'd take me here for dinner, and here we are.

I envisioned one big orgy. But Uncle Joel agreeing to bring me tempered my expectations.

I'm not sure why I wanted to come. Maybe I just wanted to piece together what Harrison grew into, what he is today as compared to yesterday.

Uncle Joel squints behind his spectacles and his index finger traces one side of the lip of his cocktail glass. Thoughtfully, he says, "Back there, people create and define the relationship that works best for them. There are rooms that allow a variety of lifestyles." He sips his scotch and adds, "The members here wish to experience their lives in deep connection with another. Isn't that what we all do in life? Seek connection?"

"That's a romantic spin." I've always loved my uncle. In second grade, when asked to use the word "jolly" in a sentence, I wrote, *My Uncle Joel is jolly. In fact, he's the jolliest man I know, jollier than Santa.* My mother took a photo and sent it to him. My homework sentences were typically a single sentence, but Uncle Joel inspired me.

True to form, he chuckles. "The great object of life is sensation. It's not enough to exist. We must sense our existence."

I chew on the edge of my thumbnail and wrack my brain. "Who said that?"

He shrugs. "Who knows? Doesn't matter. Still true."

"Are you saying that's why you come here?" I glance at the black door. "Why Harrison comes here?"

"You'd have to ask Harrison. Curiosity brought him here." The wooden toothpick perched precariously between his lips shifts up and down. "Loneliness and horniness might have contributed."

"Is horniness even a word?"

Once again, he shrugs, entertained. He's easily entertained. "Welcome to modern times, my dear. If you can get the gist of the meaning from the word, you can use it. There's an entire website dedicated to new words created by anyone with the audacity to use them."

I pull out my phone and type it in. I set it back down on the table. "It's a word."

He grunts. I take the disgruntled noise to mean he'd prefer to believe he created a word.

"Does Jolene know you're here?"

"You mean at this moment, or do you mean in general?"

"I guess in general."

"Yes. I met her here. That's why she's destined to be the love of my life. The muse of my soul." He pushes back his empty plate and gestures to a waitstaff member. "I'm meeting her shortly. Would you like to explore the back rooms?"

My throat gets tight. Dust on the polished concrete floor chafes me and I crave a shower.

"That's okay." Strolling through an orgy with a relative? No, thank you. I force my gaze off the floor and find he's as jolly as ever with a full-blown grin. "I'm good."

"Still virtuous," he says.

"Would you stop saying that?"

"If you want to be with Harrison, you may need to expand your horizons."

"I don't want to be with Harrison." He doesn't believe me. "That was a lifetime ago." His expression doesn't change. "I ended things with him. Remember?"

"I remember," he says as a waitperson brings him a leather folder, and he signs his name on a slip. "As I recall, you favored the rational. Sometimes as we age, we embrace love over reason."

I leave him with a roll of my eyes. And he chuckles.

He's right, of course. Partially. Harrison and I were accepted to different medical schools. If we stayed together, we would've been hundreds of miles apart during the most challenging academic time of our lives. And we were young. I loved him with all my heart, which meant I loved him enough to end things before they got bad. Before stress and guilt turned our love into vitriol. Because the line between love and hate is thin. A life truth I bore witness to over and over again until I withdrew from the hate.

And yes, after med school, and after residency, I embraced love over reason. Or, in retrospect, love is an inaccurate descriptor. What I felt for Warren was contentment. Hope for the next phase in life. Every part of my rational being knew a relationship with a partner in a practice I joined was unwise. But I did it anyway because I thought we could grow into more; we could grow old together and be happy enough. I let myself risk it all and jump off the proverbial cliff. And crashed.

Now I'm on life support. And it remains to be seen if I'll come off it. My twenty-two-year-old self was spot on. It's my thirty-something self that lost all reason.

Outside, streetlights cast a glow over the alleyway. It rained recently, and mist rises from the pavement into the cooler night air. A car approaches, headlights on. It's not a cab. I haven't ordered an Uber. I wrap my arms around my middle and stride into the night. A walk is what I need.

Fifty-five minutes later, I'm in the Menlo Park neighborhood. Two men sit on a park bench near the museum. Both smoke cigarettes. Cars are parked all along the street. The hum of conversation from a nearby restaurant with an outdoor patio floats through the air.

Harrison and my uncle live two blocks apart. I should go to my uncle's, remove my shoes from my sore feet, and settle into a warm, relaxing bath. But as if pulled by an uncontrollable force, let's call it irrational intention, my steps lead me to Harrison's front door.

Thirteen

HARRISON

Pop. Pop.

The dull sound barely cuts through the screen cacophony.

Pop. Pop.

Ding. Dong.

My doorbell. Someone's at the door. I check the time. It's late. That's the reason I didn't call Ian. His wife's exhausted by the end of the day. Pregnancy is doing a number on her.

I run my fingers through my hair, attempting to put it back to rights.

"Hello?" I call. I don't have a peephole. My neighborhood is safe, but still, I don't get unexpected visitors. Maybe the occasional neighborhood kid trolling for donations for school or some shit, but that's on Saturdays.

"Harrison? It's me." The voice vibrates through me. My gut drops as if I'm in free fall. The instinct to retreat strikes hard.

But I'm a man. I outgrew those weak tendencies. There's no excuse for being ridiculous. So, I twist the knob and let her in.

"What're you doing here?"

"Just walking."

I glance down the street as a passing car rumbles by. "Walking from where?"

"TMPT."

"Are you out of your mind?" My neighborhood's safe, but there are some sketchy, barely occupied streets between the warehouse district and here. "It's almost…" Well, it's not that late. It's not quite ten.

"I was concerned about you." She shrugs and wraps her arms around her waist, shrinking into herself. She appears smaller. Fragile.

Her curls are pulled back into a thick ponytail. One tendril falls free from the binding, falling from her temple to below her ear, and a small, round, gold earring glimmers. In the dim light, dim because I didn't bother to turn on any lights, the violet irises that haunt my dreams bear a mahogany undertone. "You left and…" She shrugs and looks down at the doormat. "I don't know. You seemed bothered."

"You know me. Reactionary. Seeing you there caught me off guard."

We stand awkwardly, me barring the threshold, arms crossed, her focused on the black rubber mat that I should've replaced years ago.

I let out a breath and scratch my head with a vigor I don't feel. "Well, now you see for yourself. I'm fine."

"Is someone here?"

"Why would you ask that?" *Why do you care?*

"I thought I heard someone."

I peer down the hall. My craftsman home has a classic configuration. A hallway with a dining room to one side, opposite a mirror image room across the hall, both road facing, and at the end of the hallway, I tore down walls to create an open living area and kitchen. My bedroom is up the stairs.

Muted voices float down the wide hall. "It's the television."

"You?"

It's true. I'm not a fan of the tube. "Do you want to come in and see?" I say it not as an invitation, but to chide her for doubting me. I've never lied to her. Ever. I hope she hears the edge in my tone and steps back, then heads down the street, leaving me in peace.

"Sure."

Dizziness inflicts itself upon me. Back in med school, I would've immediately diagnosed a brain tumor. Maybe tomorrow I'll draw some blood and check the white blood cell count.

"Are you going to let me in?"

The little warning voice screeches, but I've established the voice is senseless. I won't fall for her twice.

"Harrison?" Her questioning tone has me clenching my teeth.

I glance down the street, still incredulous she walked several miles at this time of night. "Where's Joel?"

"With Jolene."

I might as well let her in or I'll look like I'm not over her, like I'm harboring a grudge. I step back, and she enters. The door hinges squeak. The door clicks closed. "Have you met her?"

"No. Not yet. But she's definitely been at the house when I've been there."

She grimaces. I rock back on my heels. Having her here in my home is surreal. Other than Amelia, no woman has come here. We stand there in the dark. Awkward as fuck. "Well," I hold an arm out, gesturing down the hall, "come in."

Her footfalls sound behind me on the wide plank oak floor I installed before moving in. We pass through the living area, past the television, and out onto the screened in back porch. I can't sit inside with her. I need fresh air, shrill crickets, and a breeze.

"I like your home. It's what I'd always envisioned it would be. Lots of plants and books. Very different from your office."

"What's your home like?" I sit down in an armchair, leaving her a choice of a sofa or another armchair, or the hammock on the end of the porch.

She selects the sofa.

"I'm homeless at the moment." There's a hint of despair in her tone that the small smile she offers doesn't eradicate.

"Tell me about that." I am curious. What threw the driven Zuri Lennox so off course?

She crosses an ankle over a knee. It's not a ladylike stance, but it's all Zuri. She's wearing wide pants that hang like a skirt, but in the position, the exposed smooth skin along her ankle and calf gleams in the moonlight.

"There's not much to tell. I'd been living with someone. Now I'm not."

Breathe. There's no reason to be surprised she lived with another man. If anything, I'm surprised she hasn't been married. But, no, she distrusts the institution of marriage. Considers it a farce. *Pessimists are never disappointed. Therefore, marriage is for optimists.* Her words back then created the illusion of brilliance.

"What about you? You're not with Amelia, but are you living with anyone?" She glances around like someone's going to step in from the shadows.

"No." She's the only woman I've ever lived with. The only woman I ever wanted to share my life with. But I'm different now. I was an optimistic youth. No more.

"You have a nice size back yard. It's bigger than I would've thought."

Menlo Park, the area where I live, won me over because it feels like the suburbs in the middle of a city. I can walk to restaurants, for coffee, or to the Menlo Museum. But to say any of that out loud would feel superfluous and artificial.

"When we were together, did you have BDSM fantasies?"

I smile because that's my Zuri. She digs in the dirt like a gardener. "No. You were my fantasy."

There's no harm in admitting the truth to her. She completed me. Back then.

"You're so full of it." She shakes her head and bites her lip.

I lean forward and click on one of the battery candles for added light.

"I answered your question. My turn. The guy you were living with. I take it he's the reason you're here now?" My chest squeezes at the idea that someone else captured her love more deeply and truly than I could. She does an odd nod and shrug combo, confirming my theory. "What is his name?"

"Warren."

"Is he eighty?"

She laughs. But I'm rather serious.

"It was a family name."

Ah, yes. All the crap names that won't die are family names. "What was it like having sex with a man named Warren? Did you shorten his name?" The joke pinches, since she shortened my name, but she's laughing, so I keep on. "War? Is that what you called out?"

"No." Her smile is wide, but her eyes are sad. She lets out a loud sigh. "He was a colossal mistake."

"Hmmm." I shouldn't ask, but I shouldn't have let her cross the threshold, so here's to all the shouldn'ts. "On the colossal scale, where did I rank?"

Her smile falls, and our connection, the one that flowed between us ages ago, the one that lets me know when she's near, heats. My palm flattens against my sternum, massaging the pain point.

"You were never a mistake." She swallows, and I can't breathe. "With you, I did everything right."

Fourteen

ZURI

Can't he see it? I gave us the best chance for friendship. The kind that spanned decades. The smartest path to avoid mutual destruction.

"Being with you was never a mistake. Those were some of the best days of my life. But ending things wasn't a mistake either. Eight years long distance isn't doable." Not combined with our hours.

"We could've ended up in the same residency program."

He's out of his mind. But that's Harrison. Forever optimistic. If I'd led a semi-charmed life, I too might be optimistic. "Four years long distance before residency. You would've ended up resenting me. Hating me. Or one of us would've dropped out of school, and then that would've been worse."

"You have so little faith."

I'm a realist. But he's not. "You're a dreamer." His expression says he doesn't see the issue. "It's not your fault. You can't fathom love going sour." His hands grip the ends of the armrest, like he's holding himself in. "They're suing each other again. Or one is suing the other. I think Dad's suing Mom, but I could have it wrong."

"What on earth could they sue over so many years later?"

Fair question. My gaze lifts to the ceiling and the motionless overhead fan. I stopped following the court proceedings years ago. "Does it matter?"

"Wasn't their divorce finalized like fifteen years ago?"

"But then they had to fight over assets." They also fought like crazy for custody of me and my sister. Both asked me to testify at the trial for custody of my younger sister, but I refused. "It's something to do with inaccurate disclosure of financial information in an earlier trial and a request for court expenses to be covered."

"At this point, your parents could have earned a law degree."

My parents dwindled their savings paying lawyers over the years, a sore point, given doing so required emptying their kids' college savings accounts. Fighting over who should contribute what to our college educations would have been debated in court, except the court doesn't get involved after a kid is eighteen. Therefore, they refused on grounds the other should pay, and my sister and I ended up paying our own way. Which is fine. Plenty of kids pay their way through college.

"Your parents are unbelievable."

"These cases don't move fast." I peer at Harrison, over the large, battery-operated candle on the coffee table. Doesn't he see? That's what happens when relationships go bad. It all goes to hell.

"It's almost like they keep suing to continue contact. Like it's too painful to completely cut ties and move on."

I scoff. Leave it to the idealist. Mena got it wrong. He's the romantic. "You would say something like that."

We sit there in the semi-dark, surrounded by Harrison's lush back yard, silently trading arguments.

And it hurts. The accusation in his expression, in his stance. He may never see it, but I ended things *for* him. If things got tough,

Harrison would've quit med school or postponed it or transferred the first year he was able. I couldn't let him sacrifice his dreams, not when the chances of our relationship surviving through med school and residency were so slim.

He's the idealist, but I'm the realist. And as the realist, I sidestepped the slippery slope from love to hate. If he'd tried, our friendship could've continued. Texting, maybe even connecting over breaks. Who knows? Maybe I suffered from naivete.

"What's with your lawyer?"

I cover my eyes and let out a sigh. "You really don't want to know." And I don't want to share my mistakes. "Uncle Joel says that TMPT is all about people making connections. Have you made lots of connections?" Hanging between us, the question sounds unintentionally accusatory. "I'm just curious. I…didn't expect…" Back then, Harrison seemed sold on monogamy. "I'm just curious."

"Connection is the word Joel used?" He runs his fingers through his hair. It's shorter than it used to be, and he's got a couple of days growth on his jaw. Even unkempt, he's model-worthy. Classically handsome with a devilish aura. It's easy to see why women swarm around him with desserts. "Leave it to Joel to get poetic. I'd say it's about finding like-minded people for sexual release without the burden of dates or relationships." He rests his head on the armchair and closes his eyes. "But I suppose he could've been talking about some other aspects of the club. Amelia, for example, found a deep connection with someone."

"Kind of like Uncle Joel and Jolene?"

"Yep."

I get up and stroll across his back porch. There's a shelving unit against the back of the house. It's bursting with shade plants in pots, but it's the pot at eye level that amazes me. "Oh, my god. You still have it."

The misshapen brown earthenware pot earned extra credit. For the class, we only had to make a coffee mug, which was, truth be told, hard enough for someone who'd never touched clay before. But Harrison loved plants. I earned an A in the class thanks to that bit of extra one-on-one time with the instructor creating my handmade gift.

My thumb trails the uneven lip. "You should've thrown this out."

He joins me at the shelves, enveloping me in his heat. I crave resting against his strength. I'd like nothing more than for his arms to wrap around me and for him to tell me he's still there for me, that I can have him back in my life. I've missed our friendship so much. After I've had too much to drink, I sometimes imagine there's a physical hole in my heart created by his absence. But the organ doesn't work like that.

His thumb swipes the ugly brown glaze, carefully avoiding colliding with my fingers. "I forgot I had it."

The explanation makes sense. He owns dozens of pots. I'm sure somewhere in his house he has a window filled with bottles of water propagating plants. He steps back, and in my peripheral vision I see his hand cover his forehead like he's in pain.

"You made it for me. Of course I still have it."

He sounds defeated, and my heart aches. It aches for what we had, for what I did to keep us on the best path forward, for the pain we've both felt over the years. My palm falls to his chest, and I close my eyes, feeling the deep, comfortable rhythm of his beating heart. In turn, a tremor passes through my ribcage, as if his proximity to my heart awakened something deeper within me.

It's a silly thought. Cognitively, I recognize the absurdity, but I can't bear to step away, to risk breaking the connection. *Connection.* There's that word again.

The rough pad of the base of his hand caresses my jaw, and I lean into his palm, resting the side of my face in his hand. My eyes are closed, and I don't want to open them. I don't want to see accusations or hurt, I just want to feel his warmth and breathe in his earthy scent.

He tilts my chin up. Warm, soft lips brush across mine. A tender caress. My knees quiver, legs weak, heart palpitating. I remain here, surrounded by him, and lose myself in these sensations. This feeling of being alive in a memory. I could stay like this, with him, forever.

Fifteen

HARRISON

Adrenaline courses through my veins, alighting my skin with awareness. My heart pounds. Her scent, a light, sweet aroma, surrounds me. Emotions bubble within. I can't label them, but the burn in my eyes and the ache in my chest tell me tomorrow I'll need to define them.

My eyes close, and I focus on the sensory impact. How her curves feel beneath my hands, her silky strands between my fingers. Her soft inhalations. The brush of the tip of her nose along my jaw. The shivers down my spine.

"I've missed you."

Her whispered words are a balm. *Say it again.*

She can never understand my heart, how she owns it. She'll never understand that, to me, she is oxygen. It's as if I've spent the last ten years on an OR table, flatlining, and no one could do anything. Her words, the idea that she missed me, that she regretted what she did, is akin to someone clapping paddles on my chest. A resuscitation.

With my eyes closed, like a blind man, my wandering hands rediscover dips and valleys and curves through touch. Her smooth forehead, the soft skin of her temple, her high cheekbones, the softness of her cheek, to the dip in her chin. My thumb ravels along her elegant throat, and her pulse vibrates through me.

"Kiss me."

Her words sound like a plea. And I freeze, hovering over her, the choice before me.

My lips have brushed hers, over and over. Over her face, her throat, her clavicle. She tugs at my shirt, and the smooth pads of her fingers touch my side. Skin on skin.

I've wanted this. Dreamed of this. Convinced myself I would never see her again.

And yet, here she is. In my city. At my practice. In my home.

My eyelids flutter open. Elizabeth Taylor eyes. I've never met another woman with them.

Her fingers heat my neck with transcendent pressure. In her eyes, I see both the question and the desire.

It's sensory overload, and I have lost all power. Reason submerged by sensation.

She opens, and I accept. God help me, I accept. I shouldn't, but I do.

My tongue touches hers, softly. She tastes like honey, vanilla, and mint. Our kiss deepens. Tongues dancing. Relearning a once familiar routine.

My energy responds to her. It always has. Jesus. I'm so screwed.

She grinds against me just the way I like. She fucking feels divine. I press her against the wall, and she tugs at my shirt. I take over for her, gripping the bottom and tugging it over my head. She looks up at me like she's just unwrapped a present. The tip of her tongue passes over her swollen, wet lip.

"Like it?"

I work for this body. The slight nod she gives me, while her fingers canvas my chest, makes every fucking hour in the gym worth it.

"You weren't like this before."

Damn straight. When she and I dated in undergrad, I didn't even know where the on-campus gym was.

She dips her head and takes my nipple into her mouth. Her tongue swirls, and I hiss. With hooded eyes, she twists my other nipple between her thumb and index finger.

"How much time do you spend in the gym?"

"A lot." If I'd been fitter back then, would she have left?

Her fingers and mouth roam, teasing me, taunting me into action. But I shouldn't. I've traveled this trail, and it culminates in painful, thorny briars.

Her nails comb through my hair. Her hips undulate, the slow movement titillating against my groin. Against the ridge of my rock-hard erection.

She guides my lips back to hers, and the confusion weighing me down dissipates. Suddenly, all I want is her. Only it's not a want. I need.

And so does she.

I tug on her skirt, lifting it higher. But it's not a skirt. She's wearing pants. She gets the idea and reaches behind her at the zipper. The action pushes her breasts higher, and the need to see her breasts, to become reacquainted, nearly overwhelms me. I tug at the bottom of her top, much the same way she did mine.

She takes over the top while I go back to her bottoms. I push them over her hips and let the material pool on the floor. I find her warm center and palm her silk panties. I slip the fabric aside and dip my finger between her silky lips.

She whimpers.

Her fingers find my dick, and, Jesus, they feel good.

Her pants are in a mound on the floor, she's still in a bra, my pants are down to my ankles, and she's positioning me at her entrance. It's sexy. Surreal. And I want to drive into her, but…

I can barely breathe as I struggle to process. Her leg is lifted, over the curve of my arm, and she's guiding my tip through her. And holy mother…

Condom. I let out a pained groan and let my forehead fall to hers.

"Condom."

My condoms are out in the car.

I push away from the wall, desperate for air. To think. One more second, and I'd be plunging inside her, incapable of stopping.

Her hair is wild. Her chest heaves. Her panties remain pulled over to the side, exposing her trimmed pussy and rosy, pink center.

I shouldn't be doing this. She'll move on, and she'll be all I can think about for months. She'll own real estate in my head long after she's gone, after she's dating and doing whatever she likes to do these days.

She crosses one knee over her leaning leg in a demure posture. Flushed cheeks, wild tendrils, swollen lips, plain Jane white bra, silky panties, and the smooth curve of a hip. A hip that years ago was bony is now softer and seductive.

I bend before her and palm her thighs. Nip and suck as my fingers dig into her ass cheeks and position her right where I want. I won't let this go any further. The walk out to the car will give me strength. But if tonight is all I have, if it's my one chance to possess her once again, I'm going to taste her one more time.

I press my lips against her mound, breathing her in. Eagerness and desire surge. It's as if my body recognizes hers, and every cell has awakened in her proximity. The second my tongue dips into her flesh, she whimpers and shifts her leg, giving me far more room.

God, I've missed her. It's the thought that rips through me as I lick, suck, and nibble in the places she likes, especially on her slick, sensitive clit. She tastes of the best of times…and heartache. My fingers curve into her, hitting a spot that sends her quivering and curling forward, shouting out my name, "Hair."

My hand is soaked. If I had a condom… no, it's not that. If she were going to be here, if we stood a chance, I'd move us to the bedroom and spend the entire night getting reacquainted. But to do so would be suicide.

So, I grip my pants and pull them over my throbbing dick, carefully tucking my needy self inside.

"What are you?" She's breathing heavily, but her expression grows serious as I dress. "Are you going to get the condom?" Her gaze flicks to the front door. "It's okay. I'm…" Her gaze falls down my body, as if it just occurred to her I might not be clean.

I am. I get tested monthly and use condoms religiously. But I am promiscuous. The last thing I want is to expose Zuri to something.

I brush my fingers through the wild hair at her crown and press my lips to her temple. Her fingers touch my side and I mirror her, feeling the dips of her ribs, up to her bra. I palm her breast, and my thumb dives behind the bra's fabric to the tender nipple. Her lips press to my jawbone.

We hold on to one another in the hall. Partially disrobed. As oxygen returns, so do thought processes, and a dawning awareness we fucked up. Or at least, she stiffens against me, as if she's realizing she screwed up, but it would've been my destruction. To her, it would've been sex. Maybe a night of sex and then possibly a goodbye coffee in the morning.

But there's no such thing as just sex for me with Zuri Lennox. Like an addict, I must refrain.

Sixteen

ZURI

Mornings in Paragon are quiet. The surgeries occur on a different floor, and I imagine there's more movement and life up there. Here, on the lobby floor, you can hear the stroke of keys and the occasional phone ring.

I'm doing a competitive grid on area pricing for services, to ensure the pricing Paragon selects positions them in the market correctly. It's easy, mindless work, and it's about all I can manage after last night.

Harrison insisted on driving me home after the hallway incident. For the rest of my life, I'll remember the hallway incident as equal parts mortifying and fulfilling. I didn't hear from him all weekend. Not that I expected to. He made it clear he's not interested. Well, there was evidence to the contrary. He wanted to do something, but not with me.

He'll never forgive me. Doesn't matter that my logic was sound. I was looking out for him. Doing what was best for both of us.

Being realistic about what would happen to us if we stayed together. In his eyes, I left him. And by doing so, I killed us.

We can't be friends.

It's what he said. Proving him correct, I'm in town for less than two weeks and the hallway incident occurs. What we did crossed the friendship boundary. Maybe we can't be *just* friends. And there's no point in pursuing more. He's got his roots in Texas now, and I'm…well, what am I, exactly?

In transit? Rerouted on a detour?

It's ironic. I promised myself I'd never end up in court with an ex, and yet here I am. Worse off than my parents, because my medical license might come under fire. My livelihood.

Come to think of it, I'm due an update on the status of the case. I pull out my phone and dial my lawyer, Mr. Shelton. I could email or text, but I suspect speaking with his assistant is the most effective way of reaching him. She nags him to call, whereas emails or texts lie about in the graveyard of the unread.

"Lichtenstein Law," a cheery female answers lyrically.

"Hi, ah, this is Zuri Lennox. I'm calling for Mr. Shelton. Is he available?"

"Hi, Zuri. He's at court today. Can I take a message?"

"Sure. I was just wondering…" What am I wondering? "Does he have an update?"

"Oh." Papers rustle.

It's amazing to me that people still use so much paper. Medical offices will one day be mostly paper free, but perhaps law offices shall continue to sacrifice trees. There's still a lot of weight placed on paper contracts and, in my case, affidavits.

"Yes!" the woman on the end of the line proclaims with much enthusiasm. "I knew I'd seen your name. I'm supposed to call you."

I spin the chair to the side, waiting.

"Oh. Yes. You have a court date scheduled."

I let out a sigh of disappointment. The bubble of hope I'd been harboring that Mr. Shelton could get it thrown out of court popped.

"August twenty-first."

I look at the calendar. "That's over three months away."

"Well, you know how summer is. Vacations and such. You're lucky he got you on the docket as soon as he did. He had to pull strings."

Right. So lucky. "Anything else?"

"No. He'll be in touch later this week."

"Okay. Thanks."

She ends the call, and I stare at the phone in my hand. This case is going to take forever.

A light rap draws my attention to the front of my desk. Gina looks down on me, surveying my laptop and its roving screensaver.

"Hi." I set the phone down and spin the chair to better face her.

"Hey." She tilts her head, and it's oddly…friendly. "Got the status update with the builders. Good job tackling the decision list."

A sense of dread hits me. If she's here, it can't be good.

"What're you working on now?" She gestures with a twitch of her chin toward my phone.

"Competitive analysis." It's busywork. They're months away from opening. "Is there something I can help you with?"

"Yes. Actually." She crosses her arms, but her expression isn't as guarded as it has been. Perhaps she's decided I'm really not planning to invade her territory. Of course, thanks to Harrison, I'm sitting behind reception surrounded by multiple open desks. It would be silly for Gina, in her luxury office, to be intimidated by me. Maybe Harrison did me a favor.

"Can you come with me?" Gina gestures to the lobby.

"Oh. Yeah. Sure."

I follow her through a hallway maze to a back supply room.

Several large boxes are stacked to the side, and there's a table with a three-ring binder.

"We just got this shipment in. Can you go through and inventory? Sometimes they don't send us the exact amount ordered, so double-check and then update the inventory book."

"You track inventory in a notebook?" I'm not a tech person, but that strikes me as wildly old school.

She shrugs. "If you want to build us something better, that would be great. Right now, I'm the only one who accesses the supplies. But it would be good to have a better system before the expansion."

"I'd be happy to do that." At my old job, everything was online. Our practice kept track of every vial, every bottle, every pill. I can reach out to our office manager and ask her what software they used.

"I figured you would." She moves to leave.

"What do you mean by that?"

"You seem like you need this job. It's not my business." She holds up a hand, as if imploring me to not explain. "But there are things we can use you for."

"Thanks." Yes, I feel a bit like a high school intern, groveling for any work at all, even if it's just photocopying papers. But, in reality, I'm more desperate than a high school intern, because I am out of high school and have serious bills to pay.

Hours later, after I've researched three different inventory management systems and spoken to two reps, I head out of the supply room to stretch my legs.

I slow as I pass Harrison's office. He's having a conversation with someone, but there's no one in his office that I can see. I peer around the corner, curious.

"Yes, ma'am. That all sounds very normal. I'd expect the bruising and swelling to continue for several more days."

He rolls his eyes, which is the Harrison I used to know. His phone lies flat on his desk, and his EarPods are in. He must be returning patient phone calls.

On the coffee table, there's a tray. It looks like it's a drawer that's set out. And there are sample breast implants. I pick one up. It's silicone, but I can't believe how soft and squishy it is in my hands.

He watches me, but it's clear he's listening to his patient. "The thing I need you to be on the lookout for is fever or bleeding around the sutures. But, based on the photos you sent, I think you are going to be very pleased with your result. You're healing nicely."

I hold an implant over my breast and raise questioning eyebrow.

Harrison's eyebrows nearly meet over his nose and his face scrunches. "You take care of yourself, and I'll see you at your follow-up." He ends the call with a press to his phone.

"No?" I ask with an implant over each breast.

"Put them back. They aren't toys."

"Someone's in a testy mood."

"Just…" He runs a hand through his hair. He's changed back into his suit, and it's a shame, because he's absolutely delicious in scrubs. But he's pretty spectacular in a suit too, especially when he's flustered.

"They're a lot softer than I thought they would be."

"You didn't do a rotation in plastics?"

"No. I mean, I saw implants in medical school. But they weren't nearly as soft."

"They make improvements every year." He's focused on his laptop now. Maybe looking through the patient portal for more messages from patients.

"If I were to get them, I'd want this kind." I squeeze one in my hand, and the thick material fills the space between my fingers.

"You don't need them." He types away. Dismissive.

I set the implants down and take a seat across from his desk. All

I have waiting for me is research. And I kind of ache to hear more about how I don't need an augmentation.

The Harrison I knew wasn't a plastic surgeon. He didn't spend day in and day out with beautiful women from all walks of life. Does the Harrison of today constantly evaluate women, picking them apart, deciding what he could do to enhance their beauty? To give them an extra boost of self-confidence? Does he have a list of improvements he would recommend to me?

"I think I could do with another cup or two."

"Your breasts are perfect." His fingers slow over the keyboard. "And you know that." The pace over the keyboard quickens. "Don't go begging for compliments. It's unattractive."

"I'm not begging for compliments."

"No?" His fingers freeze and he turns stormy gray eyes my way. I love it when his irises darken like that. My pulse kicks up a notch. The way his eyes narrow, it's like he senses what he does. Or maybe he's secreting pheromones that are altering my behavior.

Because I didn't come in here to tease him or taunt him. I break my gaze from his and push up off the chair.

Two steps later, I pause. I didn't see Harrison for the rest of the weekend, as expected, but… "We're still good, right?"

"In what way?" His arms fall to his armrests, and he leans back in the chair.

"As friends." My voice sounds meek, and it's not a good sound. But, years ago, he said no to any friendship, and it feels like I'm trying to sneak one by him.

He pushes away from his desk, sending the chair rolling back. His hand goes to his tie, and he loosens the noose. His sea gray irises lock on me. With every commanding step forward, my throat tightens.

He stops just short of me, and I have to tilt my head up to see him. "Why can't you understand? I can't be friends with you. The things I want to do to you. What I do to you in my dreams. What I fantasize over when I jack off? The thoughts I have about you when I'm fucking someone else? Those aren't the thoughts of a friend."

I can barely breathe. His presence depletes the oxygen in the room.

"And yes, I should've gotten over you a long time ago. And I did. I got over you a thousand times. But then you returned and… the thing is, I'm not sure I'll ever be over you. The only chance I have is for you to leave. Because when I'm around you, it's like time hasn't passed, and you're still mine…and damn my soul, but I'm still yours."

Seventeen

HARRISON

Zuri Lennox took possession of my soul years ago. I still remember the first time I saw her. History. Lecture hall. I saw her, and the rest of the room dimmed. She wore a hoodie sweatshirt. A good fifty percent of the campus population wore those, so she should've blended in. Her worn forest green suede Birkenstocks might have set her apart as a tree hugger, but her short, army green skirt didn't feel over-the-top granola. Her curls were wild and unkempt, partially bound by a clasp. And then, as if she could sense someone staring, she turned, and I took in those violet eyes.

I'd grown up being asked about my unusual eyes. The occasional inquisitive person would ask me what my license says, or they'd comment that they're an odd shade of blue. Some call mine gray, I call them dirty blue. Well, her eyes were like nothing I'd ever seen. Almost purple.

It wasn't until three weeks after that first day that I built up the courage to ask her to hang out.

"Any chance you want to get together after this?"

Those were the first words I said to her that didn't involve seats. Not what's your name, but by then we knew each other's name thanks to the TA's roll call at the beginning of class.

"You mean, like, to study?" She'd hiked her backpack strap farther up her shoulder, and I'd wanted to offer to hold it for her, but I thought that wouldn't go over well. She struck me as the kind of woman who not only could carry her backpack but wanted to. The kind who might be insulted by flash-from-the-past gentlemanly bravado.

I took a beat to look into those baffling irises surrounded by corkscrew curls and the freckles that crossed her cheekbones. And her lips. Glossy. Full. A light shade of pink that struck me as supremely kissable.

"I was thinking…more like a date." I swallowed and risked a glance at her face. Friendship would've been the safer tactic.

The corners of her lips lifted, and she said, "Don't you think maybe we should get to know one another first?"

"Isn't that what dating's for?"

She grinned, or really, she looked like she was struggling to control her smile, like she had this beaming smile on the inside, and she wanted to protect me from the ray of light.

"I guess it is." Again, she repositioned her heavy backpack across one shoulder, leaning against the weight. "Let's get lunch. Dutch." She paused, apparently reading my reaction. I was a freshman in college and didn't think twice about what she was saying. All I cared about was she didn't shoot me down. She said yes. And I'd been as excited as the day I won the rocket launcher competition in seventh grade.

Growing up, my parents always told the story of how my mom had been crossing an intersection in Santa Monica, and my dad pointed to her and told his buddy, "That's the woman I'm going to marry."

I've always suspected Dad was viewing the past through a rose-colored lens. Like maybe in reality he said, "She's hot. I want to meet her." And over time and memory obfuscation, the phrase evolved. But I never asked him point blank. Because that story made my mom beam. And as a kid, I liked the romance of it; this idea that he looked across the avenue, below a flashing green arrow, and knew to his core she was the one. Over the years, I've wondered if maybe I wanted so much for that story to happen to me, too, that when I met Zuri, when I looked into those crazy colored irises, I inserted myself into the dream.

After all, she left.

And now, here she is, once again. Once again tossing around the friendship word. Only now we're not freshmen in college. We're thirty-something adults. With history and enough baggage to fill a 747. Sinewy scar tissue binds my heart together.

And yes, I should've gotten over you a long time ago. And I did. I got over you a thousand times. But then you returned and...the thing is, I'm not sure I'll ever be over you. The only chance I have is for you to leave. Because when I'm around you, it's like time hasn't passed, and you're still mine...and damn my soul, but I'm still yours.

"I'm not trying to be cruel," I say, finally breaking the silence and bringing us both back into the room. "I could try to make your life hell. That had been my goal. Originally. But I need you to go."

A lone tear escapes, and it cuts across my chest, severing veins with the precision of a scalpel.

She lets out a gasp, then pulls her shoulders back and breathes deeply, tucking away her emotions. It's a very Zuri thing to do. "I can't go back right now. But I promise you, I will. And I'll stay out of your way as much as possible. I just need this income. For right now."

I remember what Ian said, that I could offer to invest in her practice, but she's never wanted my help. She's always been too stubborn, too strong-willed, too determined to make it on her own. It's like when her parents set her on her own at eighteen, they inadvertently welded determination into the fiber of her being, and now the thought of not doing it on her own threatens to break her welded spine.

I'm the lucky one. My parents loved each other until the day my mother died. And I don't have any loans because I'm a trust fund kid. Over the years, I've admired Zuri's determination. What my grandfather would've called gumption.

It's pointless to offer. Even so, I say, "You know, if you ever need money," those wide eyes flash, and my heart cinches, "anything, really. If you ever need anything, all you have to do is ask."

She offers a soft smile. "Same goes to you. Even, you know, with you needing me in a different state…if you ever need anyone, ten, twenty, fifty years from now, if I'm alive, I'm here for you."

As she leaves the room, all the tension leaves with her. I should've frosted the office windows with the click of the remote and angrily fucked her over my desk. Claimed her one last time. Reminded her she not only used to be mine, but that she loved being mine.

But the problem is if I did that, all that pain would return tenfold. I observed the destruction in my friend Ian recently. That complete sense of despair. The aching chest. The feeling that the only answer is to drown oneself in alcohol. A desperate need to escape.

I'm older now. Sure, I might have toyed with being an immature jackass, but I didn't go far down that road. I'm still not going to go tell her she can have her office back. But there are things I can do. Things that will help her, *my friend*, when she needs it, and that will help me by giving her the freedom to return to the life she wants.

Back at my desk, I pick up my cell and dial my financial advisor.

"Mr. Freedman's office. How can I help you?"

"Can I speak to him?"

"He's in a meeting at the moment. Can I have him call you back?"

"Sure. This is Harrison Ramsey."

"Oh. Dr. Ramsey. Hold on just a minute. I think he might be available."

I spin my chair to face the portrait behind my desk. There's a hint of freesia in the air. A vestige of Zuri's perfume.

"Harrison." Mike's deep, booming voice cuts through the line. "To what do I owe the pleasure? Everything okay?"

"I need you to do something for me."

"Sock it to me."

"I need you to pay off Zuri Lennox's student loans."

"Okay. Do you have the account information?"

"No. I'm hoping you can figure out how to get that."

"She won't give it—Wait. Is this the same person you dated in college?"

"We lived together. Yes."

"Harrison. Why don't you just write her a check?"

"She won't cash it. Plus, I don't know how much she needs. I'm guessing it's over half a million. Can you run a credit report and see how much she owes on credit cards?"

"That's...Harrison, this isn't how you—"

"Can you do it or not?"

"I'd need her social and—"

"You have all of that. She's in my will, remember?" At this point in time, she's the primary beneficiary. It's not like my dad needs any money.

"I'll see what I can do. They don't make it particularly difficult to pay bills, but this isn't advisable. You understand that, don't you? This isn't how you get someone to love you."

My gaze lifts to the smooth white plaster ceiling. To someone like Mike Freedman, I'm out of my mind. And maybe I am.

There are some loves that never let you go. They linger deep in the crevices, like roots taking hold on a rocky cliff. That kind of love can survive in the harshest of conditions.

"It's not about winning her over," I tell Mike. "It's a favor." And self-preservation. "She's got a lawsuit going on back in Minnesota. Can you see if you can uncover anything about that? If you can figure out who her lawyer is, contact him and tell him to direct all future bills to Freedman Financial."

"So, you want to pay her legal bills too? Are you doing this anonymously?"

"As much as possible. She'll probably figure it out. Just pay what you can."

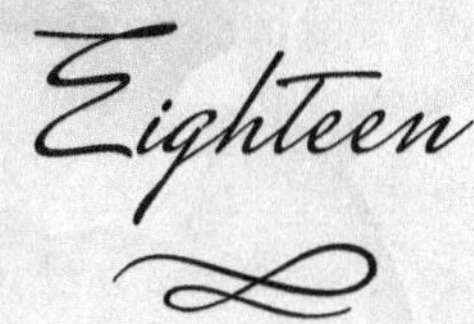

Eighteen

ZURI

"There she is." Uncle Joel stands in front of the reception desk, beaming down at me. "Did you say goodnight to Gina?"

That's an odd question. But looking around, almost everyone is gone, and I don't remember saying goodbye to anyone. I'm sure I did, but it's like I've been driving a car, and I obviously traveled distance, but I don't remember the road.

I probably look like I'm the most diligent employee in the place, but ever since leaving Harrison's office, it's like I've been moving through a foggy haze. My progress has been limited.

"Come on. Shut down that laptop. I'm taking you to refuel."

I do as he says.

"Why do you look like hell? What's going on?"

"Nothing. I'm fine." The leather strap of my tote bag digs into my shoulder, and I shift it without lifting my gaze. Uncle Joel's questioning stare follows my every movement. I don't have to see it because I sense it.

"Is that why you were splashing water on your face in the bathroom?"

"Who told you that?"

"Gina."

Hmm. I don't remember her being in the bathroom. I snap the laptop shut and decide to leave it. I won't attempt to work or study tonight.

"I'm a little dazed." The blank expression he's giving me prompts me to expand. "So I splashed water on my face." I refuse to tell him I was crying. I shouldn't have been crying.

We drive back to Uncle Joel's house and walk to a nearby Mexican restaurant. We're seated outside on a nice patio that over-looks the street. As the sun sets, the heat settles. Most others would choose the comfort of the indoor air conditioning, but Uncle Joel correctly senses I need to be outside.

My phone vibrates as we're seated. The name on the screen jolts through me.

Warren: Did you move?

"What is it?" Uncle Joel asks.

I close my eyes and breathe in. *I am strong. Snap out of this fog. Gain control.*

"Zuri? Are you okay?"

I shake my head to wake up. God, I hate myself sometimes. "I'm fine. It's douchebag McGee."

"What's he want?"

I hold up my phone so he can see the text. "Wants to know where I am, I guess."

"You haven't spoken to him?"

"No, my lawyer advised against it. All communication is to go through lawyers."

"You know that case is going to either get thrown out or settled before it goes to court."

"Why would you say that?" We have a freaking court date.

The waitperson arrives, and my uncle orders us both margaritas on the rocks with salt. I chug about half of the water in my glass before the waitperson leaves our table.

"The case is scheduled for August." He blinks. "August twenty-first."

"What does your lawyer say?"

"It's an assault case." I shrug. "I mean, it's property. But no, since it's my first offense, he's not expecting prison or anything like that. His biggest concern is that Warren might take it to the medical board."

"But you're out-of-state now." I'm not sure why that will help. If Warren wants to be vindictive, it won't matter what state I'm in. Sure, my lawyer loved the idea of me moving far away, but it's my understanding that was to ensure I didn't cross paths with Warren. It's imperative I avoid doing anything that might be construed as intimidating.

Our drinks are delivered, and as my uncle lifts his margarita, he gestures to the phone lying on the table. "You going to answer him?"

"I'm not supposed to."

"You know, if you can win him over, this whole thing could go away. If he tells the prosecuting attorney that you two have worked everything out, it's almost guaranteed your charges will be dropped."

God knows the repairs to Warren's precious overpriced boy toy are penalty enough without the add-on of lawyer fees. Oh, and unemployment.

"I can understand not wanting to work things out with him," Uncle Joel says.

"He's an asshole." A fucking cheater. I trusted him. Against my better instincts, I risked everything for him. And it did not go well.

"So are all my ex-wives, but trust me, it's better if the two of you can find civil ground."

"Are you still friends with your exes?"

He dips a chip into salsa and nods. "I am. Not besties, but cordial. Probably helps we don't have children or anything to continue fighting over. I mean, Natalie and I had a dog, and that dispute got pretty brutal. But Whistler died, and…we're friends now."

I chomp on a chip, and a thought hits me. "Do you think that's why Mom and Dad still fight? Because Lila and I are still alive?"

My sister currently lives in Amsterdam as a writer and a waitress. I hardly ever hear from her, but that's partially because of the eight-year age difference. I left for college shortly after Mom and Dad separated. She lived through it, bouncing between homes. I don't blame her a bit for taking off to another country.

"Nah." He sips his margarita. An amused look plays across his features. "There's a fine line between love and hate. Your parents have a passion that's unparalleled. The fight and make up thing worked for them. Until it didn't. And they hired devilish, greedy-ass lawyers. Satan's spawn. Pretty sure they keep putting random ideas into your folks' heads. Milking the cash cow. But, regardless, that's their drama. You know I love them both, but I'm happy they don't live near me."

Me too. My parents are batshit crazy. But I'm too old to be using parent issues as an excuse for my behavior. Warren's text taunts me.

"What's the harm if you text him?" The text must be taunting Uncle Joel, too.

I could call my lawyer and ask his opinion, but that would probably be another $150 added to my bill.

"Just act appropriately." Uncle Joel urges. "Always remember anything you put in writing could be read in court to a judge and jury."

I pick up the phone and tap.

. . .

Me: Yes

After we order our food, Uncle Joel's face morphs as he steeples his hands.

"What've you got going on there?" I wave my index finger around his contorted cheeks and lips.

"Ah, I should be direct, shouldn't I?" He smiles, and his cheeks rise to the rim of his gold-rimmed spectacles. "Just get it out there. Don't pussyfoot around it."

"Definitely do not pussyfoot."

He crosses his arms and rests them on the table, over the placemat. "How're things with you and Harrison?"

"I've been wondering how long it would take before you asked me."

"I don't want to pry."

"Of course not." I give him a not-so-heartfelt grin. "But when would you have the time? You and Jolene have quite the sex life, and that must be attended to."

He chuckles, and it's quite possible his cheeks flush ever so slightly. "You hear us, huh?"

I wave a hand like it's no biggie. "The pillow muffles the sound."

"Oh. It does, does it?"

I take a long swallow of my margarita, to the point there's only ice remaining. I don't really want to talk about my uncle's sex life. But I also don't want to talk about Harrison, so I hold up my glass at a random waitperson walking by. She stops at our table.

"One more for you?" I nod, and she turns to my uncle.

He says, "Yes, please, Sasha."

"You know the staff here?"

"It's within walking distance." He shrugs. "The beef carnitas are…" He holds his thumb and index finger up to his lips and makes a smooching sound. "And Harrison?"

"We're friends."

He immediately brightens. "That's great."

I let out a sigh. The weight on my chest, the cloud around my head, it all says things are anything but fine. "Friends who still need space."

"You don't look happy about that."

"I'm not." I risk a glance up from the plate. "But I have to respect what he wants. He basically told me he can't…doesn't want me around."

"He's not over you," Uncle Joel drawls the words, like he's weighing them.

"Ha." The haughty sound spews out before I snap it shut. "I'd say he's over me. He just…" God, I'm so confused. He ate me out the other day but refused to fuck me. And why would he? He can have anyone. He probably has everyone at that ritzy club of his. But that's not what this is. It's not about sex. Boring sex or red-hot sex. It's about… "He'll never forgive me."

And that's the crux of it. We love one another. That became clear today. If disaster ever strikes, he's my call and I'm his. But he'll never forgive me for making a choice he disagreed with. It was the best thing for him, but he'll never forgive me. He'll never trust me.

My life is such a cluster. I don't trust myself. Why would I ask him to trust me?

The concern pouring across the table touches me, and I pat my uncle's arm. "Don't worry about me. I'm going to get my footing, and I'll be fine. But I won't stay at your practice. It's not fair to Harrison. He earned his place there, and…" I let my words drift. Uncle Joel created a position for me, and I'll forever be indebted to him, but it's not my long-term solution.

"How're you liking Texas so far? You always said you'd never move here."

"I said that, didn't I?" I swirl the fresh margarita around, watching the lime green liquid slosh around the sharp ice rectangles. "Never say never, right?"

"Now, that is something I agree with!" He clinks his glass against mine right as a text comes through.

Warren: I have some things of yours. Can I drop them off?

I can't think of anything he has that I would want.

Me: Give whatever it is to Goodwill.

I stare at that text and decide it's not particularly conducive to smoothing things over. So I delete it, and type.

Me: Thank you. But that's okay. You can give whatever it is to Goodwill.

I set the phone down and watch as the bubbles emerge. I suspect that ol' Warren doesn't like me not coming straight out and offering him my address. He's the type of guy who doesn't like not getting his way.

Warren: A Burberry winter coat and scarf. To Goodwill?

. . .

Shit. He gave me that coat, and it's probably the nicest coat I own. Not the warmest, but hands down, the most expensive. It was probably in the trunk when I rammed a baseball bat into his precious baby.

Warren: I'd keep it, but Sherry prefers I return it.

Of course, Sherry prefers to not have any memory of me around. After all, Sherry and I were friends. I introduced them.

Me: I don't want it. You can throw it away if you prefer.

I hit send but then quickly reread the text as my heart rate kicks up a notch. The last thing I need is to send something that will make me appear bitchy or mean to a jury.

Warren: You and I both know you're going to need this coat come winter. Just give me your address and I'll drop it off.

It's really bugging him that he doesn't know where I am. That's what this is all about.

"Be nice," Uncle Joel says. He can't read the screen, but he can probably read me.

Me: I moved to Texas. I don't need the coat. Please send my best to Sherry.

. . .

Satisfaction fills me. That is an artfully articulated fuck you that his lawyer can read to a jury. I set the phone down, quite pleased.

"And now that you've dealt with Warren, can I bring up Harrison again?"

All my satisfaction leaves with the meager breeze. "There's really nothing to say."

He gives me a sad puppy dog look. If he was asking me for a treat, I'd give it to him. Anything simple, I'll do. But if it has to do with Harrison, it's not simple, and it's out of my control.

HARRISON

The woman in the back tilts her head back, cheeks flushed, palms flat on the table. The man beside her is sitting so close no one wonders what's going on. He's warming her up for what's behind the door, but what strikes me most is how intently he's studying her, lost in observing her pleasure. Sure, fingering her in public strikes some as lewd, but that's why people join clubs like TMPT. Safe from judgement, these two explore the world intimately together. They live out their fantasies safe from exposure.

"Dr. Ramsey, is everything okay?"

Roxanne, the bartender, draws me away from gawking at the lovers, and I lift my glass of water and knock back the remnants. Condensation drips down the glass and leaves a telltale rim on the black counter.

"I'm fine."

"Would you like something to drink?"

"No." I shake my head and dig my fingers into the pretzel dish. "How're you doing? Still loving working here?"

Roxanne is a relative newcomer to TMPT. A bartender by night, by day she's in grad school. With jet black hair cut in an angled bob tinged with neon blue dye and a small lip ring, she's got an edge, but her smile is babydoll sweet. I'm sure she gets hit on by the club members all the time. Or she would if it weren't against the rules.

"I do." Her pitch rises, and she smiles, flashing a set of perfect white teeth. "Pays better than any job I've ever had."

"People respect you?" From what I've seen, the members here are always respectful of staff, but you never know. She's a bartender, and it's easy to imagine some jackasses might take the two-drink max policy out on her.

"Never had a problem." Her eyebrows rise in emphasis, and then she leans forward, closer. I suppose she's leaning into the bartender as a therapist line of work. "It's unusual for you to sit out here for so long. Is Amelia meeting you?"

"Just me tonight."

The leather-wrapped door taunts me. I know what awaits, but I'm not drawn to it. And it's all Zuri's fault. The moment she entered the conference room, she fucked with both my heads.

Roxie wipes the bar down, but she stays close. It's a quiet night.

"How's school going?"

"It's summer." She says it like that means something. "School's fantastic."

"What're you getting your masters in again?"

"English Lit." She smiles, slowing the white rag as she wipes. "With a specialty in the romantic period."

"That's right." I glance back at the loving couple. Now it's her hand that's under the table. "So, are you an Austen fan?"

"I like her for her wit. The female perspective. But I'm more of a Byron girl."

"Individual freedom? Social justice?"

"You got it. Gen Y baby." I nod. "I didn't take you for a lit fan."

"I read. Not so much the classics anymore, but..." I twist on my stool, looking to the door, preparing mentally for what I will force myself to do to eject Zuri from my head.

A man enters the club and approaches the bar. I take that as my cue to get to it. I rap the bar with my knuckle and depart.

But when the leather cools my fingers, my gut sinks and twists. I'm not into it. And this is supposed to be fun. This is my entertainment, my release. If I go back there and do something I don't want to, I won't like myself. My frame of mind is so unsettled I'm not even sure I'll achieve an erection.

I stride across the restaurant and escape into the night. There's another bar, Jack's, that Ian and I used to go to all the time. I wander inside. There's a spotlight on the small black stage, but no one sits on the stool. They're between sets and it's a slow night, with only about ten or fifteen patrons scattered about.

I ask for tonic water with lime. I don't recognize the bartender, and John, the owner, doesn't seem to be here tonight. No one here is familiar. Less than half a year ago, I knew the entire staff, and every time I entered, I'd recognize at least a couple of the folks.

It's unsettling. My life is unsettling. I pull out my phone and glance through my notifications. A few news articles populate, but nothing piques my interest.

I tap the messages app. Type in Zuri's name, and her number pops up. I haven't texted her in years. Does she still have the same number? Did she block me like I blocked her?

Me: Is this still you?

I still have the same number, but lots of people change their numbers. I have no idea why. Seems like a total pain in the ass thing to do, but there are a lot of things in life that are a pain in the ass.

. . .

Zuri Lennox: Y

Across the bar, a woman at a high-top table makes eye contact. She offers a timid smile. Nothing too flirtatious, but she tilts her head as she talks to her friend, and I get the sense she wouldn't be opposed if I spoke to her. But I don't have the energy.

I could sit here and text back and forth with Zuri. I'd look like any other jackass sitting at the bar glued to his phone. But no, right now, in this funk, I want to go retro.

Less than fifteen minutes later, I'm standing in front of Joel Lennox's house, looking up at the windows, wondering which one is Zuri's. The downstairs lights are off. It's late, but not outrageously late. Ten thirty. A golden light filters through one upstairs window.

Me: You up?

Zuri Lennox: Y

Me: Come outside

A sheer curtain flutters, and a shadow flits by the window. Less than a minute later, the front door opens.

"What're you doing? Is everything okay?"

No, Zuri. Everything is not okay.

"Was in the neighborhood." I offer her a slight smile. "You gonna buy that?"

She steps forward and sits on the brick step. She's wearing long pajama pants in an oriental print and a black tank top. Her curls are pulled back, and her face is freshly scrubbed. The no make-up look was her standard go-to in college, and my body, my heart, pulls toward the familiar. God, I miss those years. I'd give anything to go back to that window of time.

"I'd invite you inside, but Uncle Joel's already at it." She pats the steps. "Come sit."

"What do you mean by he's already at it?" I don't step forward. My heart's reacting, and I need a minute to breathe.

"The noises. You'd think at his age he wouldn't have sex every single night."

"He and Jolene?"

"I guess so. I have yet to meet her."

I haven't met her either, but that's not surprising. I glance up at the house. "Which bedroom is his?"

"Why? You planning on throwing rocks up at my window sometime soon? Want to make sure he's not home?"

I've never thrown rocks at Zuri's window, but there were movies from our past where the characters did so. And back then, Zuri would be beside me, very often under me, before the movie or show was over.

"Does Jolene park her car in Joel's garage?" There was no car in the driveway when I parked.

"Not sure. Never thought about it." She twists, glancing over her shoulder to the garage, then back at me. "What's up?"

Slowly, I step forward, one foot in front of the other, until I reach the steps. I sit down beside her, looking out across Joel's Bermuda grass lawn infested with crabgrass and dandelions. Joel needs a better yard service.

"I can tell something's wrong. You know how I know?"

Because it's late at night and instead of fucking myself into oblivion, I'm sitting on your doorstep? I side-eye her. I won't dump that shit storm at her feet.

"The skin, between your eyebrows." She places her index finger above her nose, between her two slightly misshapen brows. Only

Zuri could screw up her eyebrows and have a charming result. "It wrinkles when something's bothering you. I guess you don't use Botox?"

"No. I don't. But you know who does?"

"Like, half of America?" she answers, wry as ever.

"Dr. Narcisse."

"Seriously? I wouldn't have pegged that."

I shrug. "He's a perfectionist."

"I'm sure Dr. Chandler does, too." She looks thoughtful. "I'd bet my Uncle Joel does. It's not a big deal."

"Do you ever use it?" Lit by the moon, her skin appears luminescent.

"Like I can afford it. I can't even afford gasoline these days."

That sort of makes me chuckle, but then I do math in my head. "You've gotten your first paycheck, right?"

"I have. But I have a lot of bills."

"You've always got a lot of bills." Back in the day, she stressed over bills. "Don't dermatologists get some kind of discount?"

"Wouldn't help me. And I'd need to be a practicing dermatologist." She leans down, hugging her knees. "Things I never thought would happen. Ya know? Finally, having school and residency behind me and being broker than ever."

"Does that mean it's all ramen? No splurge for cereal or mayo sandwiches?"

"Have you seen the price of bread?" She's so deadpan I can't help but chuckle. "Nah, Uncle Joel has a relatively stocked kitchen. Of course, living with him takes about the same hit to my self-esteem as moving back into the parents' house."

"Knowing you, you earn your keep." One thing Zuri Lennox is not is a freeloader. "I'm guessing you do, what? His laundry? Clean? Probably not his lawn." His lawn is a mess of weeds and bare spots.

"I do what I can. But he has a cleaning service. He didn't want to let them go temporarily. But I do cook for him and clean up in the kitchen, and obviously I wash and fold his laundry if he brings it into his laundry room." She holds an arm out, gesturing into the night. "I steer clear of his bedroom. Given the noises, I don't want to know what he's got going on in there."

"If the noises get to be too much, I've got two spare en suite bedrooms. You're more than welcome to one."

"You were just telling me I need to leave the practice as soon as possible." She looks aghast, as she should. And to be honest, I'm taken aback by the offer myself.

"I guess…it's like I told you. If you ever need me, I'm there." No matter how much it hurts or ungrounds me.

A car passes in the street out front, a hum of engine and wheels over asphalt, temporarily providing the bass to the shrill crickets and frogs.

"Harrison, please know I never meant to hurt you." I stare up into the broad spanning canopy of the live oak on the right side of Joel's lawn. "I did what—"

"Can we not?" I interrupt. "Let's let the past lie dormant."

"What do you want to talk about?"

"Well, how about who are you today?" I don't need to look at her to know my question rings hollow. "Or, how about this? What're you doing it all for?" I bend and pluck at a brown-edged blade of grass. "Back in the day, we worked our asses off to be doctors. Now, we're doctors. So, what're you doing it all for now?" It's a question I sometimes ponder. "Why do you get out of bed?"

"To pay my bills."

That's a copout answer.

"What?" She widens those eyes, eyes that in the moonlight could be mistaken for mahogany. "Hate to break it to you, Harry, but this is adulthood. It's not all about a dream. At least for those of us, you know, who don't have to worry about…" She doesn't bother finishing the sentence. She doesn't need to. She was going to say something along the lines of money or survival.

"I'm over feeling guilty for that, you know."

She glances up, perhaps surprised by my defensiveness.

"It's not my fault I was born into a wealthy family, any more than it's your fault you were born into a dysfunctional family."

Her lips twist, but she acknowledges my truism with a simple, "True."

"There has to be something more than paying bills. What do you love these days?"

She lets out a sigh and wraps her arms around her knees again. "I'm not sure there's anything I really love."

"Not buying it." I call that bluff because that's just not Zuri.

"It's felt like that recently." She reaches for a small stick and digs into the moss between the bricks on the path. "I kind of got my heart smashed. And I'm recovering."

God, I hate hearing about her loving someone else. But I've been there. My friends have been there. And talking about it helps. "What did he do?"

"He cheated."

"Dumbass."

"It's not so much that he cheated. I mean, that was an asshole move. But it's that he knew how much I valued my career and my reputation and how hard I fought ever dating him." She drops the stick and looks up at me. "I mean, I really fought him. Said no a million times before ever agreeing to a date. And all because we worked together. And then, we're together like six months, lived together for less than a month. Everyone knew we were a couple. And only then does he go and—"

"He's an idiot."

"I've thought a lot about it. I mean, you know, since learning about the club that you and Uncle Joel are members of. And I think if he'd said he wanted us to have an open relationship, I would've agreed. But I would've wanted it private. Or…who am I kidding?" She lets out a sigh and palms her forehead. "I wouldn't want my colleagues to judge me for being in an open relationship. I would've been terrified they'd find out."

"He cheated on you with someone from the office?"

"A nurse. So fucking cliche. My friend. I got her the job there."

"He had everything, and he threw it all away. He's the dumbass here, not you."

"Thanks for that. Still, in retrospect, I was angrier at myself than at him. Poor decisions. I should've known better. Should've been a better judge of character. Been more practical."

We sit like that, approaching midnight. My chest tightens and loosens, all with a dull, throbbing pain. I could get up and go home, but I don't want to. There's no other place I'd rather sit in silence.

"What's it like?"

I have no idea what she's asking about, so I twist and push my eyebrows together, silently asking for a little more information.

"An open relationship?"

"Ah." My lips spread into a smile. It's one of amusement, not happiness. "You mean life at the club?"

"Well, yeah, whatever it is. How does it work?"

"For me? I can't speak for everyone."

"Well, yeah, for you."

"It's a place to meet people, Zuri. Without expectations. No relationship outside of sex. That's what it is for me. I haven't committed to anyone. Not since you."

My words are weighted and heavy. And it's not what we agreed to. We agreed to let the past lie. "So, tell me. The Texas boards and certification process. Where are you on that?"

"I thought you wanted me to leave."

"I don't own the state. If you need someone to run questions with..."

"You'd help me?"

"Not a lot going on in my life these days." It's an admission, and it's also a method of playing down what I'm offering.

"So, other than uninhibited sex, what else do you do these days?

Gardening? What's a typical day away from the hospital like for Dr. Harrison Ramsey?"

"Is gardening the same as yard work? If I spread mulch, is that gardening?" This is the kind of pointless banter we used to excel at. Our conversation circles around nothing of importance for hours. It's after one a.m. by the time I walk in the door and head to my bedroom. I don't bother turning on any lights.

Twenty

ZURI

Life has taken on a regular pattern evoking normalcy. It's been over a week since Harrison stopped by Uncle Joel's house. He hasn't visited since, but we acknowledge one another when our paths cross in the office. The state certification test is the weekend after next, and I've been spending most of my free time studying for it.

On the way to the break room for my third cup of coffee, I notice Harrison in his office, staring down at the lightbox at a patient's scan. I tap lightly on the doorframe to get his attention.

"You're not in surgery?"

"Patient ignored instructions. Thought a doughnut wouldn't really count as eating." His attention remains focused on the scan.

"Does that happen often?"

"More than you would think."

I step closer. He's laser focused, still in scrubs. His thick, dark hair is ruffled, like he's run his fingers through it multiple times today. His arms are bent, which slightly flexes his biceps. It's easy to see why women fall over themselves for him, because he's gorgeous in a handsome, classic way. And seeing him in his element, as he problem solves, lost in a patient, well, this is when he's at his sexiest.

The closer I get to him, to the view of the lightbox, the harder it is to breathe. My heart pitter-patters along in a silly, girly way. Cognitively, it's featherbrained. But I suppose even my disciplined, jaded soul is susceptible to the McDreamy of the plastic surgery world. I didn't appreciate him when I had him. My one consolation is I'm not alone in that sentiment. There are plenty of others who don't appreciate what they have, and back then, I was young.

"What're you studying?"

"Tomorrow's surgery." He holds up a photo of a model and glances between the photograph and the scan. "She wants this nose."

I can't tell much from the scan, but he's clearly skeptical. "You don't agree with her choice?"

"Not feeling good about it, no."

"Do you suspect body dysmorphia?"

"Who am I to say? So often, I don't see faults where patients do. Beauty is subjective. You know this. And if a change can make someone feel better about themselves, that's powerful. Consider the butterfly effect. A stronger self-esteem can have profound implications over the years."

"Yes, but you still have doubt. Trust your gut. Patients come to you for your expertise. While it's true that we can look in the mirror and, thanks to the wonders of plastic surgery, change what we don't like, it doesn't mean that we should."

He lowers the photograph. His brow furrows and his jaw flexes. He's genuinely troubled. But those eyes, when he turns them on me, the effect is to suck the hard-earned oxygen right out of my lungs. Time stills, and the connection between us, the one I used to always feel, pulses. It's as if the molecules between us are speeding up, bumping into each other frenetically, forging a meta-physical connection.

His long, thick lashes, wasted on a man, fall. His attention returns to the scan, our brief connection broken.

"Who am I to decide if change is warranted? Her life has improved so much since getting her cleft palate fixed. Her mom says she has a ton of friends, but it's more than that. She's gained self-confidence. Over the last year, she's transformed into a different person. Maybe this nose…hers is slightly crooked. Maybe it's the last change she needs—"

Knock. Knock.

We both turn to the doorway, and Jessica Chandler asks, "Am I interrupting?"

"No," Harrison and I say in unison.

"Zuri, can I ask a favor?"

"Anything."

Harrison flips off the lightbox. "Sorry, ladies. I need to go prep. Feel free to stay behind." His navy scrub top falls short of his waistband, and the scrub pants drape the globes of what I know to be a muscular, finely shaped ass. Gorgeous. He's gorgeous. I have yet to enter the hospital, but I'd bet every single nurse sighs as he walks by.

"Not you, too," Jessica snaps.

"Not me," I assure her. "What's up?"

"You want to stay away from him," she says, crossing her arms over her middle. She's also in scrubs, only her scrubs are white with dancing hearts sprinkled about. "He's the definition of a player."

"So I hear." Sadness presses down because he wasn't always like that. But perhaps playing the field was his destiny.

She narrows her eyes, studying me. She's a little older than I am, but not by much. Her skeptical gaze has me shifting in my flats all the same. With an exasperated sigh, she waves her hand and says, "You do you. Look, do you have time today to meet with my daughter?"

I have pretty much nothing but time. "Sure."

"She was crying this morning over acne. I don't think it's that bad, but you know teenagers. And my dermatologist doesn't have any openings for a month. Can you take a look at her skin? Maybe discuss her skincare regimen with her?"

"I'd be happy to."

She pulls out a phone from her butt pocket. "When can I tell her to come in?"

"Anytime." Jessica's gaze lifts from her phone to me. "Really. I don't have any meetings today. I'm spending most of today prepping for the certification exam. Which, you know, I'm not certified in Texas?"

"Oh, yeah, I know. But I think you're fine to recommend what to wash her face with, right?"

Jessica's expression is one of total degradation. Which is a little infuriating because dermatology is a damn competitive field. It's not surgery, but I didn't want surgery. And actually, I do perform minor surgical procedures.

She finishes tapping on her phone and slides it into her back pocket.

"Okay. She's swinging by before she goes to volunteer this afternoon."

"Where does she volunteer?"

"Humane society down on Alameda Road."

"Oh, nice. Has she been begging to adopt animals?"

"That was part of the deal when she volunteered. She's not allowed to ask me to adopt anything. She'll be off to college in less than a year, and I'd be stuck with it." A slight smile plays across her lips. "But that's not to say she won't be showing you pics and trying to sell you on a pet."

"Well, she can try all she wants, but I'm a transient. Can't take on a pet when you don't have a home," I say to Jessica's retreating back. There's nothing quite like someone walking away while you're speaking.

"My daughter's name is Molly. She'll ask for you. Wait." She pauses a foot outside of Harrison's office. "You're behind reception, right?"

I nod.

"You can use my office." Her gaze travels behind me, around Harrison's office. "If you don't want rumors starting, I wouldn't spend too much time in here."

Right. Rumors. The root of my fear back in Minnesota.

Less than an hour later, when I'm on my laptop, answering questions on a practice test, Mena distracts me.

"Molly. My goodness, you have grown up."

"Hi, Mena." A young woman approaches reception. She's wearing a sweatshirt that falls mid-thigh, completely covering what I'm assuming are shorts somewhere high up skinny tan legs. Stick-straight brown hair is tucked behind both ears.

"How're you doing?"

"Good," she says unconvincingly.

"Your mom's still in surgery," Mena says as I snap my laptop closed and stand.

"I'm here to see a Dr. Lennox? Ah, Zurney Lennox, I think Mom said?"

"Zuri," I correct. "Your mom said we could meet in her office."

I open the door to exit the reception area and meet her on the other side. The skin below her eyes is puffy, and I can see a couple of inflammation areas along her T-zone, but overall, her skin looks remarkably clear. There's one red, angry zit on her chin.

"Are you not a doctor?" Her expression is tentative, nervous even.

"I am a doctor. But I'm not a part of this practice." Nor will I ever be, but that's not relevant at the moment. "Come on back. You know, when I was a kid, I had the worst acne. Your skin looks really good."

"Is that why you went into medicine?"

"Because of my acne?" I think back to my days spent popping zits. "No. My mom helped me get it under control pretty quickly. Back then I used Neutrogena. Have you heard of it?"

"I've been to a drugstore. I read magazines."

The attitude in her tone has me cracking a smile. A teen indeed.

I flip on the light switch to Jessica Chandler's office. Her name plate outside clearly states it's her office, but I haven't been inside. Light gray walls give it a fresh and modern aesthetic. She's arranged silver frames artfully on one corner of her desk, and there's a low cabinet unit with matching silver frames. All the photos are of Molly, although there's one photo with Jessica and Molly, and another photo with Jessica, Molly, and a man I presume is her father. But maybe not. He could be her stepfather.

There's a furry white rug sprawled over the center of the room, and the furniture is a soft pink suede. The rose colors add a decidedly feminine air to the room. All across the coffee table are spiral bound notebooks that presumably hold patients' before and after photos. Molly and I won't be needing those, but I lead the way to the seating area and turn on a table lamp.

"Why don't you sit here so I can get a better look at your skin?"

She does as I ask, and I run the pad of my thumb over her smooth tissue, tilting her head in the light to get a better look at the inflamed skin below her eyes. If I were back in Minnesota in one of our examination rooms, I would ask my PA to run and get me two small cold gel packs.

"I have normal to oily combination skin," she says.

There are slight indentions around the inflamed pimple near her lip. "Have you been trying to pop this?"

"Yes."

"Don't do that." I sit back in the nearby chair. "Tell me about your skin regimen."

"I use Cetaphil to wash my face and an Aveeno moisturizer and

Clean and Clear for acne flare-ups." She lifts her eyebrows. "Not that it's working."

Her skin actually looks great to me. I wouldn't lie to her about that. "What you're using should work. If someone needs something stronger, I'll often recommend a line called Proactive, but…" I lean forward, running my finger pad over her jawline. "I'm a little worried that might be too strong for your skin. Are you by chance menstruating right now?"

Hormonal fluctuations can be brutal in teens. I tilt her chin to get a better look at the bridge of her nose. Her cheek is wet. Her eyes are glassy. Tears overflow.

And just like that, all the pieces fall into place. She's not crying over an inflamed pimple.

"Do you need a tissue?" She shakes her head, but I'm up anyway, searching Jessica's office.

"I don't know why I'm crying," she sniffles. "I've been so emotional. Crying nonstop."

"And your mom saw you this morning?" I ask, careful to keep any judgement from my tone. There's a tissue box in a drawer filled with implant samples, and I remove the box from the drawer and deliver it to Molly. She promptly pulls out a tissue and blows into it.

Ever so slowly, I lower myself to the chair near Molly's. Her gaze is on the floor, and those tears don't show any sign of slowing. Inside, I ache for her. But I barely know her. I'm not someone she would naturally open up to, but here we are.

"You know, I once had an accidental pregnancy."

Those eyes flick up to me. Her lashes are damp and the skin around her nose is flush.

"I was in college. Freshman year."

"What did you do?"

I exhale, debating what I should say. Those tears keep falling, and I see so much of myself in her. She needs honesty.

"I terminated the pregnancy. Within days of missing my period,

I took Mifepristone. It's a pill." She covers her nose with a tissue.

"Have you talked with your mother?"

"I'm not…" Her eyes widen with fear, but then her face falls. "You're my doctor. You can't say anything, right?"

"I won't say anything to her. But you should." I don't have a medical file on Molly. But my guess is she's sixteen or seventeen. No older than seventeen. "You have options, Molly." A fresh bout of tears fall, and her shoulders tremble. "You may feel like it's the end of the world, but it's not. Talk to your mother."

"I can't." Her voice cracks and the words come out like a whine.

"Yes, you can. She loves you. More than anything, she loves you."

"No. She won't. She'll hate me."

"Honey, she's your mother. She could never hate you."

"She will. You don't know her. Not like I do."

I can't argue that point. I see her mother around the office, but she's never joined us for drinks after work. We've never shared so much as a discussion about a television show in the break room.

"I don't know your mother, but I can look at her office and tell she loves you. Look around."

"Are you a mother?"

"No." She squeezes her lips together and stares at me. I've no idea what she's thinking, but I'm certain she needs to talk to her mother. "Honey, having a child is a big decision. Talk to your mom. I understand it's terrifying. But—"

"No. I'm not telling her. And you can't either."

My head swirls. I'm out of my depth here.

"You're my doctor, right? I have doctor-patient confidentiality."

In a normal state, she'd be right. But god knows what the politicians in Texas have legislated concerning matters like this. And I'm not positive I'm legally her doctor in this situation. *Jesus fucking Christ. I need to consult with another lawyer.*

"Honey, you've got to talk to her. Let her in. She'll want to be there for you."

"No. You can't tell her. A friend of mine is getting me a pill. The same thing you did."

Right. But I went to a doctor.

"Where's your friend getting it?" She blows her nose. "What's her source?" I shudder at the thought of her getting a pill from some guy on a street corner.

"A friend's mom. She's helping me. My mom never needs to know."

"But, honey, she should know. This should be something—"

"You don't know my mom." She's staring at me head on, but those tears are still flooding and wetness pools on her chin.

I'm not sure what else to say, especially given my mother doesn't know and I have never regretted handling it without her knowledge.

"Do you regret it?"

My heart cinches, and it's hard for me to swallow. "No," I tell her. "It wasn't the right time for me, and I don't regret it." Harrison and I decided together. A flash of memory, of him holding me that night, curled up in the twin bed of my dorm room, quakes through me. A vivid image follows the flash. Student health. Bright white walls, fluorescent lights, the laminate floor, the scent of sanitizer. We went together to get the prescription. "I regret the birth control method I chose. I was on the pill. After that…" I lift my gaze to Molly, but she's not looking at me. She's holding soaked tissues up to her eyes. "After that, I went to student health to get an IUD. They're much more reliable. The American Academy of Pediatrics recommends it now as the best birth control for those who want extended birth control protection." My voice has taken on a doctor's intonation.

"Do you think I need a parent's signature to get one?" she asks. On the coffee table before her is a pile of spent tissues.

"In this state?" Those eyes finally lift, filled with so many emotions. She understands me, and I don't need to say more. "Molly, I know how scared you are, because I was in your shoes.

But I can't emphasize this enough. You should talk to your mother." A thought occurs to me. "Or your father. A parent."

"Maybe I'll talk to my dad," she mumbles.

"And, honey, if you decide to take a pill, don't take anything unless it's in the packaging and you can confirm it's exactly what it says it is. Okay?" She stares blankly at me, a tissue below her nose. "There's scary stuff out there. On the streets."

"My friend's mom is getting it." She says it angrily, like I'm questioning her, and I suppose I am.

"Okay. Just…" She looks at me with this expression like she can't believe what I'm insinuating. "When I did residency, I did a rotation through the ER. Any pill you take should come from a reputable pharmacy. On the street, pills can be laced with chemicals that should never be ingested. Just…" She's young, and she feels invincible, and I want more than anything for her to talk with a parent who will take her to a doctor. "If you don't want to talk to your mother, then talk to your father. But someone. Please."

She sniffles, scoops up the pile of tissues, and walks them to the trash can. "You're going to tell my mom that I need to keep doing the same skin care routine, right?"

"Yes. Your skin care routine is sufficient. You don't need any prescription medication."

Twenty-One

HARRISON

Fragrant rosemary overwhelms all other scents and stains my skin as my clippers trim the thick bushes bordering the screened-in porch. A scattering of fireflies twinkles in the oak's shadow. The drip line clicks on, sprinkling cool water below the mulch, a much-needed defense against the omnipresent Houston heat. I swipe the cathartic sweat dripping from my brow.

"Harrison?" I hear her before I see her.

She rounds the corner, still in work clothes, simple black slacks with a white sleeveless top.

"Yard work?" She sounds surprised.

"I don't think of it as yard work. It's meditation." Yes, my T-shirt has sweat marks and soreness tweaks my back muscles, but my evenings in the yard soothe.

"It's so hot." Sweat pearls along her hairline and frizz over-whelms her curls.

She sweeps her hair up off her neck, putting a band around it and twisting it into a messy bun.

"Not a fan of humidity?"

"Are you cooking tonight?" She stares down at the discarded rosemary stems.

"If I didn't trim this back, it would become too leggy." I back up, setting the shears down, and remove my gardening gloves.

"Something worrying you?"

All these years apart, and she still knows me well. Although, back then, I repotted plants since we didn't have a yard. "This is my normal." I tell her the truth, but not the whole truth. I don't want to do the surgery on Maya. "Doesn't mean anything's wrong."

Off in the distance, thunder cracks through the air.

"Thunderstorm might hit us after all." The crickets' shrill cries intensify. "You want something to drink?"

"I don't mean to impose. But I need to talk to you about something."

"Come. Sit." I lead her to one of the wooden steps that lead up to the back porch. "What's up?"

"I had something happen today, and I'm not sure what to do about it. I wanted to talk to Uncle Joel, but he's not home. I assume he's staying with Jolene tonight."

Joel is a piece of work. I stretch out my legs. The knees of the khakis I'm wearing are soiled, and I stretch to brush off some of the dirt.

"I saw a patient today."

"You're not licensed."

"Right. It was as a favor to someone."

"Jessica's daughter?"

"How'd you know?"

"She came to talk to you in my office. What's wrong?"

"I can't really say now. It needs to be anonymous."

"Doctor-patient confidentiality?"

She nods. She's worried. Her downward gaze and the tense line of her lips give it away. Whatever's wrong, it's not acne. Jessica's been having issues with her daughter, but… "Did her daughter open up to you about something?"

"She did." She purses her lips, and it's as if it's painful to her.

"You barely know her, and she opened up?" Zuri looks younger than she is. Maybe her bedside manner is companionable.

"I don't know why she opened up to me," she says, as if she can read my mind. "I think it was just something that's really bothering her and she's having trouble keeping it in."

Damn. "She's pregnant?"

Zuri looks off to the side, to the far end of the yard. Another bout of thunderclaps. A rain drop splatters on the brick, followed by another, and then the deluge hits.

I jump up, and the screen door creaks as I hold it for her. The pitter-patter of rain overpowers the crickets and frogs, and the temperature descends.

On the sofa, I study Zuri. She never answered me, but she didn't have to. Jessica has complained about a guy her daughter is seeing and has worried that she hasn't been focused on grades. And didn't she skip school recently? "Where'd you leave things with her?"

"Encouraged her to talk to her mom. Or her dad. Told her her skincare regimen is sufficient."

"I'm not sure patient confidentiality is in place." I consider Jessica. Type A. Driven. Religious. One of the few surgeons I know who attends church and mentions it. "You've got to tell her."

She crosses her arms and sucks on her lower lip. "Do you think?"

"Did you talk with her about options?"

She says nothing, but she doesn't need to because I can read her averted gaze and the guilt playing across her features.

"Jesus, Zuri, this is Texas. What did you tell her?"

"I told her about me. What I did."

"What we did."

Her eyes, dark in the dim light, flash to mine, but quickly look out as a flash of lightning coats the yard in light. "I never told my parents."

"You were a college student. Over the age of eighteen."

I haven't paid close attention to the legal bullshit in this state. Ian made a few references that he might have to leave Texas to get the best medical care for his wife, Sunny, as she's an older mother and there's always a risk of complications. This isn't a normal state. I'm pretty sure I heard something about a doctor could go to jail for mentioning abortion options to a patient. That has to be doubly true for an underage patient. "You're gonna need to consult with a lawyer."

"I figured." She lets out a sigh. "I'm a dermatologist. This shouldn't even be something I come across."

She sits there, looking forlorn and sad. I pull her to me, onto my lap. She rests her head against my chest, and I hold her. I close my eyes, reveling in the surge of sensations coursing through me, radiating from my heart to my extremities. I've missed her. Missed this.

"Do you ever regret it?" Mixed in with the downpour of rain, it's hard to hear, but I hear her question.

"No. Neither of us were ready." I hardly ever think about it, but when I do, I recognize it made us closer. We were freshman, dating, having fun, but also quite aware that unlike so many of the others in our dorm, for us, for our futures, we needed to care more about our grades than parties. And after that happened, in the spring of our freshman year, our relationship strengthened. "Sometimes, I wonder if our experience made you more determined to become a doctor. Maybe to prove to yourself that it was worthwhile."

"Hmm."

Her hum is neither disagreement nor agreement. It's a point I might not have ever considered, except that she threw away our relationship in pursuit of her career.

"Bringing a child into the world is a big decision. We weren't ready. Neither of us wanted it. Those reasons are enough."

"I agree." My lips brush the top of her fuzzy hair. The scent of her shampoo is new. In college, she used an apple-scented shampoo. Now, there's a subtle hint of mint.

"Do you remember when we used to say that we would still have that child? One day?"

Of course I remember. Boy or girl, one day I wanted a child with her eyes.

The warmth flooding my chest transitions to a dull, deep ache. Outside, the storm has transitioned to a heavy, peaceful rain. The scent of earth permeates the porch. She lifts her head. In this light, her irises appear deep blue, and those lips, full and soft, beckon.

She shifts in my lap, and our lips press together. Instant remedy for the ache. Every atom in my body quivers. Wanting her, needing her. She opens, and I taste her, feel her. She's home for my wayward soul. But this isn't real. This is temporary. She'll move on, and I'll be left devastated. More so than before.

My arms wrap around her, incapable of doing anything else, but a part of me, the deepest part of me that must survive, pulls back. My breaths are forced, heavy and deep. She looks up at me, questioning. And I purse my lips and whisper into the rainy night, "I can't."

No matter how much I wish it otherwise, I can't go through it again.

When I crack the door open, in the aftermath of last night's thunderstorms, the fresh scent of earth tinges the air, the humidity is cut in half, and bright blue skies are on the horizon. If only my insides could match the sky's luminosity. With every foot pounding onto the pavement, my chest grows darker and heavier.

The irony isn't lost on me. I can fuck nameless women into

eternity, but I can't bear to do more with the woman who remains in my dreams, no matter how hard I've tried to forget her. And since she's closer, down the street at night, in the office by day, if I wake and remember a dream, she's always a player. Always present.

When I greet Mrs. Hernandez and her daughter, it's with forced congeniality. Mr. Hernandez isn't present, as he has a project that requires his oversight.

"I told him I'll text him as soon as she's out of surgery." Mrs. Hernandez holds her daughter's hand and smiles up at me. She's treating Maya like a child, but at seventeen, she could be mistaken for twenty-three. But, I suppose, she could be thirty-three and a parent will still be a parent. "Do you think I'll have any trouble getting a signal? He wants to check in, too."

"There shouldn't be any issues in our facility." We're doing the surgery in our outpatient facility. "I think what you're thinking of is the hospital. There are definitely issues with cell signal at Houston Memorial."

I put my hand on Maya's shoulder. "You ready for this?" *You sure you want to do this* is on the tip of my tongue, but I'm in such a foul mood it would probably come out sounding like I don't think she should do it, so I go for a joke. "Let's see. It's Raquel Welch's nose we're going for, right?"

"Who?" Maya's eyes widen and she lets out a nervous laugh. She's playing along with my bad doctor joke, but there's a hint of fear. The bad doctor joke works better with breasts. "We want to make them smaller, right?" asked when the patient is there for breast implants.

"Now, seriously, you've both reviewed the model I prepared. And you understand there's no guarantee of the final result? We'll fix this bend in the bridge of your nose and correct the slight nasal deviations."

I look Maya directly in her dark brown eyes. My gaze falls to the slight scar on her lip, more evident since she's not wearing make-up. She's come a long way. Of course, I thought I'd come a long way, but based on last night and my mindset this morning, I'm surviving. I haven't come far at all.

I leave Maya in the hands of our nursing staff and the anesthesiologist. Before prepping, I visit Mrs. Hernandez one more time. It's the usual conversation. I tell her I should be done in one to two hours. I estimate the surgery will be done in under an hour, but I always provide conservative estimates, as I don't want a loved one panicking in the waiting room.

As I scrub my hands under the water, my chest is heavy, my thoughts dark, but I breathe deeply. It's time to push everything else away. It's time to change someone's life.

Twenty-Two

ZURI

"This day is dragging."

Mena's cheery voice invades my mental space. Rather than hit pause on the online practice test, I hunch my shoulders and reread the question.

"Zuri? You okay?" Reluctantly, I hit pause.

"What did you say?"

"Is everything okay?"

"Yeah. Absolutely." It's clear as day that I'm lying to her, but I'm not going to get into it when I'm sitting at an open desk in a space that opens into the reception area.

"I'm gonna go get a Diet Coke. You want anything?"

"Nah. I'm good." I hold up my water bottle. "Thanks, though."

"You sure you're okay?"

"Yes. Just studying."

She slides off her stool. "Will you cover for me? We aren't due for anyone else for like an hour, but if anyone comes in?"

"Yeah. Sure." The smile I'm wearing doesn't feel real, but it's sufficient. Ever since last night when Harrison nearly forced me into his car to drive me home, a heaviness has weighed down on me. The strained silence, the tortured expression, it's too much. Moving down here was selfish. An act of desperation, but selfish all the same.

And then there was the kiss. Heart-warming. Tender. Passionate. If it had been up to me, I would have stretched out on that sofa and kissed him endlessly. But it's not up to me. He has other places to be, other things to do. And we can't go back. In life, there are no re-dos.

My cell vibrates on the corner of the desk. I flip it over and see a familiar Minnesota area code. Thankful Mena is temporarily absent, I answer with, "This is Zuri Lennox."

"Zuri, this is Kelly." Kelly's a few years younger than I am. She's a part-time assistant working in the network's HR department, but she's someone I consider a friend. But she's also HR.

"Hi, Kelly."

"How are you?"

"I'm fine." The repetitive phrase is like a ringtone playing over and over. "How're things there?"

"Well, can you meet up for a drink?"

"Ah, Kelly, I'm not in Minnesota."

"Oh. Where are you?"

"Texas."

"Oh. Well, do you have a minute?"

"Sure."

Rustling sounds enter the receiver. It sounds like Kelly is moving.

"Have you spoken to Warren?"

"No."

"Maybe you should."

"My lawyer advised against it." And come to think of it, why is HR asking that question?

Kelly's voice drops to a near whisper. "From what I'm hearing, he's thinking about dropping the charges."

"Kelly, it's not up to him. The DA has to drop the charges. The court case is already on the docket. End of August."

"It's weird they're even pressing charges for a first-time offense. You know that DA is a friend of Warren's. If he backs down, they'll drop the charges."

"That would be lovely." If the charges are dropped, I can begin the job search. There's no point in looking for a job with a criminal suit hanging over my head.

The door to the reception area opens, and Mena enters, a drink in hand and a smile. I flutter my fingers in a wave.

"Warren ended things with Sherry."

"That doesn't mean all is well." Yes, I'm pointedly vague because Mena's listening.

"Well, you didn't hear it from me, but there's a meeting with the partners later this afternoon. And the head of HR, for, like, the entire network, is attending."

"I doubt that has to do with me." Mena glances back at me, and I raise my lips in a smile.

"I wouldn't be so sure. We have to decide if we're going to replace you or hold your position until the end of your leave."

My leave. The way she says it, you'd think I'd taken vacation time.

"What're you doing down in Texas?"

I lower my head, my gaze set on Mena's back. She's playing solitaire on the computer.

"I might move here permanently," I admit to Kelly.

"What?" she gasps. "You want to move to the south?"

"Well, no. But I need a job. I have a connection here. I'm taking the state certification exam next week."

"Seriously?"

"Yes." It's hard to not snap at her. I don't know what these people really expected me to do when they put me on an indefinite unpaid leave. "How're things with you?"

Mena pushes up off her stool and leans forward, looking out into the lobby.

"They're good. I miss you." Her comments are eye-roll worthy, given Kelly and I hung out once every other month, tops.

As Kelly fills me in on the office minutiae, Mena exits our area and enters the lobby. From my desk, I watch as she wraps her arms around Allie, and then Allie dabs her eyes with a tissue.

"Hey, Kelly? Can I call you back?"

"Yeah. Sure. How about I call you after the partner meeting today? I'm telling you, I think this whole thing is going to blow right over."

"You got it," I say absentmindedly and end the call.

I lean out into the lobby and ask, "Everything okay?"

The disquiet in Mena's doe-eyes has me waffling between going back to my desk to give them privacy, or shifting forward, offering comfort.

My feet remain glued in place. Outside, cloud cover dims the bright sun. An afternoon storm approaches. Allie sniffles as she closes her eyes. She might be crying.

"What's going on?"

"We lost a patient this morning."

My stomach falls into the pit of sick. In the last year, I haven't heard of anyone dying. Even the skin cancer cases I've referred to oncologists have thrived. But during residency, patients sometimes died, and the best way I could describe the sensation is the pit of sick. It draws everyone into a nauseating abyss. But it's also the circle of life. Except, most of what they do here at Paragon is elective.

Who is on the tip of my tongue, but it's an inappropriate question. I won't know them, anyway.

Allie blinks and inhales. She stretches out her fingers. "Okay. I'm getting out of here. I need some fresh air."

She forces a small smile and turns, heading out into the parking lot. Mena folds her arms around her waist. I step up to her and put an arm around her shoulders.

"You okay?"

I have to imagine they don't lose many patients here. I mean, any time you do surgery, there's always a risk. But, from what I've observed these last couple of weeks, Paragon's patients are healthy and would bear low surgical risk.

"Yeah. But it's sad. That little girl was so sweet."

"It was a child?" My mouth drops open in disbelief. That's the worst. My chest aches, and I brush the butt of my hand against my sternum, as memories of my rotation in pediatrics rock through me.

"Well, she was seventeen, but I met her several years ago. She came in for a cleft lip."

"It was Harrison's surgery?"

She slowly nods.

"Where is he?"

I take off toward his office, not waiting for her answer. His office lights are off.

It's the surgery he was nervous about. The one he didn't want to do. I know it to my core, and deep within, I know he needs me.

He's not in his office, so I grab an Uber, and in under ten minutes, I'm out of the car and running. His front door is locked. There are no lights on in the house, but he's here. I feel it. I sense him, and he's hurting.

I round the house. The garage door is open, and his car is parked inside. The knob twists on the side door. It's open, and I push inside.

"Harrison?"

He's sitting on the sofa. There's a bottle of bourbon on the coffee table in front of him. The top's still on and there's a dry highball glass beside it.

His eyes are red-rimmed, but his cheeks are dry. Devastated. Broken.

"I had to tell her mother." His head bows. "Her father was off working on a client's irrigation system."

Words won't be of service, but I wrap myself around him, holding him. I hope it's not his fault, but I won't mention fault… can't mention fault. In residency, we learn the hard way that sometimes, despite our best efforts, patients die, and it is our fault. Everyone makes mistakes. We're all human, regardless of our profession.

I bury my face into his neck. His arms lie limp, and I grip him tighter, wishing I could take away his pain.

"Cardiac arrest." His voice cracks, and I squeeze harder. "Fifteen minutes after. In recovery." He falls back against the sofa, bringing me with him. "The anatomy of her throat was slightly altered from prior surgeries. But…it doesn't explain. I did an emergency tracheotomy, CPR."

He closes his eyes, and I breathe in relief. It wasn't his fault. If it happened post-op, it wasn't his fault. She's still dead. A tragedy. But it will weigh differently on him.

"There's no such thing as a routine case." Those are the words of one of my med school professors, and I don't know why they fall out of my mouth at that point in time. But they do.

"She died getting a fucking nose job."

She knew there was a risk. I think it but can't say it. To a seventeen-year-old, death feels improbable. One in a thousand equals "not me" to almost anyone. The trouble is, one in a thousand isn't the same as zero.

"And I knew. I felt it in my gut."

I clamber onto his lap, straddling him. I cup his jaw with my hands, gently but forcefully, needing him to hear me. "No. You can't do that to yourself. You questioned if she'd be happy with the results. Doubted her goals were achievable through elective surgery. That's very different from sensing she would die." He slowly lowers his head. God, he looks lost. So lost.

And then, somehow, his lips are on mine. Soft. Open. Needy. The skin along his jaw is rough. He tugs me against him. Closer.

He's the one who breaks us apart. His breaths are rapid.

"I need you," he says, and my heart cracks.

"I'm here." My eyes mist. I rock against him, attempting to get closer. His lips caress my throat, and his hands are everywhere.

"Fuck. I need to lose myself in you." He breathes it out, half plea, half demand.

I answer by lifting my shirt over my head. As my bra hits the floor, I wipe an errant tear away.

Twenty-Three

HARRISON

She's here. On my lap. Touching me. Eviscerating the weight holding me down. Breathing life back into the depths. My drug of choice. My addiction. Zuri.

Her pulse beats beneath the tender spot on her neck, the spot that makes her arch her back and moan. Her skin is smooth and silky. I trace the planes of her back, the terrain of her waist, and the slopes of her breasts. Time stills as she rocks against me, the pressure painfully divine. When I take her nipple in my mouth and twirl my tongue around her buttery soft peak, a wave of dizziness hits. We're in a fever dream, and I never want to wake.

Her fingers toy with the buttons on my shirt. I hiss from her touch, like a brand on my skin. My fingers travel up the length of her spine, to the nape, into her unruly hair. I send the binding across the room and gently tug on her curls, exposing the long lines of her neck. I suck and kiss my way to her lips.

We explore with long, searching kisses, mixed with short, frantic ones. I want everything all at once, and simultaneously I want to freeze this moment in time. To remain in this shelter, never to emerge. I need her.

My fingers fumble with the button on her slacks, and she swipes them away. My breath halts, and I look up into those familiar, stunning eyes, questioning. She licks her swollen lips and shifts on my lap, sliding back on my thighs, giving herself room. Her hair falls forward as she tugs at my scrub pants.

A gentle smile lights her face, and she clambers off me. "I'm going to take care of you."

Assisting her, I lift my hips, letting her remove my pants and my briefs. My erection bobs in the air, achingly hard and extremely needy. Mesmerized, I watch as she kneels on the floor before me, palms on my thighs. Again, she licks her lips, and I swallow hard.

She grips me at my base and flattens her tongue, licking my shaft until she takes me in. Consumes me. My head hits the back of the sofa, and my eyes roll back in my head.

"Fuck."

God, I love this. I've always loved her mouth. The warmth, the tightness, how she cares for me, doing something for me. The base of my spine clenches as she bobs up and down, my hand lightly on the back of her head. But she's too good, and I'm too close.

I pull her off me and urge her to stand. It's my turn to undress her, and I do. She stands bare before me, and I palm her ass, guiding her sweet center to my mouth. She's so wet, so turned on. And god, I love the taste of her. Smooth velvet, hot and wet and oh so sensitive. She tousles with my hair, curling over me as she quivers, her nails grating my skin. I dry my mouth with kisses along her pelvis and up her smooth belly.

"I've missed you." Her words wrap around my heart like an invasive vine. A flowery, thorny vine, one I would be wise to pluck before it roots, but one I'm powerless to hinder.

With one hand on my shoulder, she presses me back and straddles me. Her fingers wrap around me, and she hovers over me, pressing my cock against her sex. She lowers her hips, and my crown disappears. *Consumed.* I look up into those eyes, and I swear every atom in my being vibrates. She stretches around me, a repossession of what has always been hers.

Hot. Wet. Tight. Sublime.

"God, I've missed you." Tears prick my eyes. At the moment. At my confession. Who the fuck knows why, but emotions bubble up and I flip her onto her back, taking control.

Her legs wrap around me, but I slow myself, pulling one calf up to my chest, nipping at her ankle, and slowing my rhythm. And oh, god, the sight of me moving in and out of her. This is what we should always do, what we never should have stopped doing. She feels like no other. My thumb brushes over her trim black curls. With every press of the pad of my thumb, I watch those violet eyes flutter, the strain of her lips, the bend of her throat. She tightens around me like a vise, and those eyelids close. I grip her hip hard.

"No. Eyes open."

She does as I command. Time stops. For a fraction of a second, she's all I see. My soul swims within hers, and I crash over her as the most powerful orgasm of my life rips through me.

We cling to each other as we gasp for air. Outside, a crow squawks. A distant emergency siren sounds through the house. And I collapse against the corner of the sofa, bringing her with me, my shelter from the reality encroaching upon our sanctuary.

She presses her lips to my chest, and I toy with her hair as I listen intently to the departing siren. A city sound. We're in the middle of the city.

She shifts, and I slide out of her. She smiles down at me, a soft, loving smile, and I reach between us, fondling her breast, loving the quiet intimacy. And then I look between us, and it hits me.

"I didn't use a condom."

She relaxes into my chest. "It's okay. I've got an IUD."

"I'm clean," I say into her hair. I always use a condom. She's the only one, Jesus, in so many years.

"I know." I hear her smile.

"How do you know?" I ask as I tease the curve along her hip.

"Because you'd never hurt me."

I tighten my hold on her. She's correct. I would never willingly hurt her.

But as if needing to prove the reverse isn't true, she stiffens in my hold and stretches. Her palm pats my chest, and she moves away.

I attempt to hold her in place, but she pushes up with a "Gotta go to the bathroom."

I watch her naked backside pad to the bathroom down the hall. Goosebumps rise over my damp skin. And all the flowery, poetic bullshit thoughts from her earlier drift out the screen door into the evening sky. God, I hate reality.

Twenty-Four

ZURI

The cool countertop presses into the heels of my hands. Afflicted with lightheadedness, I push against it for stability, avoiding the mirror. I close my eyes and breathe deeply, seeking to gain control of the unwieldy turmoil rocking through me.

I love Harrison. I never stopped loving him. Hell, I ended things out of love. Everything I've done, I've done for his own good.

And he's survived. More than survived, he's thrived. He's not the same man I knew eons ago. We've both moved on. Different lives. But what passed between us was more than sex. Our love still exists. I felt it.

Would he want to change his life to be with me? Would he really give me a second chance? Am I being naïve?

Women adore him.

Leave him cakes.

We call them the romantics.

That portrait hanging in his office, she's a former patient.

158

A fling? A fuck? Is there a difference?

All the quips about Harrison and his activities float around the room. He's got a new life, there's no doubt about that. Would he be interested in more than sex with me? In more than a temporary reprieve?

My muscles weaken as the thoughts roil, and a deep exhaustion falls over me like a veil.

Finally, I meet my gaze in the mirror. I'm a total fucking wreck. Sex-crazed hair. Smeared mascara. Swollen lips. Emerging red splotches along my neck and décolletage. Thin lines crease the corners of my eyes. Three wrinkles stripe my forehead. My eyes burn.

This is crazy. I'm standing naked in a bathroom questioning everything. The person with the answers is sitting beyond the door.

The worst he can say is that no, he doesn't want more. He doesn't think he can forgive me. Or hell no, he's absolutely not giving up his sexual freedom. All valid possibilities. All within his rights.

I just need to talk to him. If he doesn't want me, or us, I'll be okay. I'll survive.

With one last look in the mirror, I pull off an elastic binding from my wrist and pull back my hair. I run the tap and clean up the mascara.

"You okay in there?" Harrison's deep, comforting voice offers the last bit of reassurance I need to step outside.

It's Harrison. No matter what, I'll always love him.

He's sitting on the sofa. Beside him are my clothes, neatly folded. He's wearing the pants to his scrubs and nothing else.

I reach for my clothes, and he says, "You can change into something of mine. If you want."

With one leg in my panties and one out, I pause, glancing up at him.

"You're going to stay the night, right?"

I continue getting dressed because it's awkward standing in the middle of a room naked. This is it. Once I'm dressed, we need to talk. Ask the hard questions. And maybe they won't be so hard. He's asking me to stay the night.

"Your phone vibrated. I thought it was mine, so I went around hunting for the sound." He gestures to my phone, sitting out on the table. I'd had it in my pocket.

"Would you rather have a T-shirt of mine? Or we can shower, then order in?"

My throat feels sore, raw.

This is probably too soon for me to ask him what he wants from this. We had sex. He does this with women all the time.

But of course I'm not all women. He and I share a history. He understands that we're close. That we can too easily hurt each other. He didn't have sex with me earlier because he felt it, too.

As I argue with myself, I reach for my phone. My pants are on, but the button is undone, and I've strapped my bra back on.

This is Harrison. Be normal. Real. He's asking you to stay. That's a good sign. I click the phone. There's a voice message. I click on the icon and read the transcribed text.

Hi, Zuri. This is Lynne Westinghouse from Human Resources. If you could please call me. The board has reviewed your case and has determined they would like to end your unpaid leave and would like for you to return to work as soon as possible. Please call me back to discuss your return date.

I stare at the message. Kelly was correct. A fog clouds my brain.

"Everything okay?" Harrison asks.

He leans over and reads the message on the phone. Or at least I think he does. The screen darkens in save mode.

"Guess I don't have to take the certification test next week."

"Do you know what happened? Why they're welcoming you back?"

"Maybe the DA dropped the case? I haven't heard from my lawyer, but I'm pretty low on his priority list." Given how I have to hound him for any response, I'd say I'm on the bottom of his to-do list.

"And what case did the DA have against you?"

He's confused. As I suppose he would be. "I allegedly bashed Warren's car with a baseball bat."

"Allegedly?"

I roll my eyes and my hand. "Temporary insanity when I discovered he'd been cheating on me for a lengthy amount of time."

"You cared for him that much?"

"No." I suck on my lower lip, weighing how to explain it to Harrison. "At the time, the anger was directed at him. But it was really anger at myself. I should've known better. Should've seen the signs."

His expression softens in understanding. I rub my tongue absentmindedly over my front teeth. If I'm supposed to be back at work next week, there's a lot I'll need to do. Wrap up the project, clean up my room at Uncle Joel's. I'm sure there's something I need to do about the test next week. Cancel in advance so they don't mark me as a no-show. If they even keep records of that. I'm not sure.

"So, that's it. You're moving back?"

"I mean, it's my job." I avert my gaze, looking anywhere except at Harrison. "I don't have a job here. Remember?"

He's the one who didn't want me to work at Paragon. He's the one who said I'd need to find a job somewhere else. Maybe take over a retiring doctor's practice. And god, I have all of those bills. Tuition loans, lawyers.

Harrison's gaze falls to the floor. He's bent over his legs, forearms on his thighs, hands hanging limply down. I want to sidle up to him, to hold him, but his posture warns me off.

Fear courses through me. But I've got to get over that. It's words. A conversation we need to have. The truth is there. Do I have the courage to unearth it?

"Unless, maybe…" I wait for him to say something. He doesn't, and my insides plummet. "I mean, if you wanted me to stay—"

"You hate Texas."

He's right. I do. I don't want to practice medicine in this backward state. For me, this state is a last resort. "Would you ever want to leave here? Would you ever be open to…"

His lips scrunch together, and his eyes narrow. "To what?" He finally, finally raises his gaze. "To following you around the country? If you remember, there was a time when I was willing to do just that. And you told me no. You believed resentment would haunt us. Do you…" He blows out air. The sound is loud and angry, and he pushes off the sofa. "What do you want for dinner? It's going to take a while for anything to get delivered. We might as well order it now."

That's my answer. I reach for my blouse and tug it on. He's still not over what happened so long ago. Or he doesn't want me to stay, and he's putting up a wall, so it's my fault. It's always got to be my fault. Never can it ever be his fault.

I find my shoes and shove my feet into them as I finish tucking in my blouse.

"You don't want dinner?" He's in the kitchen, phone in hand.

"I should probably get back to my place." I shake my head in frustration. "Uncle Joel's." I lift my phone in explanation. "Need to return the call. You know, figure things out."

"Sounds good." He drops his phone and steps up to his refrigerator. Without me here, he'll probably eat leftovers.

I head out through the screen door, and he calls after me, "Zuri, thanks for coming today. I needed…" His words trail, or maybe I just don't hear them.

"No problem. What happened isn't your fault. But you know that." I have no idea if he heard me, but he's going to be okay. He'll be fine.

Twenty-Five

HARRISON

Joel had Mena clear my schedule for this morning, and he found others to cover my afternoon consultations. The decision without talking to me hit like a slap. Like a judgement. Like he was saying I couldn't handle another surgery.

But about two hours into my drive to Austin, the rage simmered, and I have to admit I'm relieved both the breast augmentation and abdominoplasty are rescheduled for next week. The visions flicking through my head alternate between Maya, lifeless, and her mother's agony. Between Zuri taking me, and Zuri walking away. It's no wonder my chest aches. I can't imagine being anywhere other than flying down the open road this morning.

Ian told me to come on down. He's on call this afternoon, which means he'll probably be working. But he told me where the key is. His family has this ranch outside of Austin. It's been in the family for three generations.

He and Sunny are buying a place in Austin so he can be closer to the hospital, but they're keeping her place, a small piece of property that borders the Duke ranch. I've got my choice of places to stay. I can stay at Sunny's house, or at the Duke family's home. His brother, Oliver, built his own house somewhere on the property, and the family house is empty most of the time, as his parents spend most of their days at the beach now that they're retired.

As I turn off the paved road onto Duke Road, a dirt road with a light coating of gravel along the middle and the sides, the navigation ends. Given the nav believes I'm in a vast area of green with no roads, I opt to pull into Sunny's house. It's the first house on my left, and if I recall correctly, the family house is several minutes farther down. Plus, I need to use the facilities.

And I need space, but I didn't come here to be alone.

Sunny's house is a simple ranch with a three-rail wooden fence separating the yard from the pasture. There's a fig tree in the back, a lemon tree in the front, and some overgrown Indian hawthorn shrubs line the front of the red brick home. The bushes are leggy at the base and need to be cut back and shaped. The bare, scorched earth at the roots of the shrubs begs for straw or mulch. But if you look past the house and the neglected yard, there's a long, rolling stretch of green leading to a line of broadleaf trees. There are no power lines, simply uninterrupted blue sky and the quiet of the great outdoors.

The key is where Ian said it would be, beneath the faded straw doormat. The screen door screeches, in desperate need of greasing. Inside the narrow house, it's tidy and comfortable. In the backyard, there's a pergola with a canopy over it and a hammock. The shade knocks the heat back and, combined with the slight breeze and my lack of sleep from the night before, it doesn't take me long at all to give in to a lazy summer day.

When I wake, the tree line hides the sun. Ian's sitting in a chair, one leg crossed over the other, tapping away on his phone.

"How long have you been here?" I ask.

"Not long." He sets the phone down on the flat armrest of a chair he's pulled over. "How're you doing?"

"Fine." It's an automated response. One Ian can easily see through, given this is the first time I've cleared my surgery schedule in my career, and it's also the first time I've ever shown up at his door—in Austin, no less—in the middle of a workday.

"Wanna go for a walk?" He's in flip-flops. My feet are bare. I removed my running shoes, the ones I threw on this morning when I left the house in knee length running shorts and a t-shirt. As I sit here, I can't even recall what I threw into the duffel bag to come here after hanging up with Ian.

Ian walks over to the back door, bends, and comes back to me with a pair of worn leather sandals. "You can wear these. Just watch where you step."

"Snakes?" I ask as I slide my bright white feet into them.

"Cow and horse shit."

"Oh. Right." I'm not what I would consider prissy, but still, stepping into a large pile of steaming shit while wearing flip-flops would serve as a cherry on the top of a hellish week.

Ian lifts his hand, pointing off into the woods. "There's a creek that runs along the back property line. We can head back there, then follow the creek up a bit."

"Lead the way." Ian straddles the fence, then slings a leg over, landing on the pasture side. I follow suit. "Where's Sunny?"

"She has a maternity massage scheduled this evening. She offered to reschedule, but I told her to keep it."

"How's she doing?"

"Good. We saw the doctor last week. Everything looks good."

There's a tightness to Ian's expression as we tread through the pasture. "You're nervous, aren't you?" Because of Sunny's age, her pregnancy is considered high risk.

"Terrified," he answers.

"She's going to be fine." The words sound especially hollow after Maya's death.

"You have to believe that, right?"

I nod and feel the weight of Ian's questioning stare. I didn't tell him much yesterday. Just that I needed to get away.

"I lost a patient yesterday." It's his turn to nod. "Seventeen. Rhinoplasty."

"Damn." The lines of trees are dark, but as we approach, plenty of light filters through and our eyes adjust. "What happened?"

"God, I swear…" My eyes mist as I think back through it all. "Surgery went fine. She coded in recovery. I wasn't even there. She had…" I gesture to my throat, about to mention some of her physical variations, but this isn't a post-mortem.

"You know, that's exactly why I'm scared to death about Sunny's pregnancy. The closer her due date gets… there are no guarantees. But then I think to myself, there's a risk to every single thing we do. My brother, a few years back, was bitten by a rattlesnake not far from here. And here we are in shorts and flip-flops. But the chances of us actually coming up on a rattler are slim. And what're we going to do? Sit inside because there's a chance of getting snakebit? Never travel on a plane because there's a chance it will crash? Hell, statistically, you're more likely to die in a car crash, and it's not like anyone is going to go back to the horse and buggy days. So, yeah, I'm scared. But I'm hopeful."

"And I'm sure you are all over her scans and bloodwork at every appointment."

He smiles. It's a full smile, one that says I'm absolutely right and he's remembering good moments. "Yeah, I am. And so far, everything's looking great. She takes care of herself. She's healthy. The amnio results are all positive." The leaves crackle beneath our feet. Up ahead, there's a narrow path in pressed dirt, and Ian leads us in that direction. "You know, I don't have to tell you this, but what happened to your patient, it's not your fault. Things happen."

"She had had surgery before. I reconstructed her cleft palate years ago. This was—"

"Completely unexpected. You know, in my line of work, I see people's lives upended by the unexpected all the time."

Ian's an orthopedic surgeon. I've spent years mocking him for choosing such a grueling specialty.

"How do you deal with it?" Ian also pulls ER shifts. He's no stranger to the loss of life.

"There's not a one of us walking around today who's not going to die. None of us know how or when, but our death date is coming. It's inevitable. The only thing we can control is how we live. And living a full life is going to involve risks."

I exhale. This is Ian's way of trying to give me a pep talk. Meanwhile, I should be the one giving him a pep talk. He's the one with a wife who's going through a high-risk pregnancy.

"Earlier this week, I had to reconstruct the leg of a motorcyclist. Now, personally, I've seen enough motorcyclists become organ donors that that's not a risk I would take. But my job as an orthopedist isn't to judge. It's doing what I can to improve, or save, a life."

I get where he's going with this line of thought. Maya was taking a risk, but it was a reasonable one. And she believed her life would be improved. For as long as I live, I'll remember her. And her mother.

Ian points to several boulders lodged in a bend in the creek. Sunlight filters through the leaves, and unseen birds chirp nearby. One boulder has a level, flat surface, and Ian clambers onto it. I join him. Our perch provides a view into the swirl of the meandering creek.

"Yesterday, you mentioned Zuri."

"Did I?" I don't remember saying anything about her.

"You said she's going back?"

My throat thickens, but I nod in answer, then break off a piece of a nearby dangling limb. The dry wood splinters between my thumb and index finger.

"She's the one you dated in undergrad, right?"

"We lived together." The clarification is necessary. People need to understand that she wasn't just someone I dated.

"What happened?"

"What do you mean?"

"Things ended." He waits until I look up to add, "Why?"

"We got into different med schools."

"You dated all of undergrad?"

"Most of it." All except the first few weeks and the last few.

"Serious right from the start?"

His question has me thinking back. My mom always said I'd fall hard and fast. I'm not sure what it is about me that made her say that, but I'd have to say that with Zuri, she was probably right. Four years of college, and I never looked at another girl, at least until Zuri ended things.

"I guess freshman year we were, ya know, exclusive but not totally serious. We both rushed and neither of us thought much of the fraternity or sorority scene, so when we weren't studying, we'd hang together. Sophomore year, we weren't as into Greek life. My mom, you know, that was when she got sick. And Zuri was there for me." I pull my knees up and rest my chin on my knee, arms wrapped tight around my legs. Instead of the woods, what I see before me is my old college apartment, and Zuri, sitting on the floor, a textbook in her lap. "I'm not sure I would've gotten through that without her." Two years, it took. Highs and lows before Mom's body wasted away. "I would've taken time off, but Mom insisted I stay in college. Wanted what was best for me. Said there was no reason for cancer to derail my life, too."

Mom pushed me away, and Zuri took me in. Gave me normalcy. Strength.

"That was when you guys moved in together?"

"Our senior year. Mom passed toward the end of junior year."

"So, when I met you that first year of med school, you were fresh off the breakup?"

"Yep." I send the blunt stick twirling into the creek.

"That explains a lot."

"What do you mean?"

"You were pretty morose."

"Was not."

"You never laughed. Drank a lot."

I'd been miserable. "It's a miracle we became friends, huh?"

"Luck of the draw on lab partners, I guess. Plus, you had an extra bedroom and were willing to let me move in."

That memory brings about a smile. He'd been living with an anthropology grad student he found through a want ad. Nice enough guy, but he liked his music loud and didn't seem to need to study the way we did. Ian would show up to class with dark circles below his eyes. When I told him I had a spare bedroom, he'd looked at me like I was a savior.

"You still love her, don't you?"

"Why do you say that?"

"Because…seeing you now reminds me of the way you looked our first year."

"How's that?"

"Like you need to be on meds."

I chuckle. But it's not funny. "I'm fine."

"You still love her." He says it as a statement, not a question.

"I'll always love her." I told her, too. Love doesn't change reality.

"Have you asked her to stay?"

Using the small remnant stick in my hand, I scrape the boulder I'm sitting on. "It's not like that."

"How is it?"

How to explain something I barely understand myself? "Well, for one, we aren't dating. I've got my life here, and she's got a life back in Minnesota." She was only here because of a breakup with another guy she was living with, but somehow that piece doesn't feel important enough to verbalize.

"You know, we're not in med school now. You guys could do the long-distance thing. See what happens. My brother, Oliver, he did long distance for like a year before they agreed one of them would move."

"Zuri won't do long distance." She doesn't believe in it. God knows I begged her before. "Besides, I've got a full life here."

"You mean TMPT?"

Ian's been with me to the club. He used to be the friend I brought along when they gave out guest passes. "No way am I giving it up. The place is a man's dream." I'm living the dream.

"You're so full of it." He pushes up and jumps off the boulder.

"What do you mean by that?"

"Why is it always easier to see through other people's bullshit than to see your own?"

"I'm not bullshitting."

"Bullshit."

I push off and land a few feet from Ian. A stick jabs into the side of my foot. "What're you talking about?"

"We've been friends now, what? Ten years?"

"Yeah."

"You don't date." I open my mouth to argue, but he says, "You fuck. You shut yourself off to anyone. Even Amelia, by the way. She's the only one I've ever known you to fuck that you kept your friendship with. But even her, you held back. Kept her at arm's length."

"There wasn't... We weren't that attracted to each other. It was a drunken—"

"Look. It's not a bad thing. You love Zuri. Sunny's dad was just like you. Her mom died, and he never gave another woman a chance." He steps forward, like the conversation is done. "Come on. It's going to get dark soon."

"And the snakes will come out?" The grass is several inches taller, significantly taller than most lawns, and a pitch-black shadow darkens the gaps between the blades.

"I was thinking more that we won't be able to see the horse shit."

I scan the pasture. "Where are the animals?"

"Sunny doesn't have any right now. Sometimes Oliver will use the paddocks over here if he has an animal that needs to be isolated."

We're about halfway through the pasture when a light comes on in the ranch house. "Sunny's home."

I plod along behind him.

"Why don't we see what Sunny thinks about it?"

"No."

"Why?"

"She lives in Minnesota."

"Have you talked to Zuri?"

Frustration and something I can't quite name merge, and it has me gritting my teeth and regretting I drove out here.

"Look. I get being scared." He waves a hand toward the one-story ranch. "But one life." He holds an index finger out. "One. Get on the plane. Ride the horse. Join the club. Do whatever it is you want to do. But for you, in case your head's too far up your ass to see it, for you… that's talk to the girl."

"She's practical. Minnesota is her best career option. Returning to the practice, proving herself." I've given this thought. Her hatred for Texas is anecdotal. And she'd never support me moving to Minnesota, because she would say that I would grow to resent her. Her voice plays inside my head, saying exactly that.

"Maybe. But are you really going to let her move back without at least talking to her about possibilities?"

Twenty-Six

HARRISON

The trip to Austin helped. Ian shared a few stories of patients he lost. Morbid, yes. But, like gallows humor, good for the battered, guilty soul. There's a reason most med schools have an annual night where they regale the biggest, and often deadliest, mistakes of their residents. It's a twisted method of maintaining a grasp on one's sanity.

I called Zuri on the way back, but she didn't pick up. I've always believed I could sense when she's nearby. On the three-hour drive home, I put those absurd powers to the test. Attempting to sense if she's still in Houston or if she's already loaded up and begun the drive back to Minnesota. Thanks to highway stop-and-go traffic, I don't arrive in Houston until early evening.

She could be long gone. Or she could be here and refusing to answer my calls. But I don't think she'd refuse to answer my calls. And if she was driving by herself in a car, she'd pick up. If she's home packing, it's conceivable my calls met with bad timing as she wouldn't carry her phone with her while toting heavy suitcases or boxes. I pull into Joel's driveway instead of mine when I get back into town, because I need to know if she's still here.

I find Zuri and Joel sitting in his back yard at a round outdoor table with peeling black paint on a moldy brick patio.

There's a bottle of wine in an ice bucket on the table, and condensation covers the bottom section of both of the stemless wineglasses. Joel smiles widely as I approach. I cannot say the same for Zuri.

"What're you two up to?"

"Spent the day going to art museums and walking around. Showing our Zuri here all the things there are to love about Houston."

"Art museums? No NASA?" I train my eyes on Zuri.

"Stayed in the area. Besides, you know me and lines." Joel's still smiling, apparently oblivious to the scowl on his niece's face.

But I'm not. And her displeasure at seeing me is curious. "I called a few times on the drive back from Austin."

She blinks rapidly. Something I said surprised her.

"You went to Austin?" Joel asks. "Feeling better now?" Joel's smile slips, and he looks at me with both concern and empathy.

"Needed to get away." I pull out a chair, and the cast iron legs grate the bricks. "Did you hear anything else from Mrs. Hernandez?"

"You mean like from a lawyer? No, but anything like that will take time. And autopsy results."

Of course, Joel's right. Besides, I'm sure Maya's parents are grief-stricken and shocked. The anger stage hasn't kicked in yet.

Call me heartless, but as I take in Zuri, it's hard for me to care as much about a case that's out of my control and in the past. I still care, and it still hurts, aches in my chest, but the present is of greatest importance. "Are you all packed?"

"I didn't know you were out of town this weekend."

"Needed to get away," I repeat. My heart spasms as those unforgettable eyes wash over me.

"Tell you what. I'm going to go see Jolene. She's been blowing up my phone. See you two later." He picks his chair up and sets it back in line beneath the table. "Don't leave in the morning without saying goodbye."

Zuri nods and slips on the sunglasses that had been sitting on the table.

"Did I interrupt something?"

"No." She wiggles her fingers in a goodbye motion to Joel.

"Can you get out?" I call to Joel.

"Yeah. Where you're parked is fine."

Silence descends as we watch the flaming red Ferrari reverse and spin onto the neighborhood street.

"When're you planning on leaving?"

"Tomorrow morning."

Her answer shouldn't surprise me. After all, I was thinking she might not even be here.

"They wanted me to be back in the office on Monday. But I asked for a week. It'll give me time to drive back, meet with my lawyers and, you know, find a place to live." She twists a blade of grass between her fingers, and I sense there's more to it.

She's really going back. I'll never see her again. Or maybe I will, in another ten or fifteen years. We'll be in our forties or fifties. What will that look like?

Lights flicker in nearby back yards. The tinkle of a bike bell sounds in the distance, and the low hum of a car engine passes. "Well, do you need any help loading things up?"

That's not at all what I came here to talk to her about, but we've been through this before.

"I have one suitcase. It weighs a ton." She lifts one shoulder. That's all she has for me. That's what we've been reduced to. "My other bags are light."

"Lead the way." I stand, and the chair's leg sticks on an off-kilter brick. Instead of sliding backward, the chair crashes loudly. I can't help but think it's a metaphor for how my insides feel. And it's all my fault. I should've kept my walls up.

I follow her through Joel's house. He's a packrat. There are stacks of magazines, newspapers, and books on almost every surface. I count three different pairs of spectacles sitting in unexpected locations. One by the table near the front door. Another on a stack of books. A smudged lens peeking out of the raincoat hanging from a peg in the hallway.

"This way," she says, and the steps creak beneath her weight.

She's wearing a navy miniskirt and a white cotton sleeveless blouse. The skirt falls mid-thigh and hugs her curves, highlighting the graceful sway of her hips as she ascends to the second floor.

There was a time when I fully expected I would never leave her side. That I would be with her until climbing stairs caused us issues, and we both yearned for a one-story home. And yet here we are.

The bedroom she's been staying in at Joel's is spartan. There's a bed with an iron headboard, one small bedside table, and an oval multicolored rug. Two closed suitcases rest in a corner, and one smaller open suitcase lies between them and the bathroom door. I'm sure tomorrow, after she wakes, she'll pack up her remaining toiletries, zip up the suitcase, and leave.

She strolls to the two suitcases and places her hand on the larger, heavy one.

Ian told me to talk to her. It's now or never.

"Would you consider staying?" I know the answer. It's a pointless question.

"Here? In Texas?"

In response, I just stare at her. What else would I be asking?

"I need to get back…I can't leave things the way I did. I need to at least get a couple of years under my belt before I open a private practice or leave for a different group."

She's answering the question like she's given it a lot of thought. Her conclusions are the same as mine.

I could offer to move, but that would be asinine. We aren't dating. Everything between us is history. Buried in the past.

"So, I guess that means tomorrow is goodbye?"

"We can still talk. Unless you feel like we can't."

I step forward, closer to her. I need to touch her, and so I do. My thumb brushes her cheek. Her breaths are uneven. My gaze falls to her chest. She's not wearing a bra. The material of the top is thick, but not so thick as to disguise the peaks of her nipples.

"Can we be friends?"

The answer to her question lodges thick in my throat.

"Can we be together? One more time?" My gaze travels up her chest, to the short chain with a glittering pendant, along her graceful neck and her heart-shaped face. I raise her sunglasses and fall directly into those novel irises.

"One last time, for memory's sake?" I'm repeating the very words she uttered to me so long ago, the night I moved out, refusing to return until she had packed and gone. It hurt so much.

Her palm flattens on my shirt, lighting up the skin beneath. But it's her other hand that answers me as she cups my erection, then caresses me over my jeans.

"I'll take that as a yes."

"You get hard so easily." She says it like she's in awe.

"Around you, yes, I do."

I pull on the cotton strap, tugging it down her upper arm until the smocked top falls over one breast. I cup her breast and flick my finger over the hard bud. "Looks like you're turned on, too."

"Should we, ah…" Her gaze cuts to the bed, but I back her against the wall. Reading me well, she helps by removing her top. And I bend to my knees. My fingers spread across her thighs, and I push higher, pushing the hem of her skirt up as I go. My mouth cups her over her silk panties, eliciting a moan. I loop the elastic band with my fingers and tug down, dragging the panties over her thighs and knees until they pool at her ankles and she demurely steps out of them.

"Skirt on or off?"

My pulse quickens as she fingers the blue plastic button and unzips. The skirt follows the panties to a pile on the floor.

I palm her ass and bring her center to my mouth. My tongue slips inside her silky smoothness. She gasps and curls forward, and I thrust a finger into her. She's fucking dripping.

Pumping in and out of her, she quivers and moans. As if she's reading me, she places one lean thigh over my shoulder, spreading herself to me, and I take my dripping finger along her slit to her tight, puckered hole. And press. Sucking and lapping her clit, with one hand working her tight vagina and the other pressing into her back channel, it doesn't take long before she's exploding around me.

And it's not until then, when I rise from the floor, that I claim her lips. She fumbles with the button on my pants, but I tear her hands away, lifting them over her head, flat against the wall as I ravage her mouth. She mewls and squirms.

She wants to be closer, and so do I. But I need the control. So I spin her around and place her hands flat on the wall.

"Keep them here," I command. "And spread those legs."

My fingers drip with her juices. I grip my shaft and stroke, then slap a palm against her ass.

"Lean forward. Ass out."

Her curls fall over her shoulders, cascading downward, as I drag my tip through her. I close my eyes, willing myself to remember, seeking control that doesn't come. With one hard thrust, I'm deep inside. She's tight. Hot. Fucking perfect. The feel of her breasts in my hands, her back to my front, her tight fucking channel.

"God, you feel so good."

And then I'm moving. I'm living. Inside her. With her. Jesus, she feels so good. The best. The absolute fucking best.

Our skin slaps. The scent of sex surrounds us. Her skin glistens in the waning daylight. My fingers spread her trimmed curls, searching for her sensitized cluster of nerves, and when she pulses around me, quivering, I know I've found it. Nirvana.

She screams, and the orgasm that rips through me momentarily blinds me.

We stand there, me clutching her as she supports us with one palm flattened on the wall, our breaths out of sync. My pants are around my ankles and the bedroom door is wide open behind us. This is living.

Out of nowhere, a realization hits me. We live every day. We fucking die once.

She twists in my arms, and laughter bubbles up from within her.

"Sexy look?" I ask, guessing I look like a bonehead with my pants around my ankles.

She presses her lips to my sternum and her arms rest on my shoulders. Her fingers curl through the hair on the nape of my neck. I close my eyes, reveling in the feel of her. I love when she does that. It's the best feeling. My dick twitches. He wants her again. But it won't be for the last time. It can't be.

"Zuri?"

"Hmm?" She nibbles my neck. Her breasts press against my chest, and I palm her ass, keeping her close.

"This time we're going to do long distance. We're going to see where this goes."

"But..." She pushes away, and there's confusion in her expression. She's unsure. But I'm not. We could talk more about it, but doing so runs the risk she'll talk us both out of it. So, I lift her, and she lets out a squeal. I step out of my pants, kick off my briefs, and deposit her on the bed. I don't know what's going to happen. But damnit, today isn't my day to die, so I'm going to live.

Twenty-Seven

ZURI

It's the way he looks at me. Like I'm beautiful. To him, I'm beautiful. And desirable. He spends his days improving women and men. Altering features to achieve the desired result.

That's how he spends his days. And I guess I assumed he'd see things he wants to change in me. A little filler on the cheekbones. In the lips. A smoother forehead.

But no, there's pure hunger in those eyes. His hair's in disarray. From my fingers. That body of his is luscious, his care and discipline evident. And as he crawls on the bed, prowling to me, I notice his arousal. It's not my imagination. He wants me. Again.

His fingers wrap around my ankle, and he places it to the side. We're on top of a thick, silky comforter. It looks expensive. Like nothing I've seen in a store, which means we probably shouldn't risk staining the charcoal gray silk. My ass slides against the smooth material as he positions my legs. I push up on my elbows.

He nibbles along my calf, up my thigh, and gets that mischievous grin. I'm wet. Really wet. He just had me. But that doesn't stop him.

He wants me.

One finger fills me, followed by another. Those eyes, locked on mine. Attentive. Possessive.

He dips his head, and my head tilts back, my eyes rolling into the back of my head.

Yes.

The man definitely knows how to use his tongue.

How did I ever walk away from this?

He's attentive. And patient. That's the Harrison from the past. It's who he is, deep down beneath the veneer.

But when he spreads me wide, spreading my juices, and he pushes past a barrier he's never crossed before, my closed eyes snap open.

"Okay?" he asks.

It's uncomfortable. But it's also naughty. Sensations curl through my sex because he's not neglecting anything. No, he's working me from every angle. My muscles tighten once again. I relax into the fullness. It's the graze of his teeth over my clit that has me curling forward, blinking into yet another orgasm.

As he crawls up the bed, his lips cover my belly, my breasts, and his tongue twirls over my nipples. His erection presses against my thigh. I reach between us, fondling him.

He groans. I push his shoulder, urging him to shift onto his back.

"What do you want, baby?" It's a question, but it's also a tease, because he knows. He knows exactly what I want. I shiver as I take him, sliding down over his hard width.

He palms my breast with one hand while the other rests on my hips. He'll let me do exactly what I want, but I know him. When I'm too erratic, too far over the edge, he'll raise his hips and drive into me. He'll take over, guiding us both when I lose physical control. I trust him. I'm not sure I've ever trusted anyone as deeply as I trust Harrison.

Maybe trust and love go hand in hand, especially when it comes to intimate moments. The bed creaks. The headboard softly bumps the wall. He raises his hands, and I link my fingers through his, holding on for balance as I roll my hips and he thrusts upward. It's a dance from the past, one I've missed. Tears leak from my eyes as my body combusts and Harrison pulses within me.

A sheen of sweat covers us both. I lie over him, half on his chest, half beside him. One leg languidly over his.

"Wow," I say, breaking the silence. His chest rises and falls like he ran a marathon.

"Yeah, I'd say."

I nip his chest. "I've missed this." I'm unsure if it's an admission or afterglow small talk.

"Me too," he says, and I playfully slap my hand over his nipple.

"Yeah, right," I tease. "I know all about your sex club."

He covers my hand and adjusts me, forcing me to look at him. "Is that going to be a problem? Do I need to…I should take you."

"What?"

"We'll go. It's this mysterious place to you. It can't be something that comes between us. I'll take you. The unknown frightens. And you don't need to fear anything." He lifts my finger to his mouth and toys with it between his teeth. Then he presses his lips to the bitten skin. "This is what we're going to do. We're going to lay here and cuddle because I need to."

"Oh, you do, do you?"

"Yes, I do. You know this about me. I love nothing more than to have your naked body clinging to mine."

I nod because he's looking at me like he expects a response.

"Then we're going to load up your stuff in my car. I'm going to purchase a flight for you, a couple of days from now."

"I've got to–"

"I'll ship your car back."

"That's so much money."

"Do I look like someone who cares about the money? This is what I want. Give me what I want. Can you do that?"

My teeth sink into my lower lip as I consider this. It's a lot of money to me, but it's not to him. And it is what he wants. And I'm not emotionally ready to say goodbye. Not after our afternoon. "Okay."

"Back at my house, we'll shower. I'll take you to dinner at the club."

"I don't think I have anything to wear–"

"It's Saturday night. Yes, it's counterintuitive, but there are no open rooms tonight. We can have dinner. I'll take you upstairs. To a private suite. I need you to see that what that place was…is…I'd give it all up in a flash for you. You can think of that place as a modern-day Tinder for me. Safer than Tinder. More upscale. An app I'll more than happily delete from my phone. Because you're who I want. No one else makes me feel like you do."

"And how do you feel when you're with me?" I'm teasing because if I didn't tease, I couldn't bear the seriousness of the moment or of what he's saying. It's too much. Too heavy. And too good to really be true, right?

"When I'm with you, it feels like nothing else matters. Like I'm exactly where I'm supposed to be. Like I'm home."

Twenty-Eight

HARRISON

"Turn around."

I do as she says, closing my eyes as the handheld pulses hot water over my shoulders and down my back. "I'd ask where you learned all your new moves, but I don't want to know."

Hot water pulses down my spine. My muscles are languid. Nearly noodles. The showers at the club have the same handheld, but there's no point in telling her that. In the years we've been apart, I haven't been a saint. I won't pretend otherwise.

My dick is heavy, coming to life after an afternoon of bliss. I spin her around, forcing her to drop the handheld so I can massage her scalp, applying shampoo, then conditioner. The two overhead showers rain down over us.

"You getting sore?" I ask, my lips hovering over hers. My tongue traces the line of her lower lip, and then I nip. My cock's still in my hand, and I drag the tip through her slit. The shower pours around us. If she's sore, we can go to the club another night this week.

She pushes up onto her tiptoes and grips my shoulders for balance.

"It's worth it." Those eyes. They're light with happiness. Pleasure. Life.

I back her against the tile and kiss her. Slow. And hot. This, us together, it'll never get old. Nothing has ever felt as right as this. Because it's not just sex. I crave her. My soul needs her, because years ago some part of me became hers, and the only way for me to achieve fulfillment is to be with her, like this, our atoms colliding.

The water is cooling by the time I've delivered an orgasm with my fingers and she's worked her magic over me, too. I wrap her in a towel, then drape one around my waist. Her nutmeg hair glistens ebony, soaked with water that drips from bendy ends. I direct her to sit, open a drawer, and pull out a dryer and a brush.

She narrows her eyes. "I thought you said you don't bring women back here."

I'm gonna need to do something about her insecurities. "I don't. Dad's come to visit, and he brings women."

"Plural?"

I laugh, push her chin up to close her mouth and pinch the end of her nose. "No. One at a time. He's been in a few different relationships over the years."

Dad's another one. Like me. Or maybe I'm like him. The Ramsey men give their hearts away, and they're never the same.

"How is your dad doing these days?" We've talked some about it, but on a surface level. She closes her eyes as my fingers tousle with her soaked strands and the blower's heat changes the texture from smooth to coarse.

"He's surviving," I answer as honestly as I can. Which is what, if I'm honest, I've done for the last ten years. "He travels a lot. Sometimes with someone, sometimes alone. He pops in for visits. We talk weekly. But he drinks more than he used to."

"Do you go home often?"

"What home?" She twists in the seat. "He sold the house the summer before med school. Almost everything from the house is in storage." One day I'll need to go through the boxes. Salvage our family photos. Although, a lot of those are digital. But there are a couple of frames I remember that I'd like to have. A shawl my mom wore. Dad said he saved her jewelry, and I suppose one day, when the time is right, I'll give it to Zuri.

Violet eyes catch mine in the reflection of the mirror. "It still hurts, doesn't it?"

I force a swallow, dig into the drawer and find a clasp for her hair, then twist the bulk of it into a top loop.

"It does. But less."

When I lost Mom, I lost Dad too. Sure, he's still here. But he's a shell of the man he once was. "You won't be able to tell a difference when you see him again," I tell her. "But, at times, it feels like it hurts him to be around me."

Her hair twists around the brush, and I flip the air back on.

"Are you straightening my hair?"

"I am." She used to love when I did this for her. If it's up to her, she lets it air dry. But she loves the way it feels when I dry it, something I discovered the one day I accompanied her to get her hair cut in college. I went feigning boredom but watched intently. Saw the pleasure having someone dry her hair delivered. And I figured it out.

The brush I'm using isn't perfect. It's got a smaller barrel than I'd prefer to use. But the hairdryer is top of the line because I dry my hair. I like the way it feels too.

"Harrison."

"Hmm?" A smooth section of hair falls against the slope of her neck. I need hairspray.

"Your father loves you. Don't ever doubt that."

I meet her eyes in the mirror. "I know."

"He's healing. You were already out of the nest."

"I know," I repeat. And I do. If I'm honest with myself, I leaned on Zuri to heal, back when Dad had no one. And then, when Zuri left, I wallowed in my world.

"The next time I speak to him, I'll get a visit on the calendar."

The corners of her lips lift. Her fingers find my forearm, and she squeezes. She's right, of course. Dad isn't getting any younger. I should reach out.

After her hair is dry, she opens her suitcase and stands over it, perusing the folded piles.

"May I?"

"What?"

"Go through? Pick out something for you to wear?"

"You can try. A lot of my stuff is in storage because I wasn't certain I was moving here permanently. And…I don't really think I own anything to go to a sex club."

I bite back a smile. She probably doesn't. A fact I derive far too much pleasure from. Now that she's mine again, I can buy her any attire she needs.

But, as I finger the tightly packed clothes, I find the black skirt and pale silk camisole I remembered her wearing one day at the office. Then I dig out a pair of strappy heels. She hasn't worn these around me, but I'd had a feeling she packed something like this. She used to have a thing for packing heels on trips and never wearing them.

"Here you go."

"Really? If I threw on a blazer, I could wear this in the office."

"Correct. I told you; we're going to the restaurant tonight. This works."

She's toying with the edge of her lip. I lift her chin, brush my lips against hers, and reassure her. "You're beautiful. You're perfect. Every man there will envy me. And if they don't, they should. We're going to have a wonderful dinner, share a celebratory bottle of wine, and then I'll give you a tour and answer any questions you may have."

"What are we celebrating?"

"Second chances."

Twenty-Nine

ZURI

The small restaurant is remarkably ordinary. The bouncer behind the twelve-foot-tall metal entrance doors seated inside a closed vestibule, plus the no cell phone requirement, communicate exclusivity. The ten-foot-tall black leather doors that lead into the building hint at something more beyond. The black leather, marble, and crimson details speak of wealth. But the people inside aren't any different than you'd find in almost any expensive restaurant in Houston or Minneapolis or any major U.S. city.

I've been here before but never have I known without a shadow of doubt I'd be going deeper into the building. The nerves electrifying my stomach eradicate any hint of hunger. The glass of wine goes straight to my head, and after mere sips the dizzying effect breeds caution.

Harrison's hand cocoons mine in warmth. "You don't need to be nervous. There's nothing to be nervous about. It's just us."

But is it just us? He's spent years here pushing boundaries, doing things that no doubt would venture far beyond my comfort zone. He says he's never gotten over me, but is it just the idea of me he hasn't gotten over? The one who got away? The one he wanted but couldn't have?

What happens once he has me? Not just tonight but a month from now. A year from now. Five years from now. What happens once he sees the others he had are more adventurous, better at sex, equipped with far better bodies? I mean, sure, I take care of myself. But I'm not a health nut. I eat meat and bread and butter.

He's seen me. We're good together. But are we sex club good? Is being here going to bring back memories for him that force him to have second thoughts?

"Babe, what's wrong?" He's leaning toward me, concern flooding his expression.

There's an older couple sitting in a booth across the restaurant, heads bent close together, fingers intermingled. They look normal. Content. Wedding bands glisten on their fingers. But are they married to each other?

Harrison's gaze follows mine. "They've been coming here for years. Longer than me, actually. He was one of the men on the board who had to approve my application. He's not on the board anymore. It's a volunteer position people rotate. She's a rather big deal in the Houston art scene."

"Are they married?"

"Yes." Harrison slowly nods then repositions his chair, presumably so it won't appear we're talking about them. There are only six tables here tonight, and two people are dining at the bar. Harrison did tell me it would be slow tonight.

"I meant to each other?"

Harrison smirks and leans back in his chair. It's a maddening expression because it's one that says I'm amusing him. He thinks I'm being silly, and maybe I am. We're all adults here. Free to do what we want.

"They're a powerhouse couple. From what I can tell, very happily married."

The information should settle my nerves. A normal, happily married couple in the midst. Older, too. I'd guess they might be in their sixties. Of course, with her closely cropped straight silver hair, silver pendants, and black leather sleeveless tank, she's the epitome of class and sexiness intertwined. He's in a black jacket and crewneck sweater, and his close-cropped hair is a sheen of white beneath the flickering golden lights. His ease is reminiscent of Pierce Brosnan, the same kind of sophisticated air, only much whiter hair.

"I'm not sure why I'm so nervous." I've always been able to tell Harrison anything, and right before going into his intimidating playground doesn't seem like a good time to start holding back. "I suppose I'm worried about what you'll think of me."

"Zuri, you're the woman I love. The woman who possesses my soul. What you want to do here, what you don't want to do, none of that changes how I feel about you. You're all I need. All I want. If you don't want this, then I don't want it."

That's what he says now. But things change. In theory, my parents were once madly, passionately in love. And they ended up with a divorce saga that broke world records. Almost fifty percent of marriages end in divorce. Evidence feelings change.

"Are you going to be able to eat?" Our salads had been delivered. A basic house salad with butter lettuce, tomato slices, cucumbers, and carrot slivers.

My stomach curls. "I'm really not hungry."

"All right. Let's go upstairs. I think I know how to get your appetite to return."

"But you're hungry. Eat."

"Oh, I'm going to eat." A flush heats my skin. "And we'll order room service afterward."

He pushes the chair back and nods to the bartender.

"Don't you need to pay?"

"No." He holds out his hand, ever the gentleman. I swallow and stand, cursing my nerves and whatever part of me lacks self-confidence. For crying out loud, there is nothing to be nervous about. As he said, the communal rooms are closed tonight. We're going to a private room. There is no reason to be nervous. Yet the relay between my mind and body couldn't be less effective.

As we approach, the leather door swings open, pushed by a man in a black suit, black Oxford shirt, and slim black tie.

"Welcome, Dr. Ramsey." My stomach somersaults. Thank god I didn't drink more wine, because what I did drink rises in the back of my throat.

A pull inside me intensifies. One part pleads to step backward, to exit the building. There's no way this can be for me. But another part, a quiet part, the part I have never given voice to before, wants to step into the unknown.

I'm not dressed like I imagined people attending a sex club dress. I could wear this to any restaurant in town. Probably even to a funeral in hot weather. The rayon fabric clings to my curves, but the silk underside slips smoothly along my skin. I don't have a bra on, mainly because my one strapless bra clings too tightly, creating unsightly lines. On the off chance I'd be in front of others when the skirt came off, I'd worn a black, plain jane thong. The silky scrap of material doesn't create lines. Harrison said tonight we wouldn't be in a public room, but no matter what he said, that phrase "sex club" reverberates back and forth between my head to my belly, creating an unease that requires a sense of protection.

I've never seen myself as a sex club girl. But ever since that night when Allie and Mena mentioned Harrison frequented one, my curiosity piqued. Partly about a sex club, partly about what Harrison is into. Curious if perhaps we've both evolved in such a way that we are no longer sexually compatible. But intrigued by the idea that maybe, just maybe, he'll expand my horizons. And also, the darker part of me, the part I always fight to squelch, that wonders what if we go in this secretive place, and I love it, am into it, but he realizes I'm not enough for him. That my body is flawed. That I am too conservative, too timid, not aggressive enough.

What if I step into that hall and after it's all said and done, he's disappointed. What if he realizes he doesn't really want me?

"You okay?" He's close, so close his breath tickles my ear. And warms the skin. There's pressure on my lower back, and I know it's from his hand. Possessive…and concerned.

"Yeah. Let's do this."

His lips roll into a grin, and he tilts my chin up to look at him. "Nerves?"

"No," I lie. False bravado works wonders. Can he see through it? Possibly. The man behind the counter in a cheap uniform-issued suit? He can't see through my facade. He doesn't know me. I step forward, chin held high, arms back, and ignore the twinge of pain in the pads of my feet. Heels aren't something I wear often, but at the moment, these five-inch beauties are my armor.

"I'm going to give her a tour before we head upstairs. The rooms are empty tonight, right?"

"Yes, sir," he says. He's an older gentleman, older than Harrison, and it feels odd to hear him call Harrison sir. There's a woman dressed in a black dress and wearing a black suit coat behind the counter with him. The tops of monitors can be seen along the edge of the counter, and she barely spares us a glance.

"What's on the monitors?" I ask the second the hallway door closes behind us. Can she see in the rooms upstairs?

"Hallways and elevators. Discretion is promised. They ensure private elevator rides, and if someone requests it, ensure no one passes someone else in a hallway."

"But that doesn't make sense. There's an open restaurant."

We're passing through a drab hallway with black-painted walls and a polished concrete floor.

"Not everyone feels comfortable eating in the restaurant. There are private exits." I glance up at him, and he's smirking. It's the look he gets when he's trying not to laugh.

I push his ribs. "Don't laugh at me."

"I'm not. I swear." Up ahead, the hallway splits around what appears to be an octagonal room with glass panels. Harrison slows in front of the oddly shaped room. "I was just remembering a friend who used to wear a wig in that restaurant."

I consider that. "Amelia?"

"Don't tell her I told you. She'll kill me."

"Did you…" I can't finish the question. The area between my ribs seizes. He told me he'd fooled around with her, but…it's one thing for him to have been with someone nameless. Another for him to be with a woman who engenders jealousy.

"No." He's calm. There's no trace of a smile. "Amelia and I are just friends and have been just friends for a long time."

"But she comes here?"

"She's a member. But, to my knowledge, Liam was the first person she's been with at this club and remains the only member she's been with. You seem to think this is solely about promiscuity. And for some, that's true. But for some, it's an intimate experience. Something to be shared only with a loved partner. The couple in the back of the restaurant?"

"Yeah?"

"They've been coming here for at least fifteen years. Inaugural members. Happily married for I think maybe twenty-five years."

I shift from foot to foot, uncomfortable beneath his studious gaze and lecture tone. I breathe in deeply, inhaling a faint lemon scent.

"They've been cleaning."

"Sanitation is important." He presses against a black plastic panel and a purple strobe light in the center of the octagonal room lights. Black leather wrist restraints hang on metal chains from the ceiling. In the center, there's a waist high octagonal table. To the side, there's an oddly shaped black leather chaise.

"What's this room?" I try to imagine how many bodies could fill the space and what they would be doing. I don't see whips or any torture devices.

"It's a room for those with voyeuristic preferences. There are buttons inside. You can tint the glass so you can see out while playing or keep it so you can't see out. Imagine that there are others watching but not actually know."

"Hmmm." Harrison and I once, years ago, had sex in the library stacks. Lots of people did, or at least, those were the rumors. I remember how exciting it had been. The thrill that someone might walk in, that we might get busted. But what if someone had walked up? If they'd walked up when I'd been right on the edge, would we have continued? Not stopped, just let someone watch?

I'd had that dream, or fantasy, more than once. Was that what this was? A safe space to play that fantasy out without the threat of winding up in a police station?

"Does it appeal to you?" He brushes a strand of hair behind my ear, and the touch sends tendrils of anticipation down the side of my neck and straight to my clenched sex.

"In theory, maybe." A tiny voice inside me tells me to speak. If this stands a chance of working, I have to communicate. "I used to fantasize that someone walked in on us in the library."

He palms my ass and in one fluid movement presses my body against his side. "Me too."

There's mischief in his eyes ,and that tiny voice squeaks *oh, no.* "But I don't know that I could actually do that. Windows set to one-way or two-way… I just…"

"You'd be surprised what you're willing to do when the mood is right." He presses his lips to my crown. "I'm not taking you around here to tell you what I want. I'm giving you the tour to sate your curiosity."

"What's your favorite thing to do?"

"You." He says it simply. Matter of factly.

"Have you been in here?" He guides me around the room, and I peer across his chest, staring into the purple haze as if I expect lovers to appear.

"No, I haven't." His brow furrows. "Never struck me as something I wanted to do. But, also, this room is typically reserved by partners. I never planned anything ahead of time. Never had a regular partner. But that's another advantage of the club." We've arrived at another black leather door, and he pushes it open. "Everyone is tested monthly. Condoms reign supreme. It's safe."

"Safe." The word blows out through my lips as I take in the expanse of the room. It's clear there are groupings of furniture in the room. Some areas are leather sofas, some chaises, some leather crosses. A swing hangs far across the room. There's a long bar but it looks like a place to rest against. Maybe to lean against and talk. Or do other things. "How many people are in here at one time?"

"This is the room that's the most like a club. Pounding music. Strobe lights. Water. Lots of water. The other rooms are for smaller groups. How many?" His lower lip bulges out as he gives it consideration. "Most I've seen is maybe twenty-five, thirty people. For big events. But people are typically in clusters. Most of the smaller rooms are off this one."

I try to visualize it. The grunting. The pervasive smell of sex in the air. Strangers watching strangers fuck. Repulsion circulates in my gut.

"I'm not sure I could do it." Does that admission make me less attractive?

"Beautiful, you can do anything you set your mind to."

But what if I don't want to?

"Let me show you the suite."

His fingers lightly trace the line of my jaw. And those eyes. Concern. Caring. Desire.

It's all there. In his gaze.

I want to experience this with Harrison. The love of my life. Past. Present. Future. *Maybe...*

Thirty

HARRISON

Her pupils are dilated, her palms damp. Fingers chilled. She's nervous. But she doesn't need to be.

I wave the plastic key card, and the lock clicks. Her fingers still interwoven in mine, I push down on the door lever and push it wide, opening it for her.

There's nothing to this place. It's a well-stocked private room. That's all.

I'd be just as happy back at my house, but she's curious. She's built things up in her head. Expectations. Fantasy and reality may collide, as long as fear doesn't act as an oxidizer, leading to an explosion.

Her fingers trail the silky comforter. The skirt she's wearing rounds the globes of her ass, and I crave placing my erection solidly between those globes. Her naked, beneath me, sprawled out on the bed. Mine to play with. To tease. Torture. Thread the line between pain and pleasure. Over and over again.

The demure skirt hangs nearly to her knees. But in my mind's eye, she's naked before me. Her every curve memorized.

She opens the glass cabinet door and fingers a black leather paddle then lifts it; one eyebrow raised in question.

"Paddle."

"People re-use these?" I fail to suppress a chuckle. Which is fine. I don't normally laugh in this place. I don't normally use these suites. But with Zuri, I'm right where I want to be.

"I requested the room to be stocked. Everything in here is new. Except the furniture." I glance to the corner of the room. "The cross. The chains. The sheets are washed. As is the duvet cover."

She lifts an anal plug. It's a trainer. Small.

"New," I answer her unspoken question.

In this room, she's calmer. She lifts a black leather flogger and trails the tendrils over her palm. She's almost too calm now. Did she and Warren play? A wave of jealousy grinds my teeth.

She looks around the room. Thick velvet drapes cover the window. Candles flicker in vases. The overhead light casts a golden haze.

"We can shower first, if you like." Water calms her. Soothes her worries.

"Do you want to shower?"

"I wouldn't mind scrubbing your nipples."

"You think they're dirty?"

"No. They're delicious. But a good scrub would sensitize them. I could pulse the water over you. Bring you to the edge." Her breath catches. I think she likes the sound of that. "Or there's a selection of oils in the dresser. I can slick you up. Work through those tight knots."

"But what about my nipples?" She slips her nail between her teeth. Coy. She's playing with me.

"Trust me." My gaze flits across the nipple clamps placed on a shelf. "I have ways."

My hand falls on her zipper. She glances over her shoulder. Curiosity and concern blend in her expression. "What is it?"

"Is this BDSM? This room here? These toys."

I sink into the edge of the bed, pointedly looking up to her.

"Bondage. Discipline. Sadomasochism. That's what you're asking about." Her teeth sink into the lower part of her lip. My dick twitches. "Is that why you're nervous?"

"I'm not–" She backs into the shelves. They shake with the force of the collision. "I guess I've always been vanilla." I like hearing that far too much. I wouldn't have a problem if she'd developed additional tastes, I just don't treasure the idea of her and dipshit Warren exploring together. Hell, I don't want to think about that part of her past, period. "And I'm wondering…" she reaches behind her and lifts the paddle again, "are these things what you're into? I don't see a whip, but–"

"Zuri, come sit." I pat the mattress. "Let's talk."

She does as I ask. Those violet eyes are dark, her pupils enormous, from the dim light, certainly. Possibly fear. Or maybe she's turned on.

"At its core, BDSM is a power exchange. It's not something I've delved deeply into. I could have, easily. But I've used this place for hookups. Safe, consensual, noncommitted hookups. The problem at its core for me is that whenever there's a power exchange, there's a connection formed. And I didn't want the connection. I wanted release."

I study her, looking for judgement. I'm not going to apologize for my behavior since she left me. It worked for me. But if the unknown might be an issue for our future, I'll share whatever is needed.

"So, you're not a Dom?"

"I have personality traits that lean dominant. Would I like to explore your limits? Yes. I'd like to push your body to the edge." Those violet eyes glance at the cabinet. "The edge of bliss. Not pain. I'm not a sadist. I don't get off on causing others pain. I would never want to hurt you. Ever. The toys I selected for inclusion in this room are all for pleasure."

"The paddle?"

"Not to hurt you." I push off the bed and reach for the flogger. "Hold out your hand." She does as I ask, and I drape the tendrils over her palm, then across the exposed skin along her wrist and arm. Goosebumps rise. "Feel good?"

She nods.

"Vibrators are on the bottom shelf. To tease you. For extra stimulation."

"And the butt plugs?"

"You know what they are." I narrow my eyes. Back in college, she and I did not explore any anal play.

"Of course I do. I get emails. Watch movies. Read books."

"If…" I pause, waiting for those violet eyes to return to me, "… it's something you want to explore, we would start small. There's stretching involved. Preparation."

"It's something you like?"

It is something I like, but I don't have to have it. Will she trust me? Only one way to know.

"It can be pleasurable. For both parties. But, if you're not interested, I don't need it."

"What do you need?"

"You." My heart's exposed. I can't possibly be more honest.

Her fingers glide over the silk comforter and her gaze roams the room. "This isn't exactly what I was expecting. I mean, obviously downstairs was an off day. But it feels…"

She's searching for the word. "Why don't you let me show you what you can feel? Why don't we explore together?"

"Okay."

"Stand up." Obedient, she stands. "Turn around." Once again, I lightly touch her zipper. "If anything makes you uncomfortable, tell me. Is there anything you don't want to do?"

"Like what?" I'm standing behind her, but I'd bet she's staring at the chains.

"Blindfold?"

"That's fine. You've done that before."

She's right. We have. I love that she remembers.

"Handcuffs?"

"Maybe not today?"

"Not a problem." I step forward until her back is pressed to my front. I palm her breast, over her belly, down her thigh, and use the tips of my fingers to inch up the hem of her skirt. She squirms. Her ass against my erection forces me to close my eyes and breathe deeply. "Can we take off these clothes?"

"Mm hmm."

I nip at her ear. "Words. In here, I need words."

"I thought you said you weren't a Dom."

"I'm not. Not practiced, at least. But I know enough to know that consent is critical. For that matter, I don't plan on doing anything to you that will require a safe word, but let's create one now. What will yours be?"

"Like...I say it and you stop doing whatever it is your doing?"

"Exactly like that." Her skirt is cinched to her waist, and I palm her sex. Her thong is damp. I slip it to the side. "Baby, you're drenched."

"Yes."

I smirk. She'd completely freak if I asked her to add the word sir. But even without asking, she sounds submissive. I let the skirt fall back over her thighs, brush her hair over her shoulder, and tug the zipper on her camisole down, baring her smooth back. There's a mole below her shoulder blade. One I remember. I bend and press my lips to it. The camisole pools at her feet. The skirt follows.

"No bra." I reach around her to massage her breasts, tweaking her nipple. "I like it."

She stretches her neck to the side, and I nip and lick my way from her shoulder to the sensitive area below her ear. Just the way she likes.

"What did you decide? Shower or oil?"

"What would you prefer?"

I pinch her nipple. Hard.

She squirms, and her ass against my hard cock elicits a groan.

"You tell me."

"Shower."

This will be fun.

I lead her to the oversized marble walk-in shower and flip the water on. I've never shared the shower here with anyone. But there are multiple water sources. Three mounted into the wall. Handheld faucets. And an overhead rain shower.

She shifts from foot to foot, one arm timidly draped over her chest. I begin disrobing. "Remove those panties."

She slides them over her hips, and they drop to her feet. She's nude before me. Trimmed, dark curls cover her sex.

"You don't wax anymore?"

"Not where I want to spend my money." I undo my cufflinks and set them on the sink. I flip on the fan. We're going to steam this room. My fingers fall to my belt buckle, and she blocks them. "Let me."

I lift my arms, letting her know I'm all hers.

"Does it bother you? Would you prefer I wax?"

"I love you smooth. I love your curls." My pants fall to the floor. The belt buckle clanks against the marble. Her fingers wrap around my erection over my briefs. I bend, reaching for her, spreading her curls, slipping a finger into her heat. Then I suck her juices off. "I love you any way I can get you."

Her cheeks flush pink. My briefs fall to my ankles, and I step out of them. Steam coats the glass.

"I believe our shower is ready."

Thirty-One

ZURI

The triple showers pound the tile, amplifying the nerves rioting inside me. My throat is dry and tight, but a dull throb pulses in my core. Obediently, I step into the shower. Hot water pebbles my nipples. I angle my head upward, stepping beneath one of the streams, letting the water cascade over my face and chest. A cleansing beneath a waterfall.

We showered mere hours ago. He took care of me. Caressed me. An intimate, sweet experience. This feels erotic.

Harrison maneuvers me between the streams so water pulses against all sides and I face a slab of marble. His erection prods my lower back. A loofah presses against my belly, then up between my breasts. Foamy white suds spill down my thighs, pooling in the water circling the gold circular drain.

"Palms against the wall. Spread your legs."

Harrison said he wasn't into the Dom thing, but his tone meets my expectations for a Dom. Obedient, I obey.

The loofah traverses my body. The pale white of my skin transitions to pink. The rough material scratches my nipple as Harrison dips a hand between my thighs.

"Baby, you are wet. Those lips are swollen." His shaft presses against me, evidence he's in a similar condition. "You excited?"

I open my mouth and drink in a swallow of hot water. Water splatters, and I close my eyelids to shield my eyes. His thumb circles my clit, and my knees quiver.

He removes his hand, and I moan. My legs are shamelessly spread, my ass out, reaching for him, wanting him. My bullet hard nipples couldn't be more aroused.

The loofah falls to my feet, and Harrison's palms cover my breasts, soothing the loofah-roughened peaks.

"Step up," he commands.

A rumbling sound blends with the shower stream. He's pushed a teak stool in front of me. It's a small rectangular stool, and it lifts me to the perfect height.

I stand on it, and his dick moves from my back to between my thighs. Looking down, his smooth crown peaks between my legs, just below my sex.

Keeping one hand flattened against the marble for balance, I use the other hand to play with him, to guide him between my folds. He alternates between pinching my nipples and soothing them. Hot water streams over both of us.

I press back, thrusting my hips, letting his subtle movements rock his tip against the bundle of nerves. It's erotic and sexy.

"I love how this feels." His chest presses to my back.

"I should make you wait. Tease you. Work you up. But I don't think I can."

I lean forward and slide his tip from the front to the deeper part of me, taking in his velvety crown.

"You don't want to wait?"

"No. Now."

And he surges forward, filling me. I tilt forward, off balance.

"Both hands," he grunts. "On the wall."

Multiple shower streams, hot water, smooth marble beneath my palms, and Harrison filling me pushes me into sensory overload. He reaches around, flicking my clit. When his finger flits away, hot water surges over the sensitive skin, only to be drummed by him. He hits that coveted spot deep within. Over and over. His teeth bite into my shoulder. He pinches my nipple. He slaps my mound as he thrusts so deep I swear he rams my cervix, and I shatter. My knees bend, and he's holding me around the waist.

"That's it, baby, that's it." I pulse around him as he jerks inside me. He wraps his arms around me, holding me for blissful minutes while I slip in and out of awareness.

With one arm around me, pressing me to his front, he flips the showers off. A dark gray, plush, heated towel wraps around me. With care, he dries me and smears my skin with lotion.

Steam coats the mirrors, but as the temperature falls, my sentience returns.

"Let me do you."

I lift a towel to dry him with the same care he tenderly administered. He lets me pat his chest dry but stops me.

"We're not done, sweetheart. Not by a longshot."

He leads me into the bedroom. We're both completely nude, and goosebumps rise along my moist skin from the drier, chillier air.

"Are you okay with a blindfold?"

"Yes, of course. I trust you."

Silky fabric falls over my eyes, resting lightly over the bridge of my nose. He leads me to the bed. I feel safe. At his mercy. It's a contradiction.

"You can restrain me." He says he doesn't do this with others, but there were restraints down in that room. They were also in that cabinet. I didn't think I'd want them, but every muscle in my body is relaxed. If I don't try it now, when?

Furry softness circles my wrists. My arms are placed above me.

I melt into the silky duvet. A light flutter swirls over my belly. I twist.

"That tickles."

"Do you know what it is?"

"The flogger."

"Good girl."

He strokes my nipples. Teasing.

Thwack. Swish.

"Does it hurt?"

"No. It's…nice." My sex clenches. On reflex, I perform a Kegel, squeezing my core, working myself, wanting friction.

"Does it turn you on?"

Thwack. Swish.

"Yes," I gasp.

He resorts to a random pattern of sweet torture. A soft tease interspersed with spiteful lashing. Over my breasts and between my legs.

"Roll over, ass up."

I think I'm tied, so I shouldn't be able to.

Thwack.

My sex pulses in response.

I begin to roll, only to discover my arms move with ease. If I'm tied to anything, there's a lot of give. I turn my head to the side to breathe.

"Hmm. I think a pillow might help."

I expect it under my head, but a silky-smooth object wedges next to my hips. He positions me so my ass is in the air.

"Nice. I do love your ass."

"Are you planning to spank me?" I can't help but grin as I ask. It's ludicrous. He's slapped me once or twice during lovemaking before, especially when he's come at me from behind, but the whole spanking thing has always struck me as silliness.

"Yes." It's a growl. To my chagrin, my pussy pulses in response.

The silky softness of the flogger crosses over my buttocks, between my ass cheeks.

Whap.

My right ass cheek burns. Behind my blindfold, my eyelids pop open.

"Was that the paddle?"

"Too much?"

I close my eyes. Take stock. It tingles. The soft strands of the flogger soothe.

"No, it's good."

Whap.

My left cheek stings.

He alternates the treatment. Hard blows on the crease of my bum and thigh, soothing flogger afterward, occasionally straying to my pussy lips.

"God, you're gorgeous."

I try to come up with a sexy response. It's hard to imagine I'm gorgeous with my ass propped in the air. Still, my tender skin elicits yearning and my hips rock against the pillow as I squeeze my thighs. More Kegels.

"Spread out and vulnerable," he continues. So, that's what he likes.

"Is my ass pink?"

"Yes. Is it sore?"

Swish.

"No. I can take it." *If this is turning him on, let's do more.* After all, the carnality and salaciousness has me grinding a pillow. "Spank me harder."

Whap.

I hope he can tell I'm enjoying this.

Whap.

Fuck. My skin burns. But fuck, am I turned on. The longer it goes on, the harder it is to speak. The louder my groans and guttural noises.

Then there's nothing. The cabinet door clicks.

"Are you open to ass play?"

"Yes." The words out before I give it consideration. Warm liquid oozes from the bottom of my spine down my ass crack.

"We'll start with stretching." A cold wetness nuzzles at my pulsing sphincter. There's a slight burn as my pucker stretches. He's slow. Patient. The device doesn't enter me until my body welcomes it.

Click.

Vibrations begin. Holy…

I squirm on the pillow and his warm palm covers my hip.

"Be a good girl," he warns.

I have a vibrating butt plug up my ass. I should be mortified. But I'm not. I'm loving this. Every bit of this exploration. Finding out what he likes. Discovering if I like it too. And so far? I do. Being at his mercy is freeing. Divine. A bubble of joy expands in my chest while lust twists and flames.

"Open your legs wider."

Something cold, possibly metal or glass, cools the hot entrance of my sex. The temperature variance is soothing. Enticing. Delicious.

The object presses inside me. I let out a loud groan.

The plug is tight. Far tighter than I've ever experienced. It's dirty. Filthy. And I don't want him to stop.

He could ask me to do anything, and I'd agree. Nipple clamps. Whips. Canes. Hickeys all over my throat. Whatever he wants, I'm game.

My head spins with the stretching sensation as the object between my legs delves deeper, all the way to the hilt, so deep inside me. Harrison pistons the object back and forth.

The vibrations intensify. I'm not sure if it's the plug or the dildo, but it's intense. I scream.

Harrison pulls the device out, and I gasp from the loss. Then I'm filled again.

Only this time, it's Harrison. I'm full of Harrison. Hot. Thick. Hard. Pressing right up against that spot once again. Each hit reverberates through me.

I'm screaming. Sweating. Panting.

"Please…" I cry.

"What do you want?" Harrison's voice is stern. Harsh. Fully in command.

"Fuck me."

"I think I'm doing that, sweetheart."

"Use me. However you want."

"You want to suck my cock?"

Bam.

"Take me in your mouth?"

Bam.

"Let me come all over you?"

Bam.

His fingers press and toy with my clit, and my world explodes. I disintegrate into a babbling puddle. Pleasure fragments in bursts from my pussy out to every extremity.

The plug leaves my ass, and I gasp. Harrison crashes over me, his dick pulsing inside me, his hot, sweaty front to my back.

Holy fuck. I've never had an orgasm like that.

"You are the hottest thing under the sun." Harrison lifts my blindfold. Tugs on the wrist restraints, letting them fall to the bed. But he remains over me. "God, I love you."

My eyes burn. And then he's kissing me. The pillow gets pushed to the side. Our limbs tangle. The kiss soothes the rawness. I'm not exposed. I'm safe. I'm loved.

"I want to do that again." I brush the damp strands up off his forehead.

He smirks. Takes my hand and presses his lips to my palm. "Baby, I'm thirty-five. You're going to need to give me some time. But we've got this room for the rest of the night." He takes my index finger and sucks on the nail. Sinks his teeth into the flesh.

"Of course, we don't need this room. We've got the rest of our lives."

A niggling voice in the back of my head asks if that's really true…I'm about to move a thousand miles away. The past repeats itself. But bliss pushes doubt into the Siberia of my mind.

Thirty-Two

ZURI

Blue jays squawk in a nearby tree. A couple of feathers float downward from the leafy branches. The dark feather drifts on a slow backyard breeze. The fan above me whirs, keeping the rising Houston humidity at bay.

It's been two days since our night at TMPT. Two days since Harrison and I moved my suitcases into his house. Uncle Joel couldn't have been more pleased. He acted like a proud shadchan, or matchmaker.

We ate dinner with him last night. Later today I'll meet with a car shipper who will pick my car up and deliver it to Minnesota. Harrison insisted on buying me a first-class plane ticket back.

Sipping my coffee on his tranquil screened-in porch strikes me as highly domesticated. It feels like I've slipped back in time and we're living together again. He's off to work and I'm here, hanging out at the house. It's like when we were in college, and one of us would have class while the other would stay home studying.

Those were good days, but every college student knows those

good days will end. It's in the back of your mind at all times. No one can be a college student forever. Student life is the definition of temporary. Fleeting.

I set the coffee mug down and flip open my laptop. I'm not working today, but I do need to log on and pay bills. Bills that, thanks to the grace and generosity of Uncle Joel, I can actually pay with ease. I'll resume work on Monday at the practice in Minnesota, which means my paychecks should resume in two weeks.

Damn Warren. If he hadn't forced me to get a lawyer, I could've weathered unemployment. But the ten thousand I had to pay the law firm upfront drained my savings. The squawking among the birds in the tree picks back up.

"Is that a territorial dispute up there or a lovers' quarrel?" I call out to the back yard. Unsurprisingly, the birds do not answer.

It's hard to believe I lost it over Warren. I'm a buttoned-up person. Controlled. Together. And if I'm honest with myself, I never loved Warren. I only agreed to date him and move forward in our relationship because it felt like that's what a mid-thirties professional does. It was timely. Expected. But I also took a risk with him. And it hurt. God, it hurt to discover I chose poorly.

I rolled the dice when I shouldn't have. And I'm not one to roll dice, ever. Yet here I am, on Harrison's porch. I went to a sex club with him two days ago. Maybe, just maybe, there's a risktaker within me, and I've been in denial. But am I really taking risks with Harrison? The niggling voice taunts *oh, yes, you are.* She's wrong, though. There's no career risk with Harrison.

My screen goes black. I've been sitting and doing nothing for too long. I click the keys and visit my bank's web site. Paragon's payments are reflected in my account balance, so I should be able to pay my credit card bills, student loans, and maybe, if I'm lucky, the latest legal bill I received.

I start with my credit cards. They're lower than normal since I've been down here in Houston camping at Uncle Joel's. *Bonus.*

The tab which shows upcoming scheduled payments doesn't list any of my student loans. Which is odd. I click over to see why. Blink. Blink again. It's a zero balance. All three of my student loans show a balance of zero.

I scratch my neck. Look up at the spinning ceiling fan. *Fucking Harrison.*

It has to be him. There's no way Sallie Mae made a mistake on three outstanding loans. Uncle Joel loves me, but not that much. The man didn't have children for a reason.

What could Harrison be thinking? That he has so much money he'll just pay my bills without asking? Or is he thinking that by doing so I'm beholden to him? Is it a way to ensure I don't end things again? A way of buying me?

You don't just go and pay off almost half a million in debt without having a conversation. Offering a loan. It feels dirty. Wrong. I don't have the words for it.

When did he do this? I click on the payment history and see the account was paid almost a week ago. If I opened my statement balances that they email to me, I would've seen it last week.

Last week we weren't together. What was he thinking? Why?

Was he thinking he'd pay if off to buy me? But if that was the case, he never said anything about it.

How much money is in his trust fund? *Jesus.*

My thoughts whirl with questions. I waffle between consternation and anger.

A low rumble permeates the kitchen as I pour my second cup of coffee. The garage door is opening. As if summoned, Harrison's home. He should be in surgery. The crazy thought that he got notified when I accessed my account flits by, but no, a bank wouldn't do that for him. The system doesn't work that way. Even for people with ungodly gargantuan trust funds.

The side door opens. I lean against the counter, arms folded over my stomach. On a scale of one to ten, my anger level is around a three. Annoyed, agitated, on edge, on standby to skyrocket to eleven.

"Hey." He enters the kitchen, still in scrubs. Clean navy scrubs. It's my favorite look of his. He doesn't look like a business tycoon or a billionaire playboy. No, he looks like I always imagined he'd look in residency. Down-to-earth. Dedicated. Delicious. "Surgery canceled."

"Why?"

He stops in front of me, studying me, but lifts my coffee mug and sips. "Everything okay?"

"Why was your surgery canceled?" I really hate when people don't answer me.

He blinks and his eyelashes flutter. He looks like he's waking up. He tilts his head and answers slowly, "She's sick. Woke with a low-grade fever."

Can't do surgery on someone who's sick. The explanation makes sense.

"My seven a.m. surgery went smoothly. Nine a.m. canceled. What's going on?"

"You paid off my student debt."

He backs up against the opposing counter and crosses his arms. The position flexes his biceps and the tendons in his forearms. I force my gaze upward. My attraction to Harrison has never been the issue.

"I paid your outstanding legal bills too."

"You what?"

His expression is neutral. "I told you. I'll always love you. You were stressed about finances. I have more money than I need. I'm an only child. One day I'll inherit five times what I have in my trust fund, and I already earn more in interest than you'll make in a yearly salary. What's the point of having money if you can't help those you love?"

"Harrison!" I pace the kitchen, searching for the anger that intellectually should be boiling over. But I'm oddly touched. I shouldn't be, but I am. There's a sweetness to it. Naive. Wrong. But he wasn't even going to tell me about it. It's not like he was trying to buy me. He didn't hang an offer over my head. He just did it.

"I expected you'd be in Minnesota by the time you figured it out."

I slow near the refrigerator. "And what did you think would happen?"

He shrugs his broad shoulders. "I figured I'd get an angry phone call. I might have to spend a few years shredding checks you mailed me attempting to pay me back."

I let out a loud sigh. "It's really not okay. I pay my way. My independence is important to me."

He purses his lips. His chin juts out. "I get that. You've worked hard. Your parents…" I raise an eyebrow, wondering what he's going to say about my parents. They are each highly successful, cutthroat business executives. Their careers skyrocketed after they separated. I'm not close to them. Hardly speak to them. "You did it all on your own. There's a lot of pride in that. I didn't mean to take that away from you. I just saw you stressed and…I didn't want that for you. If you want to pay me back, we can arrive upon an arrangement."

There's a smirk playing across his lips, and I fight the impulse to laugh at the unstated implication.

"Harrison." I'm firm. There's no hint of the humor bubbling inside me. Humor that absolutely should not be present.

His eyelids close. His jaw flexes. When he opens his eyes, he locks his gaze on me. "Fine. If you want to pay me back, we'll pick a charity. You can send your donations monthly to them. You'll have the added benefit of not being charged interest on the loans."

I stare at him.

"Or you can pay the money back to me. I don't need it. But if that's what you need, that's what we'll do."

He sounds resigned. Annoyed.

"I can't believe you did this knowing I'd be moving back to Minnesota."

He opens his mouth. His jaw cracks with the stretch. He's thoughtful. "I think I had it in my head I'd try to win you back. When I paid off the balances, we weren't together, but I think somewhere deep down, I don't see a future that doesn't end up with us together. And if we're together, what's mine is yours."

A recollection stirs. His old roommate who would write his name on the cereal box and the milk. "Harrison, that works for food items."

He *tsks*. "It works for everything."

He holds out his arms, and I reluctantly fall into them. Intellectually, I should be angry at him. But I can't muster the emotion. I bury my face against his chest, my nose right at the V of his scrub shirt. He smells of soap, hospital disinfectant, strong man, and, well, mine. His heart thumps against my cheek and within my chest a warmth surges.

He can be infuriating. But his heart's in the right place.

Knock. Knock.

I lift my head. "Are you expecting anyone?" Someone's at the front door, which is bizarre. All the delivery guys just press the doorbell, drop, and go. It's a weekday.

Ding dong

That's the doorbell. He exhales and looks down on me.

"Are we okay?"

I nod, and he presses his lips against my forehead. I watch his back retreat down the hallway. My chest sinks. This is where I'm supposed to be, yet I've got a ticket to return to Minnesota in three days.

"Jessica." Surprise rings through Harrison's greeting. "What's up?"

"Is Zuri here?"

"What do you want?" I roll my eyes at his defensive tone and rush down the hallway.

"Hi. I'm here," I call.

Dr. Chandler is also in scrubs. Hers are a light rose color. "Joel said I could find you here. Can I speak to you? In private?"

She's standing outside on the front porch. Harrison has his arms folded like a sentry.

"Sure. Would you like some coffee?"

"No. Thanks. I won't be long." She glances at Harrison. "I also had a surgery cancel today. Sick as well. Maybe something's going around. But I have to get back. I have a scar repair to do and then a full day after. I heard you're going back, and…" Her gaze cuts up to Harrison, who still hasn't moved.

"Come on back. I was just on the back porch. It's not too hot yet."

She by-steps Harrison. If she's here to rail at me for her daughter, or bring a lawsuit against me, at least I know someone has my back this time around.

We step out onto the screened porch. I slide the glass door closed. Harrison stands in the den, concerned. I blow him a kiss. And smile. Completely uncharacteristic of me, but I want to relay that it'll be all right. Whatever it is, we'll face it together.

When I turn away from the glass door, Dr. Chandler is standing awkwardly in front of a chair.

"Sit," I say.

"No, that's okay. What I have to say won't take long. But I wanted to say it in person."

I rock back on my heels. And cross my arms. Lots of crossing arms for a Tuesday morning.

"I wanted to thank you. You…when I first found out, yes, I'd been angry. I'd wanted to have your medical license." I grimace. That's what I feared. "But my husband calmed me down. He's good like that." She turns so she's facing Harrison's green back yard. The blue jays have quieted down, and the only sounds are the occasional rumble of a car or a burst of birdsong. "My anger was…well, at me." She spins. "I should've seen what was going on. And what happened with Molly? It was on us. On her. Really, on her." Her eyes search mine. "But not on you. You did what any human would do, and I want to thank you."

"How is she?"

"It was a false positive. She's not pregnant. She's fine."

She's lying.

"You can't tell anyone about this. You get that, right? Anyone could try to…it's what I've been trying to emphasize to Molly. The laws in this state. You might not be aware, but there's a ten-thousand-dollar bounty given to anyone who reports an abortion. She wasn't pregnant, but if someone believes she was, if they believe she did something about it, I don't want her to have to deal with that. She's in high school, and kids talk. It's just…" She lets out a half laugh. "It's surreal that we have to be worried about it, but we do."

"I was more afraid she'd get a pill from the black market. These days, with what's going on with fentanyl, I don't trust anything to not be potentially laced with–"

"No. I absolutely agree. I wish when the condom broke she would've gone and gotten the morning after pill, but apparently she's a gambler." My throat tightens. "And, false positive. She was never pregnant." She looks me straight in the eye, then softens. Her eyes are glassy in the light. "She went to her father. You know, it hurts that she was too scared to come to me."

There's vulnerability in Dr. Chandler. Something I hadn't seen before. But I can see how she'd push her daughter. It's a Type A trait. The pursuit of perfection.

"It doesn't mean she doesn't love you." Love is a complicated emotion. I wouldn't go to either of my parents with an issue, mainly because they're so involved in their own lives. But it doesn't mean I don't love them. "I'd bet, if anything, you guys will be closer because of this." She pushes her shoulders back. "False positive. I'm relieved for her."

"I hope this is a wakeup call." A soft smile plays across her lips.

"I had Molly when I was in medical school. It wasn't easy. I mean, I'd do it all over again. It was my choice. But I don't want that for her. I suppose, if anything good came out of this, now she knows that whether I agree with her choices or not, I'll always love her. I'll always support her."

The world blurs and I blink furiously, blinking away the emotion. "She's lucky she has you."

Dr. Chandler nods then looks at her wrist. "I've got to run. Just…no one can know. Something might be misinterpreted or misconstrued. I can't emphasize it enough."

"I would never have said anything to anyone."

She nods. She leans forward, like she might hug me, but she's not a hugger. As she passes me she says, "Hope to see you around. Take care, Dr. Lennox."

I watch her retreat down the hall. Harrison follows her out, but not without throwing me a worried glance over his shoulder. I give him a thumbs up signal.

It's all worked out. For me. For us. For Molly. But what a clusterfuck.

Thirty-Three

ZURI

Harrison: Chandler says hello.

Proof that this time around is different, Harrison has texted and called frequently since we said goodbye at the airport. If he hadn't completely shut down and blocked me ten years ago, would we be in this place today? Would our friendship have sustained a relationship until we could wind up doing residency together? But residency is a crapshoot. In all likelihood, we would've ended up in different states for residency too.

I tap out a quick nothing return text.

Me: Tell her hi. About to go into the office and meet with HR. Wish me luck.

. . .

It's Friday. I start back to work on Monday. It feels like a lifetime ago that the partners threw me out on my derriere. All of them lined up on Warren's side. Not that I can blame them. I had a lawsuit staring me down that had the power to affect my state medical license. Charges of criminal damage to property in the first degree.

And now, here I sit in the parking lot of a nondescript building. A far cry from Paragon's gleaming modern design. The practice is one of many offices in this two-story brick building downtown. The front doors open into a lobby with a sign that includes all the office names and the floor unit.

The door opens, and Warren steps out. My first instinct is to dive below the steering wheel. But even as my cheeks heat, the mature part of me stands my ground. This coincidence is a good thing. It's much better to face off with him in the relative privacy of a parking lot than in the office with colleagues and patients alike observing us.

In the sunlight, his closely cropped hair appears grayer, or the more accurate term would be whiter, since I last saw him. He fumbles with the coat pocket on his white jacket and pulls out a cigarette pack. He once told me he only smokes when he drinks, but given it's ten a.m. on a Friday, it's clear that's one more lie he told.

A click sounds loudly within the car when I pull on the car door handle, but Warren continues along the front of the building, heading to the grassy area on the side. All the smokers convene there. He's almost around the corner when I close the car door.

That sound, he hears. He slows and glances over his shoulder. Then stops. Between his fingers, he holds the unlit cigarette. I half wave.

His back curves slightly from years of bad posture. What did I ever see in him? Why was I willing to risk my professional reputation on a relationship with him?

He retraces his steps to the front of the building. In front of the doors, he pauses, watching me. I step forward as the doors behind him open and a woman holding a young boy's hand exits. She passes Warren without a second glance, talking to her son as she makes her way through the parking lot.

The click of a car door unlocking sounds as I come to stand before Warren.

"Hi," I say. "Thank you for dropping the charges."

"Wasn't up to me."

It would've been up to the DA. *Right.* "Well, thank you for allowing me to come back to work here."

"Wasn't up to me. I had one vote."

My stomach craters. "Do you not want me to come back to work here?"

He crosses his arms over his chest, then throws a glance into the lobby. "Come with me to talk."

His coattails jostle with his walk. Uncertain, I follow him.

By the side of the building, out of view of the entrance, he pulls out a Bic lighter and lights his cigarette. He sucks on it, then exhales.

"I'm no longer with Sherry."

"I heard."

"But we can't date again. What you did. It was seriously not acceptable."

But you cheating on me with someone on staff was completely acceptable. My teeth press together so hard my cheek muscles strain. Total bastard.

"I really am sorry about your car." There, that's an acceptable semblance of truth. I spin, ready to go talk to HR.

"Wait."

I stop. I don't turn around but bend my head, a sign to him I'm listening.

"You don't have to go. Tell me. How was Texas?"

"Good." I slowly spin to face him.

"Any interest in going to dinner tonight? We can catch up."

"Didn't you just tell me we can't date again?"

"This wouldn't be a date." He shrugs with an innocent air, but the problem is that I know his game. He takes you to dinner, orders a good bottle of wine, or two, and then when your defenses are down and you're not quite thinking straight, he makes his move. At first, it's just a kiss. The next time, his hands roam, and the trouble is, you want those hands to roam. And soon, he has you trapped in an office supply closet and he's whispering into your ear how attractive you are, how much you turn him on. How you're irresistible. But you tell him it's not a good idea. You're colleagues. And he says it will be forever. That his desire for you is unlike anything he's ever known. And then you second-guess yourself, and you say okay, until you find out you're not the only one he's taking into the office supply closet.

"I start back on Monday. If you'd like to get lunch, I'm available." That's a sound suggestion. I'll invite Kelly so we won't inspire gossip, and it'll send a clear signal that Warren and I have put the ugly saga behind us and we can work together.

He smirks. A few months ago, I thought he had a sexy smirk. Wrong. It's sleazy. I suppose as you learn more about a person, your perception of them changes. I don't really see what I ever saw in him. How I ever wanted those hands to roam.

"Lunch it is, then. Are you back in your apartment?"

"No. I found someone to sublease it. Can't really kick them out." A fake, forced smile plays across my lips. Yes, I gave up a terrific apartment to move in with him. But I was smart enough to not give it up permanently.

"Too bad. That was a great location."

Yes, it is. There's no point in continuing to talk to him, so I head around the corner and leave him smoking alone.

But a feeling of failure hits me. If I'm going to be in this practice, I owe it to myself to put us back on a professional plane. When I round the corner, he looks up from flicking ashes. His eyes narrow and the corners of his lips turn up. Amusement. Ego.

"Warren, I shouldn't have ever taken my anger out by damaging your car. It was inappropriate. But you shouldn't have cheated on me. I took a career risk by agreeing to date a colleague, and you humiliated me. That's in the past now. But I need to be completely clear. Our relationship will be strictly professional moving forward."

He flicks the cigarette to the ground and stamps it out with his toe. "Understood." He no longer looks amused. No, he's ambivalent. Which is fine. Better than fine, actually.

I head into the building with Warren a couple of steps behind me. In the elevator, I notice he reeks of cigarette smoke. Do his patients notice? How did I not notice it before? Is smoking during the day a new habit he's formed? It's not my concern.

Marcy Hall greets me with a warm smile. She's a couple of years older than I am and has two young children. She works four days a week for us. Before she came to work here, she worked for a big consulting company and apparently had to travel all the time. These are the things I remember about her as she waves my hand away and gives me a hug.

"Welcome back."

"Thank you," I say, scratching the back of my neck. I didn't expect such a warm welcome. In my mind, I expected that everyone here thinks I am the slutty psycho.

She sits behind her desk, and I take one of the guest seats. Her office is small, but a window fills the back wall, and she has a bright, cheery framed flower print on the wall to my right.

"The partners decided they don't need to meet with you." She falters and flattens one hand on the calendar stretched out across her desk. "If you want to meet with them, you can. But they didn't think it was necessary. When an assault charge was filed, we had to take it seriously. But no one believes you are a threat or a risk."

"I'm not," I assure her. "It was a momentary lapse of reason."

"I get it." She offers a quick smile. If I were to read into it, I'd say she's nonverbally communicating that she would've done the same thing in my shoes. "I'm glad the charges were dropped. From what I understand, we needed you back on staff yesterday."

Before my departure, I'd had a fairly full calendar booked out for almost a year, so I'm sure they need me. It's common for patients to book their annual check-up a year out, so it doesn't take long for a calendar to fill up. There are some dermatologists within this practice who are so established they no longer accept new patients.

She has me sign some documents and we make small talk. She's as friendly as can be. It's almost like talking to a friend, except I'm fully aware she's HR, and I've been told you can never trust HR. So I keep it professional and I'm out of her office in under thirty minutes.

In the parking lot, I check my phone. There's a text from Harrison, and I smile.

Harrison: Where are you?

Me: Leaving the office. It's all done.

I set the phone down, feeling lighter than I have in months. It's all done. So much easier than I ever anticipated. The weight of an assault charge gone. Re-assimilation into the practice I've invested two years of my life in begun. The phone lights up and then vibrates.

It's Harrison. He's calling. My car is too ancient to tie into my phone, so I accept the call but put it on speaker, leaving it in the cup holder.

"Hi there!" I'm grinning as I answer because everything is great. I tell Harrison all about my meeting with HR, and how it was such a nonevent. I'd built returning to the practice to be something that would be difficult, if not impossible. Thought people would hate me. Maybe even fear me. The psycho girlfriend who bashed a Ferrari.

"I also saw Warren." There's silence on his end as I turn onto the street that will lead me to the Residence Inn. Hopefully, I won't need to stay at this hotel much longer. I put an application in for an apartment not too far away.

"How did that go?"

"Fine. I don't foresee any issues working with him."

"Did he come on to you?" There's a protective quality to Harrison's words, and it warms my insides.

Immediately, my practical inner voice kicks off about being in two different states, and long distance for eternity, but I shut her down.

"He didn't come on to me." I remember he mentioned dinner. "Not really. But it doesn't matter. If I insist on professionalism, which I will, he'll play along."

The guy has no choice. Besides, he'll find someone else to pursue soon enough.

The turn signal blinker is loud and fills the car as I turn off into the hotel parking lot.

"Where are you going now?"

"Back to the hotel. Can I call you back once I'm inside? Are you done for the day?"

"Not quite done. And what kind of question is that? We're talking every day from here on out. Remember?"

Still grinning, I end the call with, "I'll call you back in a few."

I'm not sure where we're going or how things are going to work out long-term, but this is so much better than ten years ago when he shut off all contact. I'll take it.

Thirty-Four

HARRISON

Her expression when she gets out of the battered old Toyota is exactly what I hoped for. Those violet eyes expand with both shock and happiness. Her wide smile leaves no room for doubt. She's happy to see me.

Why the hell didn't I do this ten years ago? Just ignore what she told me and show the fuck up with the plan to keep showing up? A nagging voice, or maybe it's a feeling lodged in my chest, says she might've been right. I'm not entirely positive I'm built for eight years of long distance combined with grueling work hours.

But that's behind us. All of that is behind us.

"What're you doing here?" Her mouth remains half open, but her lips curve into a smile.

She's in a navy pantsuit with low heels, and she's blown her hair straight. It's been days since I saw her, but my skin itches with a need to pull her close. And so, I do.

"Since you didn't seem sold on long distance, I had to show you

227

how it works." She wraps her arms around my shoulders and beams up at me. "Left the office after my surgery this morning."

And then I'm kissing her. In the middle of a parking lot in front of a hotel with a view of nothing and mediocre plantings. And it's everything. She's everything.

"Wanna come inside?"

Yeah, I want to come inside, but I also want more. I want everything. I glance at her car. "You have anything else in there you're going to need?"

"No." She pulls back, scanning the parking area. "Where's your bag?"

"In the lobby. Come on."

We breeze past the reception desk, where the dark-skinned woman with full breasts and ruby red lipstick and moles on her cheeks that should probably be removed assists someone checking in.

In the elevator, a balding man in a suit with his tie halfway undone joins us, and the three of us stand silently as the elevator rises to the third floor. I squeeze Zuri's hand, and she glances up at me. There's love in her eyes. It's something I love more than the color of her irises. The warmth she bestows. Under her rays, I'm a spring bud, blossoming after enduring one long, glacial winter.

Her room is four doors down from the elevator. She presses the plastic card against the lock, a green light flashes, and we're through.

I have her up against the wall before the heavy door clicks closed. Her blouse is up, and my fingers touch the bare, smooth skin along her waist. Her suit jacket falls to the ground. She tugs on my shirt. We're a flurry of hands undressing each other.

When her bra hits the floor, she lifts her hands to her breasts and massages, pushing them together. Her thumbs brush over her nipples, and I swear I nearly explode.

With a twist of my fingers, her pants are unbuttoned. Her hips sway right, then left as she pushes her remaining clothes down over her thighs. I lift her and carry her to a center island.

The room has a small kitchenette, and there's a bed behind me. The kitchen island is a perfect first stop. I set her on it and free myself. I'm rock hard.

And then I'm inside her, moaning my relief. God, she's heaven.

She leans back, breasts to the sky, bouncing with my thrusts. Legs bent, knees at my side, she tilts her head back and her eyelids half close as she releases a slow, sexy as fuck hum. I slow my thrusts and massage her, kneading her, working her in just the way that has her coming apart and quivering around me.

Still deep inside her, I kiss her, holding her up to me.

"Hold on," I instruct, and her legs wrap around me. I kick off my pants, which settled around my calves, and carry her to the crisp, white bed.

The window opens onto an expanse of the parking lot. There are buildings across the street. I doubt anyone can see into our room, but honestly, I don't care who sees us.

And with the variety of noises coming out of Zuri, lifting her head and looking straight out the window as I pound into her from behind, slapping her ass occasionally for good measure, I don't think she minds either.

It's not until I'm on my back, and she's riding me, and those eyes lock with mine, that every atom in my body syncs with hers. Her smooth legs slide down the outside of my thighs while I remain seated deep inside her. Slowly she undulates over me, rubbing herself on me, using me in the most perfect way, and my balls tighten. Her muscles quiver, and a powerful, mind-numbing orgasm slices through me.

She lies flat on top of me, her soft breasts pressed against my chest, and I hold her tight. I'm never letting go. Ever.

Of course, that's not quite realistic. But after we've caught our breath and taken turns in the bathroom, I peel back the comforter, stack the pillows, and climb into bed, holding out an arm for her. It's early afternoon. Eventually, we'll get dressed and go to dinner.

But right now, there are things that need to be said. And I want her naked in my arms as we say them.

"Are you happy?"

She dips her head and nips at my chest. "I think that's rather obvious."

I brush back her tangled hair. She's got the I've-been-fucked-thoroughly hair going, and I have to say, it's one of my favorite looks. "That's not what I mean." I squeeze her pinked ass cheek. "Here? Is this where you want to be? Minnesota?"

Caution crosses over her features. It's the worry that's second nature to her. I head it off at the pass. "It's okay if you do. I never asked how you ended up in Minnesota. Was it a place you wanted? Or did they make the best offer?"

She waffles, clearly weighing her answer, or maybe reflecting. "Best offer," she decides. "What about you in Texas?"

"Easier to stay than go. Good job offer right where I'd been a resident thanks to a connection I had with a certain surgeon you're related to." I press her palm to my lips. Her naked body is pressed to mine, and it's the best sensation. "The reason I'm asking is that I'm going to be moving."

Her eyes widen ever so slightly, and her head begins that slow shift to the right, like she's going to tell me no. She fears resentment. Scared that one day things won't work out.

"You really don't get a say." It's taken me a while to realize it, but I have a choice in this. "I'm going to move to be near you, no matter what. Should've done it ten years ago. I can't change the past, but the future is mine." It's ours, but Zuri is skittish. "So, knowing I'm going to be moving to be near you, before I do, is there another state you might prefer? Should we do some research? If this isn't where you want to spend your career, now would be a good juncture to explore."

"You would leave Texas?"

"In a heartbeat."

"But what about Paragon?"

"We'll expand to another state. Joel supports me on this."

"You talked to Uncle Joel?"

"He's on board. This is what he always wanted to happen, you know? At that man's heart, he's a romantic."

"Maybe." She looks skeptical. I don't blame her. Some would argue that at heart he's a perv. Her eyes narrow, and I brace for her to tell me all the reasons it's a bad idea. "You'd leave your sex club?"

The way she says sex club is kind of adorable. Like it's a tantric snake requiring cautious care. And maybe it is.

"Sweetheart, let me explain something to you. I've had a lot of sex since we broke up. A ton, really." Those violet eyes darken, and I sense pain. "But it was just that. A physical act. A release. When I'm with you, it's so much more. Because with you, it's not just physical. I'm making love to you, and that's entirely different. You're the only woman I've made love to." Her brow wrinkles with skepticism. "Seriously. You're the only woman I've given my heart to. The only woman I've let in. And maybe I could've fallen for someone else if I'd let them in, but there wouldn't have been a point, because there was nothing to let them in for. My heart remained with you."

It could be a trick of light, but those violet eyes look glassy. Zuri Lennox is not a crier, but I squeeze her all the same. And then the tear falls, and I know without a doubt we're going to make it. Zuri Lennox loves me as deeply as I love her.

"You know, if you wanted to, we could go together sometime." This woman is amazing. "I mean, I wouldn't…you know…with any other man."

"That goes without saying." Sure, there are couples that swap partners, and I am absolutely okay with what anyone else wants to do. I do not judge. But no man will touch Zuri in front of me. "But there are couples who find they enjoy various aspects of the club. It can be freeing. Stimulating. Erotic."

"Spice things up?" she asks, and her nose crinkles. "A little kink every now and then to keep things fresh?"

God, I love her. "To be clear, we don't ever need to return. At least not for my needs. But, if you ever want to visit, we can. If we never visit, if I never enter those doors again, as long as I have you, I'll die a happy man."

"That's the right thing to say." She's skeptical. I hear it and understand it. That geriatric douchewaffle probably told her something similar before cheating.

"Zuri, I don't say something just to say it. But you don't have to believe me today, as long as you're willing to give me tomorrow."

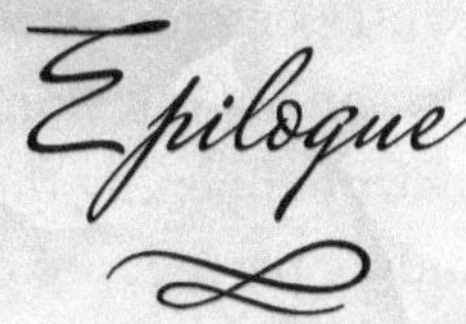

Epilogue

"Are you ready?" my husband's voice calls up the stairs, creating a slight echo down the wide white oak floor in the entry hall.

With one last glance in the full-length mirror, I check my hair and suck in my stomach. The white silk falls loosely from my breasts down to the floor in an elegant column. A single dogwood blossom from the heritage tree in the corner of our front yard adorns the pin holding strands of hair off my brow.

We purchased this new construction home close to Freedom Park in Charlotte, North Carolina. After spending ten weekends visiting cities, we picked Charlotte because of the vibrant community, the abundance of trees, and the quality of life.

Given my husband loves to garden, the home we selected has a deep back yard and a charming front yard. They removed the original trees and shrubs when the builder tore down the original dwelling. Our spec home is a blank slate to be completed as we wish, both indoors and out.

Harrison has been all about the yard. And my domestic inner

self has stepped up. The house is coming together, although the window treatments aren't in and the front of the house has a fish-bowl effect, given our front door is iron with glass panes, and an oversized glass and iron paned window graces the dining room. Well, the architect designed the room to be used as a dining room with an adjacent butler pantry between it and the kitchen, but we'll use the front room for one of our home offices.

We're five weeks away from opening the North Carolina Paragon practice. As founding partners of this location, we've agreed to abolish status meetings. We'll see how that goes.

We both are now officially licensed to practice medicine in this state, and I hope I never have to move again, because it's not a fun process. What was actually quite easy, once I agreed, was entering a marital union.

We did so in Houston one Friday afternoon when I arrived to help Harrison pack up his home. We committed to each other in his back yard beside his rosemary shrubs and drove to the justice of the peace to make it legal.

Given my parents' Duracell divorce, the divorce that just keeps on going, I was skeptical about the need to legally bind us. But, for all of Harrison's progressive ways, he's got an old, traditional soul. Neither of us are religious, but Harrison holds a deep appreciation for the cultural history and meaning behind marriage. He had his lawyer write up a detailed document that would allow me to dictate the terms of our divorce—an extensive pre-nup, if you will —that ensured if we ever dissolved our marriage, the divorce would be the quickest in the land.

I never signed that document, because I told him I had no intention of ever dissolving our relationship. We did that once before, and I refuse to go through that again. Unlike Harrison, I'm not a romantic. I expect we'll have our ups and downs. I anticipate days when we want to call it quits. But my hope is we'll dig in and work through it. My hope is we'll never be my parents. My dream is that our love will mirror his parents' enduring love. Minus one of us meeting an early death and the other one of us roaming the planet heartbroken and lost.

Harrison's dad was distressed he missed his only son's wedding. We're going to do another commitment ceremony with his father present, and tonight, we'll host a celebratory dinner.

My parents couldn't make it. My mom is speaking at a conference in Dublin, and my father missed his flight from Dubai because a meeting ran late. My sister waits tables at a tavern and said she couldn't get the time off work, not that I expected her to join us for what will really be a family meal. I suspect she couldn't afford the international flight, and offered to pay, but she and I are quite similar. Her pride wouldn't allow for me paying.

I'm glad my parents can't make it. Their hate would poison the evening.

For centuries, humans held weddings outdoors. We're following history and, in deference to Harrison's father, celebrating our union outside. Uncle Joel brought a glass for us to crush for good luck.

Uncle Joel didn't bring Jolene. He's decided open relationships are the best path forward for him. And apparently while Jolene is a real person, he exaggerated the extent of his relationship with her in a twisted ploy. He played porn loudly in his room in the hopes I would be uncomfortable and opt to stay in Harrison's guest room. His strategy was forced proximity. It turns out he's a slightly demented matchmaker. But we love him anyway.

Harrison's dad is dating someone, but he opted not to bring her. He believes Harrison's mom will be with us today in spirit, and while he cares for the woman he's dating, he's not quite ready to bring her into the family.

Harrison mentioned our plans to Ian, and he and his wife Sunny surprised us. They're staying in the Ritz, not too far away. They left their baby daughter with Ian's parents.

Harrison extended an invitation to Amelia and Liam, but Liam couldn't get away. I haven't said anything to Harrison, but Amelia's going to surprise him. She said she wouldn't miss this for the world.

I would've never invited Kelly, my friend in Minnesota, as it's so much to ask, but Harrison invited her. Her flight was delayed, so while she won't make our backyard nuptials, she'll make it to our dinner at a restaurant called Supperland. The restaurant is, ironically, housed in a building that used to be a church. We chose it because it's got the best southern food I've ever eaten in my life, and the downstairs private cellar will be perfect for our close-knit group.

It's a beautiful spring day, the perfect day for planting. Which is good because that's what we're doing. In our back yard, in the back right corner, there's a hole dug for an oak tree. After we say our vows, Harrison and I will take shovels and plant the oak. The oak tree is a symbol of strength, endurance, and longevity. Harrison believes it will serve as a reminder that our union can weather all storms if we rely on the depth, or root of our love, and, well, work at it.

When I appear on our back screened-in porch, our dog, a black pit bull and Lab mix we rescued from the Charlotte Humane Society, stands and stretches, wagging his tail. Harrison stills, and his eyes lock on me. He's looking at me like I'm the most beautiful woman in the world.

There are so many traditional wedding practices we're not following, but this is one of those traditional moments I secretly wanted. When the groom sees the bride and he's taken with her. We're already married, technically, but this moment thrills. Uncle Joel has a tripod set up, and someone's phone records.

My skin simultaneously heats and tingles. Butterflies alight within my belly. And the world falls away as my gaze locks on my groom, my partner, my husband. He's in a black Dolce & Gabbana suit, his dark hair styled and set, and my fingers itch to rough it up. A warm pulse emanates from my chest. I swear I could close my eyes and follow the connection between us, right up to his side.

It's a romantic notion. One I hope to nurture for eternity.

The End

If you're interested in Liam and Amelia's story, sign up for my newsletter and get The Club, a sizzling novella, free by visiting https://BookHip.com/XZDTPQB.

Sunny and Ian Duke's story is in Always Sunny. She's his secret fantasy, his brother's ex, and the sunshiny friend who wants a baby of her own.

Arrow Tactical Security Series

Better to See You (Wolf and Alexandria)

Sure of One (Jack and Ava)

Cloak of Red (Sophia and Fisher)

Stolen Beauty (Knox and Allison) - Releasing 2024

The Twisted Vines Series

Crushed (Erik and Vivi)

Breathe (Kairi and David)

Savor (Trevor and Stella)

Haven Island Series

Rogue Wave (Tate and Luna)

Adrift (Gabe and Poppy)

First Light (Logan and Cali)

The West Side Series

When the Stars Align (Jackson and Anna)

Trust Me (Sam Duke and Olivia)

Walk the Dog (Delilah and Mason)

Lost on the Way (Jason and Maggie)

Chasing Frost (Chase and Sadie)

Misplaced Mistletoe (Ashton aka Dr. Bobby and Nora)

Standalone Romances

How to Survive a Holiday Fling (Oliver Duke and Kate)

Always Sunny (Ian Duke and Sandra)

The Romantics (Harrison and Zuri)

About the Author

Isabel Jolie, aka Izzy, lives on a lake, loves dogs of all stripes, and if she's not working, she can be found reading, often with a glass of wine. In prior lives, Izzy worked in marketing and advertising, in a variety of industries, such as financial services, entertainment, and technology. In this life, she loves daydreaming and writing contemporary romances with real, flawed characters and inner strength.

Sign-up for Izzy's newsletter to keep up-to-date on new releases, promotions and giveaways. (**Pro-tip** - She offers a free book on her home page…just scroll down after arriving at her site.)

Want to say hi? Email her through her website or reply to her newsletter…she loves to hear from readers.

www.ingramcontent.com/pod-product-compliance
Lightning Source LLC
Chambersburg PA
CBHW020757190726

48285CB00006B/2068